Antiochus

Antiochus

by
Walter K. Price
and
John Gillies

MOODY PRESS

CHICAGO

"Year 137, month Elulu, 10th day: Seleucus (IV) the king, died. In the same month, Antiochus (IV, Epiphanes) ascended the throne. He ruled for eleven years."

> —*from a tablet listing Seleucid kings, found by archaeologists near the city of Antioch.*

"*Corpus eius cum Antiochiam portaretur, exterritis subito iumentis in fluviam abreptum non comparuit.*"
("When his body was carried to Antioch, the beast of burden became suddenly terrified and the river snatched his body and it did not reappear.")

> —*from a footnote in* The House of Seleucus *by Edwyn Robert Bevan, attributed to Granius Licinianus.*

Prefaces

The persecutions of the Jews by King Antiochus were unique for two reasons.

First, never before had a people been forced, under penalty of death, to give up their religious traditions and accept the worship of a god not their own.

Second, Antiochus's persecution of the Jews established a pattern for the future of Israel.

The days of the Antiochus crisis show, in microcosm, the events that are scheduled to repeat themselves in the last days of Jewish history.

The Jews are to suffer unprecendented persecution under a sinister figure who is to come upon the stage of history in the end days. It is my belief that that ominous personality is foreshadowed by Antiochus IV Epiphanes.

It is that conviction that initiated this book.

Walter K. Price

The events that follow occurred between 220 and 160 B.C. That period of sixty years falls within a time of biblical silence between the Old and the New Testaments.

Some scholars discard Antiochus (the name means "Withstander" and is pronounced an-TIE-a-kus) as a mere footnote to history.

The Jews did not think so. Neither did the prophet Daniel nor even our Lord Jesus Christ.

As with all historical fiction, this novel is based upon fact. Where sources differ in detail or chronology, we have had to make choices. Except for a few secondary characters who were invented, we believe we have been faithful to the historical record.

This story is frighteningly true.

John Gillies

Acknowledgments

This novel draws upon several primary sources.

The two books of the Maccabees describe the descration of the Temple, the horrible torture of the Jews, and the successful Jewish rebellion of the era.

The authors accept Daniel as prophetic prehistory, particularly chapters 8 and 11. Jesus refers to this prophecy in Matthew 24:15-17.

Polybius of Megapolis was a Greek historian who lived during the period of this story and wrote extensively about it.

Titus Livius, better known as Livy, was born in 59 B.C. He wrote 142 books on the history of Rome and its conquests; books 36 through 45 deal specifically with Antiochus and Roman politics in Asia.

Flavius Josephus was a first century (A.D.) Jewish historian and soldier, who expanded upon the Maccabean material in his writings.

John Malalas was a Greek historian who lived in

Antioch in the sixth century (A.D.); in writing about the history of his native city, he also wrote extensively about the Seleucid dynasty. His writings were translated into Slavonic and were preserved in Eastern Orthodox monasteries.

The most recent archeological work in Antioch began in 1932. The Committee for the Excavation of Antioch and Its Vicinity published several books on its discoveries through Princeton University.

Dozens of scholars, Jewish and Christian, representing many nations, have studied and evaluated this primary data, both written and excavated.

We cannot here credit them all, but we and you are indebted to them.

1

Antiochus cautiously rubbed his unshaven cheek, stretched his tall frame and arms to the point of pain, and yawned so widely he heard his jaw snap. He had slept soundly but wanted to become fully and quickly awake. His father, the king, had taught him early in life that danger too often accompanied slumber.

He saw that the two Romans were talking, and he wished he understood more of the Latin tongue.

Lucius Sempronius, the centurion who had been his guard and companion since Ephesus, had turned out to be a friendly sort.

Antiochus was not ready to judge Titus Popilius. He had met him the day before and knew only that he was a legate with some special responsibility to the Roman senate. Antiochus had noted that a smile came neither easily nor quickly to the face of Titus.

Antiochus loved life and smiled often. In fact, he

laughed as he coughed up his morning phlegm. He remembered the good times in Ephesus, after Lucius was convinced that Antiochus would not run away. Lucius spoke fluent Greek, which helped break down the barrier between captor and captive. The Ephesian wine and women were of excellent vintage.

Antiochus glanced at Titus and decided he would never make a good drinking companion.

"The Seleucid is wide awake," said Titus.

"The prince usually sleeps deeply and awakens slowly," Lucius commented, with a smile.

"He sleeps like a baby, I suppose! Well, he isn't today." Titus spat to the ground. "Look at him, Lucius. He stands there grinning like a Greek god, blond as an Etruscan. He will give us trouble. The man is too arrogant, too impertinent."

"He is a prince, legate."

"He is a prisoner. A hostage, centurion, along with the nineteen others you brought with you."

"He's not a bad fellow," said Lucius. "He's a bit wild for his age, of course. He likes his wine, and he has an eye for every passing feminine *stola*. But he is a clever lad. He observes everything. He's not afraid to ask questions, and he remembers answers."

"I doubt whether the Roman senate plans to provide an education for its hostage. You must admit that he is a poor substitute for Hannibal."

The centurion nodded in agreement.

Antiochus understood only an occasional word, but he immediately recognized the name of Hannibal and was amused.

"That crafty old viper!" The legate cursed softly

14

and kicked at the pavement. "We'll find him yet and deliver him to Rome."

The prince was ready to wager that Hannibal would never be captured. The aging general from Carthage had made a pact with Antiochus the Great. They had helped each other. The prince expected his father, for whom he was named, to keep his word.

In fact, the younger Antiochus believed that Hannibal would soon be forgotten. After all, Rome was being amply rewarded for its victory over the Seleucids. Although Hannibal had escaped, several of Rome's paramount enemies had been captured and executed. A fortune in gold would be paid by Antiochus's family over the next dozen years; grain was already being shipped to fill Roman stomachs. Furthermore, the prince knew he was in Rome to insure that his father would indeed abide by the treaty signed with Rome at Apamea.

"Do you see how he smirks, centurion?" Titus commented. "Like a pompous ass. No, not an ass—like some playful, unhousebroken puppy." The legate chewed his lower lip as he gazed at Antiochus. "I don't approve of hostages, centurion. Our usual way is the best way. When you take a prisoner, either kill him or make him your slave. Don't create trouble for yourself by making him a hostage."

"He is a nobleman—a prince, sire," said Lucius.

"Indeed. My father, the senator, has counseled me to remember that fact." Titus sighed in exasperation. "We have killed kings, and we have enslaved their sons. Why is this barbarian to become the ward of the senate?"

15

"Perhaps, legate, because his father defeated Egypt."

"And who defeated the prince's father?" Titus asked.

The centurion chuckled in appreciation.

"And Rome, today, will have its circus," Lucius continued. "I wonder how our pompous prince will fare in the triumph?"

"He knows none of the details, sire."

"And that is best for now." Titus allowed himself a fleeting smirk. "Is the animal cage prepared?"

"Indeed, legate."

"Good." Titus smiled briefly but broadly. "Feed our prisoner well. It will be a long day, and he won't be eating again until nightfall."

Antiochus watched the legate acknowledge the centurion's salute, smartly turn, and march away. He wondered when he would get to see this city called the "Eternal." He had not come to see stables and courtyards such as this; there were better stables and courtyards in Antioch. Perhaps now that the legate had gone Lucius would show him the marvelous sights of Rome.

At the time the hostage prince was boarding the twin-decked galley in Ephesus for Rome, a Jewish priest, fifteen hundred miles to the east, performed his ritual of grief.

Mattathias knelt in the ashes and debris of his former home in Jerusalem, conscious of a warmth that remained weeks after the conflagration. He had ripped his outer garment, as the ritual required. Scooping up ashes, he dumped them over his head, rubbing the residue onto his forehead and face.

16

He wept as he prayed:

> "O LORD, God of vengeance;
> God of vengeance, shine forth!"

Mattathias rocked in a chanting rhythm and then threw himself upon the ground. *Vengeance.* That was the petition of his whole being.

> "How long shall the wicked, O LORD,
> How long shall the wicked exult?
> They pour forth words, they speak arrogantly;
> All who do wickedness vaunt themselves
> They crush Thy people, O LORD,
> And afflict Thy heritage.
> They slay the widow and the stranger,
> And murder the orphans.
> And they have said, 'The LORD does not see,
>   nor does the God of Jacob pay heed.' "*

Jerusalem seemed always to be in the way of Persians or Greeks or Egyptians or Syrians. And again it was a place of desolation.

Jerusalem had long ago ceased to be free, but no longer would it be subject to the Ptolemies and to Egypt. No longer would Jewish pilgrims come to worship in the Temple from the great city of Alexandria, where scholars had translated the Hebrew Scriptures into Greek.

Now there would be a new master. Jerusalem had become part of Antioch of Syria. Instead of a Ptol-

---

*Psalm 94:1,3-7.

emy king, there would be a Seleucid monarch. Mattathias sighed as he pondered how these heathen Gentiles fought among themselves.

After Alexander had died—the great emperor who had built Alexandria, whose city and library Mattathias knew he would never see—Alexander's generals split up the empire and their descendants now fought each other.

The king of Antioch was named Antiochus—"Antiochus the Great" it was said he called himself. Construction materials to rebuild the city had been promised, especially timbers for the Temple. They would be needed.

The priest would miss seeing the pilgrims from Alexandria, but new visitors might come, this time from Babylon. Jerusalem was no longer a Judean city; the Jews were a minority in their ancient land and shared King David's capital with Ammonite and Phoenician and Greek. Mattathias believed that more Jews should come to live in the land of the covenant, yet he knew that the Jews themselves were divided, perpetuating the sins of their fathers, following after false gods, forgetting Adonai and the Torah.

Mattathias prayed that another Ezra or a Daniel might arise. Daniel! Now he would be a man for such a time as this, a Hebrew who lived among the heathen, a Hebrew faithful to Adonai. The priest would seek out the scroll of Daniel's prophecy. He would read it to his sons.

Mattathias stood up, brushing off the ashes, fearful that his appearance would displease his wife and would likely frighten his two sons. They had

18

found shelter in a small cave on the road toward Bethlehem—David's city—and the family would remain there until Mattathias could rebuild his house in Jerusalem. As he walked southward from the city, Mattathias thanked God for his two sons and prayed that Adonai would bless him with more sons. Many worthy sons of Israel would be needed in this day of spreading evil.

He began to sing, quietly at first, again remembering the words of the psalm.

> "But the LORD has been my stronghold,
> And my God, the rock of my refuge!"

His chanting became louder. Mattathias hoped the whole world would hear and heed Adonai, the God of Abraham, Isaac, and Jacob.

> "And He has brought back their wickedness
>   upon them,
> And will destroy them in their evil;
> The LORD our God will destroy them."*

The tears were gone, and his gait was strong. He was Mattathias, the son of John, who was the son of Simeon, who was the son of Hasmon. He was a priest of the line of Joarib. He was honored to serve the high priest, Onias. Mattathias quickened his pace, eager now to see his family.

*Psalm 94:22-23.

2

Antiochus ate his breakfast slowly, deliberately, and with enjoyment. The other prisoners from Syria had finished long ago and had left. The prince lingered, and Lucius seemed content to wait and remain silent.

"You have eaten enough for two of my best warriors!" Lucius exclaimed after Antiochus was finished. "Let us be gone."

The courtyard was filled with soldiers and slaves brushing and harnessing animals, dragging carts and chariots, and adding to the clamor with their earthy vulgarities.

"I thought you said traffic was banned in Rome during the daytime," said the prince.

"There will be much traffic today," Lucius replied. "I told you there would be a parade—a *triumph*."

They pushed their way past people and vehicles and animals.

"This is where we stop, Antiochus," Lucius said.

They stood in front of a conveyance that seemed strangely familiar. The prince then remembered that he had seen such vehicles all along the 350 miles of the Appian Way, almost from the marble steps leading to the harbor of Brundisium. The conveyance was a cage on wheels. There had been many of these on the road, transporting animals from Africa to the sports arenas of Rome.

"Climb in!" Lucius commanded.

The prince did not move. He was not sure he had understood, but he was certain now from Lucius's sour breath that the centurion had been drinking. Lucius loved wine and drank it copiously but cautiously. But he always drank at the end of the day, not at its beginning.

"Get inside the cage!" the centurion repeated.

The prince could not believe his ears.

"It's for animals, Lucius! It stinks!" shouted Antiochus.

"It's been washed. Get inside!"

"This is an insult, centurion. I am a prince." Antiochus towered over the shorter Roman soldier.

"Both statements are true, Your Excellency," Lucius said with irony. "The cage was meant for Hannibal, but you are to be his substitute."

"I am not Hannibal. I am a prince of a royal family."

"Think of it as an opportunity, Antiochus!" Lucius laughed. "Few men could take the place of the great Hannibal, the general who almost captured Rome."

"I will not be caged like some wild beast." The prince spoke quietly but firmly, rigid with anger,

22

aware that others were now watching.

Lucius struck the leg of Antiochus with a whip, and the prince winced at the pain.

"You will do as you are told!" Lucius said vehemently, although slurring his words. "I am told what to do. And now I command *you*. It is the Roman way." The centurion grinned with irony. "This is our day of victory, of our *triumph*. It is a holiday for Romans—a day to cheer our armies, to gasp and pant at the sight of captured treasures and slaves. It is a day to jeer and insult the chief captive of them all."

"So that is why I am here?"

"If they cannot have Hannibal, at least they will have a prince."

Lucius held the door of the opened cage. The prince stood his ground.

"Antiochus, you could be marching with the slaves. Or you could be hanging from a cross somewhere." Lucius had softened his voice and tone. "You are neither dead nor a slave because you are a royal hostage." He pointed to the cart. "Get in, lad. It will soon be over."

The prince found it difficult to crawl into the small space. He could not sit fully upright. Neither was there room to stretch out. So he sat with knees upraised and head bowed. Lucius fastened the gate and called his guards to harness the four horses that would pull the wagon.

Outside the barracks and beyond the opened gates, for as far as he was able to see, Antiochus saw chariots and soldiers beginning to bring order out of the chaos of preparation.

He heard shouts and cheers in the distance, so he assumed that the parade had already begun. His father had had such a parade after his victory over Egypt, and it had lasted an entire day and well into the night. The prince wondered if the Romans would display any elephants.

The armed forces of Antioch were famous for their elephants. The elephant was the official symbol of the realm, and the Romans ordered all of Antioch's elephants destroyed after the battle at Magnesia.

"Centurion!" Antiochus shouted. "Do we honor the Scipio brothers today?"

"We honor Quintus Fabius Labeo," Lucius replied. "The praetor of Rome. The Scipios have not yet returned."

The prince did not understand Roman politics, although he was now familiar with the words *res publica*—"public affairs"—from which the Romans created something they called a "republic." One of the Scipios had chased Hannibal across north Africa. The other had defeated Antiochus's father. One was a consul of Rome, the highest office in the land. Why were the military heroes being denied their *triumph* and a magistrate, a praetor, honored in their stead?

Antiochus shook his head and tried to make himself more comfortable. Somehow he had to find a way to retain his dignity. Now that they were moving into the parade, the prince was determined not be be just another animal on display.

He decided that he would think of other things

24

and places. His body was a hostage, but his mind was not.

The prince thought of Antioch. He had not yet seen enough of Rome to make comparisons, but Antioch was no small city. He remembered the Orontes River, the mountains to the east, and the fertile plain leading to the sea on the west. He pictured the new island palace his father had built and, in his mind, again walked through its corridors and rooms. A muscular man of twenty-two, especially a prince, should not weep, certainly not in public. Nevertheless, there was a sadness, a plaintiveness, in remembering his home.

Antiochus was becoming nauseated from the stench of the cage as well as the rocking motion of the cart. He felt he was back on the sea, sailing from Ephesus to Brundisium.

The hostages had marched up the Italian boot in eight days, walking the famous road built by Appius. Antiochus found it difficult to remember that that had occurred only last week. The traffic, bridges, mileposts, and the varied but solid construction of the road itself had merged into a blur. *Building roads is what the Romans do best*, the prince mused in his rocking cage. *They are also good at winning important battles.*

His father should never have challenged Pergamum and Rome. His father should have been content with governing Syria and Egypt and Persia. Now that Judea was also in Syrian hands, Antioch controlled the eastern shores of the Great Sea. It could have been enough. Now everything had changed, and the prince was its symbol, a royal animal paraded in a Roman cage.

"Death to Hannibal!" The cry was picked up by hundreds of voices and reverberated as an echo, heard, perhaps, all the way to the Forum where this humiliation would end.

Antiochus bowed soberly, taunting the crowds. He smiled ruefully, enjoying the joke being played upon these Romans who lived for their bread and circuses. He was not Hannibal! No man on earth could impersonate the Carthaginian.

Antiochus forced his thoughts back to Antioch and that fateful night when he first met Hannibal.

The banquet had followed the parade honoring his father's victory over Egypt.

The banquet was a sumptuous one. Dozens of guests consumed geese, shellfish, pork, and mutton. There had been green vegetables, a squash for which Antioch was well known, barley pilaf, bread, and olive oil. And, of course, there were wine and fruits in profusion.

As the grapes and plums were distributed to end the repast, the king motioned for silence and stood to speak.

"Tonight we celebrate the thirty-first year of my reign," he announced. The silence was broken by wild applause. No king of the Seleucids had governed for so long a time.

"The gods have been generous to us," the king continued. "We have reclaimed almost all of the kingdom that had been lost. Our realm extends to

Parthia and Armenia. Again we claim Judea and find ourselves at the very gates of Egypt. *El Beka*— the great Syrian Basin—belongs again to the Seleucids!" And again there was an ovation.

"What remains for us to accomplish is to look westward, toward Pergamum and Macedonia, northward to Galatia. Only then will the house of the Seleucids again be rich and secure."

Shouts of approval were mixed with the applause, but young Antiochus now remembered that even then he had some premonition that his father was being careless or indiscreet. However, surprises of a more serious nature were to follow.

"We have decided on how we shall proceed," the king announced. "First, our southern border with Egypt must be secured." The older Antiochus paused. "It is our wish that our daughter, Cleopatra, marry Ptolemy Epiphanes."

For a few moments there was absolute silence. Young Antiochus was himself astounded.

Although the Ptolemies were as Greek in origin as the Seleucids—tracing their heritage back to the conquests of Alexander—the kings of Egypt had long been rivals and enemies of Antioch. Only a few years before, the Egyptian general Scopas had been roundly defeated at Panion, the source of the river Jordan. Within recent weeks, Egypt had again been defeated, this time in Gaza. Surely such humiliations would not easily nor soon be forgotten.

"I am pleased to announce that the pharaoh of Egypt has accepted this offer of marriage and has done so eagerly."

As he listened to the cheers and laughter and

27

applause, the prince wondered how such a diplomatic triumph had come about.

"As a gift to my daughter and future son-in-law," the royal voice droned on, "I shall return the taxes from Judea to the coffers of Egypt. The land remains with us. Only the taxes will be returned, and only for a period of ten years. But Cleopatra knows that this is no small dowry!"

There was some murmuring—probably from the *satraps* and the *strategoi*—the governors and the tax collectors of the provinces—who would not relish relinquishing a single coin of tax revenue to a foreign power, unless somehow some of that revenue could find its way into their own purses. Ptolemy Epiphanes would certainly be pleased. Antiochus relished the sound of that name. *Epiphanes.* "God Manifest."

The king pounded the table for attention.

"There will be one other royal marriage."

The prince noticed that his stepmother, Euboia, stared at his father with a hard, almost cruel gaze. He did not know her well since she was young and beautiful and often journeyed with his father.

"My son will marry Laodice!" declared the king. A few heads turned toward him, but Antiochus shook his head.

"I speak of my son and heir, Seleucus!" his father announced.

The guests were standing, voicing their approval.

The idea of his sister marrying his brother did not shock the prince. Such intermarriage was common within royal families, and he agreed it was the best way of insuring the purity of the dynastic line.

28

Besides, there was no novelty to it. Laodice had already been married to one of his brothers, a brother now dead.

That brother had been the first-born, also named "Antiochus" after his father. For a time he was known as a co-ruler with his father. Perhaps he was too well liked by his subjects. Perhaps he was too ambitious. For reasons that were still secret and mysterious, his oldest brother had been murdered. His sister, Laodice, was married and widowed before she had reached her seventeenth year. The prince was given the name of his dead brother and asked no questions.

Laodice, his widowed sister, smiled demurely as she was escorted to stand beside Seleucus.

Antiochus studied the faces of all three of his sisters. Cleopatra, the oldest, would soon marry a mere boy just out of puberty, the present pharaoh of Egypt. Laodice was a year older than Seleucus, seven years older than he. She was as decisive and strong-willed as their father and probably wished she could be heir to the throne. Antiochis was a year younger than himself—quiet and often sad, but always the dutiful daughter. Many people thought they were twins. He wondered if that was why his dead mother wanted them called Antiochus and Antiochis.

He remembered his stepmother, Euboia. She looked as young as any of his sisters, and he thought she hated each of them. Now she stood with the others but did not applaud.

It all seemed to have happened so long ago. Theirs was a strange and complicated family, and the prince wondered how many of them would ever be together in one place again.

As he continued to reminisce, the younger Antiochus recalled that his father waved everyone to silence.

"There is one more announcement tonight," he said. "Perhaps the best is reserved for the last. We have an honored guest. The whole inhabited earth knows about this man. If he is not loved by all, he is feared by all. My friends, welcome Hannibal. The great and famous Hannibal of Carthage!"

Pandemonium erupted. The palace shook from the shouting and stamping of feet. The noise continued uninterrupted for several minutes. The prince had never heard or seen anything to match it in the Grand Hall of the palace.

Hannibal was known by reputation—or legend—to everyone in the room. He was the man who had nearly defeated the Romans. He had camped with his army just outside the gates of Rome itself.

The young prince tried to recall everything he had ever learned about this man who approached the king from the shadows, a distinguished-looking, white-bearded, balding grandfather who talked with the energy of one of his grandsons.

Hannibal's name was a contraction of *Hanni-ba'al*, which meant something like "the grace of Baal." The people of Carthage worshiped at least two deities. One of them, obviously, was the fertility god Baal. The other was Molech, to whom children were sacrificed, the god of fire, a god of the Canaanites to whom altars were built wherever the Phoenicians sailed their ships.

Hannibal belonged to a tribe called the *Poeni* and spoke a language known as *Punic*. Carthage, in north Africa, had been their captial.

Hannibal's father first fought the Romans in Sicily, the first of the Punic wars. Battles then followed in Africa and Spain. Hannibal crossed the Pyrenees and the Alps with his men and famous elephants. He captured the Po River Valley in the northernmost part of *Latium*. He came within three miles of Rome.

Publius Cornelius Scipio finally defeated Hannibal and his troops, winning the name of *Africanus* and the admiration of Rome. Hannibal paid the indemnities but would not surrender his person. Somehow he had eluded the Romans, who now hated him more than any other living man. Somehow Hannibal had escaped into an exile that had brought him to Antioch.

The reason for Hannibal's presence in Antioch became clearer the next day.

Those present at the war council were Demetrianus, chief of the land forces; Polyxenidas, head of the royal navy; Tryphon, the treasurer of the kingdom and father of Heliodorus, a rival of the young prince. Antipater, chief counselor and cousin of the king, was there.

Seleucus and the younger Antiochus were also invited.

The king again made clear that he wanted to fight his enemies in the West.

"The empire once extended itself from Parthia to the Hellespont," he declared. "I will not go to my

31

grave until those places again mark the width of our realm."

"You will have to fight Eumenes of Pergamum," said Seleucus. Antiochus was surprised but pleased that his brother wasted no words and came so quickly to the heart of the matter.

"Pergamum is only one kingdom among many," said the king.

"True enough, sire," said Seleucus. "Between us and the Hellespont and ancient Troy lie the kingdoms of Phrygia, Mysia, Bithynia, Galatia, and Pergamum."

"All of which were once part of the Seleucid kingdom," retorted the king.

"But Pergamum, Father, is the strongest of them all," Selecus persisted, "with strong ties to Rome."

"Hannibal has already told me this," said the king. "Tell them what you told me," he commanded the old general.

"Rome would like an excuse to help its ally. Already it meddles in Macedonia, even to the Hellespont. Rome knocks upon the door of Asia. I have said to your monarch: these Romans will not be content until they surround the Mediterranean Sea."

Members of the council were unconvinced.

"Some senators already call it *Mare Nostrum*," Hannibal continued, speaking the Latin words. "In Greek, that means 'Our Sea.'"

"Is it not clear to all of you why the Romans chased our friend Hannibal across Africa to Spain?" asked the king. "Has Rome given up any of the shores it has captured, anywhere?"

The prince could think of none.

"Then it is not Pergamum you must fight," said Demetrianus, chief of the armies.

"Are you prepared to fight Rome?" asked his admiral.

The elder Antiochus rubbed his chin hesitantly.

"If Hannibal is correct, we shall have to fight Rome sooner or later," he said. "Perhaps it should be sooner."

"There is a chance of winning," Hannibal declared, explaining that Rome was not yet prepared to maintain the long lines of supply that would be needed were it to fight in Asia.

"We would also face problems of supply, Father," said Seleucus.

"Are you already an experienced general such as Hannibal?" The king was livid.

"It would require a large army." Seleucus would not give up.

"Did I not have enough soldiers at Panion and Gaza?"

"But Egypt is not Rome, Father," said the younger Antiochus. He feared his father's wrath, but he also felt the need to support his brother.

"So now both of my sons are military advisers—and neither of you has yet been tested by a single battle!"

"They raise good questions, Your Excellency." Hannibal was smiling and tried to calm the king's temper. "You will need troops, and they must be supplied."

"We can hire all of the soldiers we need. The Babylonians will join us. The Persians will bring their horses. The Cappadocians are loyal to us. The

Gauls in Galatia would welcome a chance to fight Rome."

The king turned to his generals.

"Shall we again wage war?"

"The armies can be secured," said Demetrianus.

"We have a fleet of fifty ships," Polyxenidas declared, "and they are at your orders, sire."

"And you, Tryphon? Can we supply the troops? How strong is the royal treasury?"

"We shall miss the revenue from Judea," said the king's treasurer with a cautious wink.

The king laughed.

"But a daughter requires a dowry, does she not?" he asked. "And the Judeans will pay for this dowry!"

"There is treasure enough for war," Tryphon confirmed, but Antiochus noticed the man worked to conceal the tremor in his hands.

The decision to wage war was made by Antiochus the king on that eventful day. The seven others who were present in the royal chambers agreed with their sovereign. Hannibal would provide counsel and strategic advice. The two princes were eager to do battle.

Things went well for Antioch at first. The troops of Antiochus the Great not only reached the Hellespont but some of them even crossed the Dardanelles into Europe as well. The Syrians marched and fought through the Greek colonies of Heraclea, Iconium, Laodicea, Colossae, Philadelphia, and Sardis. The Aegean coast was occupied except for the diminished enclave of Pergamum. As the Greek colonial cities surrendered, Antiochus found governors who would

34

be loyal to him and to Antioch.

New alliances were made.

Aetolia, in Greece, was weary of feeding the Roman armies and requested help from Antiochus. Another contingent of the Seleucid army crossed the Aegean to Thessaly. In the battle that followed, the son of Publius Cornelius Scipio, the famous Africanus who had defeated Hannibal, was captured.

Naval battles were fought near Attica and the island of Rhodes. The finest sea warriors of the day came from Rhodes as mercenaries of Rome. But Polyxenidas, the admiral of Antiochus's fleet, was himself a native of Rhodes and was as inventive as his enemy. He began the practice of carrying caldrons of hot coals in the prows of his ships. When an enemy vessel was rammed, the coals were dumped, and the rival wooden gallery was soon in flames.

Rome was more involved than it had intended, and Rome's generals sought an opportunity for negotiation. Antiochus the elder made it clear he would speak to no one other than Publius Cornelius Scipio, Africanus, and a meeting was arranged in Thrace, on the European side of the Dardanelles. The Seleucid king, meanwhile, had learned that the Roman general was ill and decided it would be humane to return Scipio's captured son.

The Roman leader was grateful but adamant.

"You must stay out of Europe!" he declared.

"Only if Rome will stay out of Asia," Antiochus replied.

"Would you return Hannibal to us?"

"Hannibal does as he wishes, general," said the

king. "I will not bargain with his life."

It was clear that both antagonists had a warm respect for each other.

"We can strike a bargain without Hannibal," Scipio Africanus declared, "if you will simply leave Thrace and Thessaly."

"Then let us agree!" replied Antiochus the king.

"As equal with equal!" said the Roman, extending his hand.

Antiochus was convinced that he had won a victory. He had no desire to fight in Europe. He had regained his lands in Asia Minor. Rome had agreed, he thought, to remain in Europe. However, the agreement would be short-lived.

Eumenes, king of Pergamum, surrounded by Antiochus, would not surrender but knew he could not survive unless Rome came to his aid. He sent emissaries to Rome, pleading for help as Rome's ally. The senate concurred, sending its supreme leader to command the Roman troops into Asia. Ironically, the consul was Lucius Cornelius Scipio, the younger brother of Africanus.

Thus, one brother was overruled by the other, and the understanding with Antiochus was broken. Rome crossed the Hellespont and invaded Asia.

Antiochus was furious at the treachery but confident of the outcome. He had assembled sixty thousand battle-seasoned soldiers and cavalry. The Pergamenes, with their Roman allies, had less than half that number, according to the Seleucid spies.

Antiochus had much cavalry—both horses and camels, as well as warrior elephants and scythed chariots. His ships were anchored off Trogyllium and Ephesus and were ready to intercept the Roman retreat by sea, which Antiochus fully expected to see. Nothing would deny him his victory.

The prince would never forget the day of accounting.

The converging of forces occurred at the Hermus River, at the foot of Mount Sipylus, near the Greek Magnete colony called Magnesia. The Romans came from Thyatyra, in the north; the Pergamenes, of course, marched from Pergamum in the northwest. The seaports of Ephesus and Patara, in the south, were in Antiochus's hands.

His supply lines seemed secure. His troops were disciplined and competent. Their gold and crimson colors saturated the landscape.

The prince reviewed his father's strategy in his mind.

The elder Antiochus placed ten thousand infantry in the center of his phalanx. Those were divided into ten sections, each separated by two elephants. There were thirty-two ranks of soldiers.

Those particular elephants were selected for their size. They wore frontlets and crests. They carried wooden towers on their backs in which rode four archers and a driver.

To the right of his phalanx, Antiochus placed his Galatian soldiers and cavalry, armed with pikes and spears, armored with breastplates.

On the left he placed his light infantry, archers, and slingers. Here were placed the dromedaries—the camel cavalry—mounted by Arab archers who also wielded six-foot-long swords when necessary.

At the very center of this array, the Seleucid king placed his scythed chariots. These were deadly weapons with sharp knives or scythes attached to both ends of the chariot axles. The blades faced both forward and downward; in a charge they could amputate or impale whatever lay in their way. The king placed much confidence in his newest weaponry.

Antiochus the elder commanded the right flank. His son and heir, Seleucus, today would drive a chariot and, with Antipater, would lead the left. At the center were three trusted commanders: Minnio, Zeuxis, and Philippus, who was master of the elephants. Antiochus the younger was assigned to help the quartermasters with supplies.

Everything appeared to be in order except the weather.

The day began with a mist, which soon turned into a steady penetrating rain. The Seleucids cursed the moisture that affected bow strings and slings and the thongs used to propel javelins. The ground became soggy and muddy. Chariots and animals moved slowly and soon not at all.

King Antiochus was the exception. He led his horsemen through a rocky terrain and easily broke through the Roman lines. He moved so swiftly that he lost contact with his army.

The enemy had scouts on Mount Sipylus, who saw enough of the maneuvering, despite the poor weather, to report accurately. The rain, of course, did not affect the use of sword and spear.

It did affect the use of the supreme weapon, the scythed chariot. King Eumenes of Pergamum perceived how the chariot was, indeed, a two-edged sword and how it could be turned against his adversary. He ordered his troops to attack the horses pulling the chariots. The result was chaos.

The wounded horses could not be controlled. They reared and turned, and the bladed chariots decimated the ranks of the Seleucid armies. The elephants were frightened by the horses and stampeded. The Romans and the Pergamenes waded into the melee with sword and spear and took every advantage of the Syrian collapse.

Perhaps the day would have been saved for Antiochus if his own troops had not been the victims of their own discipline. Unlike the wounded horses, they did not break ranks. They moved forward despite the onslaught of their own battle chariots and the enemy infantry.

It was several hours before King Antiochus learned of the butchery. He had advanced so rapidly and with such success that he felt assured of victory. Too late he realized that he himself was now surrounded.

Antiochus and his two sons survived the slaughter because they had the good sense not to hold back a rout. Retreating to the Taurus mountains, they counted their losses. The king had killed many of the enemy. So had Seleucus. Prince Antiochus felt cheated and angry because he had been behind the lines, helping supply the troops. He had wanted to shed blood himself.

Nearly fifty thousand men had been killed. The Romans captured less than two thousand soldiers and only fifteen elephants. Polyxenidas, the commander of the fleet, moved his ships to Patara, disembarked, and had not been seen since in the Seleucid court. Hannibal, somehow, had escaped.

Antiochus, king of the Seleucids, had been defeated by Eumenes of Pergamum and his ally. The king cursed the gods for the poor weather and the Romans for their treachery. The Scipio brothers could not be trusted. Publius Cornelius had broken his solemn word, despite the return of his wounded son. Lucius Cornelius would soon be named *Asiaticus* for his victory. The only good the king could see was that Hannibal had escaped, and Hannibal was the chief reason for Rome's attack on Asia. The young prince was certain that his father knew more about Hannibal's getaway than he would ever admit.

The Scipio brothers remained in Asia until Antiochus sent representatives to discuss the terms of peace. Antipater, who had also survived the battle, debated the terms of the treaty, which would not be binding until verified and approved by the senate in Rome. King Antiochus signed the treaty in Apamea, a small city in Phrygia, in the center of Asia Minor.

Six months later the two sons faced their father.

"The treaty is signed and approved," said the king. Young Antiochus was shocked at his appearance. The defeat had made his father old and jaundiced.

"I must review the terms of the treaty with you, my sons," he said. "The terms are harsh, but it was not ordained for us to choose the terms. We cannot change them. Neither can we improve upon them." He sighed as he unrolled a scroll. "No matter how

40

hateful and bitter, the terms must be accepted."

Seleucus and young Antiochus remained silent.

"I have agreed to remain on the Syrian side of the Taurus mountains." There was a trace of a tear in the king's eye. "I am never again to turn my face toward Europe." He paused to see if his sons understood. "We are allowed to retain the rest of the kingdom. Isn't that generous of our Roman friends? But, nevertheless, that is no small kingdom and no small responsibility, as both of you know." He stood and motioned his sons to stand with him.

"I charge both of you, here in this royal room today, to promise me that this kingdom will be preserved!"

The two sons embraced their father and swore their commitment. Again they sat.

"The treaty demands that we pay the costs of the war. Rome is to be paid the sum of fifteen thousand talents."

Both princes looked at each other in dismay. Rome had exacted a fortune.*

"I paid five hundred talents six months ago to the Scipio brothers at Sardis. Twenty-five hundred talents were paid at Apamea, when the treaty was signed. The remainder—twelve thousand talents—is to be paid out at the rate of one thousand talents every year for twelve years."

"It is a heavy debt," said Seleucus.

"We will pay it. Our honor demands it. But, more importantly, Rome demands it."

*Well in excess of US $20 million.

"Is there no obligation to Eumenes?" asked the young Antiochus.

"Four hundred talents have been paid—a rather small amount to pay the person who brought about our defeat by calling upon the Romans."

"How will we pay such a large debt?" the young prince asked.

"In the usual manner," replied the king. "We will raise taxes. And we will rob a few temples!"

The king broke into laughter and was joined by his sons. The mood of solemn tragedy was broken for a moment.

"Are there other requirements, Father?" Seleucus questioned.

"Our remaining elephants are to be turned over to the Romans. All of them. And I shall comply." The king smiled and winked. "But the treaty says nothing about securing a new herd of elephants. That I shall also do and without delay."

The younger Antiochus was pleased that his father had not aged to the point of forgetting how to drive a hard bargain nor to deceive an enemy.

"Our fleet of ships is to be destroyed," continued the king. "We may keep ten galleys, but they cannot sail beyond Sarpedonium, except under special circumstances."

"What does that mean?" asked Seleucus.

"These galleys may transport our gold and grain to Rome. Yes, my sons, we are also to provide grain." The king stood, began to pace the floor, then returned to his sons.

"The galleys will also transport our hostages."

42

The brothers stared at their father in silence.

"This is the most difficult and bitter part of the treaty," said the king, standing now behind his son Antiochus.

"First, I am to deliver Hannibal to the Romans."

"But Hannibal has fled," Seleucus said.

"The words of the treaty state that Hannibal is to be delivered 'if he can be found.' " The king paused and placed his hands on the young prince's shoulders. "I will let Rome find its enemy. The old man deserves his freedom, and I hope he keeps it. I will not lift a finger to find Hannibal!"

"Good!" Seleucus declared with a broad smile.

"But I am to deliver hostages, and I cannot renege. There must be twenty hostages. They are to be sent to Rome to insure that the indemnity of gold will be paid as promised and scheduled. The hostages may be exchanged every two years, except for one unlucky person." The king now dug deeply into his son's shoulders. "You are that unlucky person, my son."

Young Antiochus remembered the shudder that moved up and down his spine. He could sometimes feel it still.

"Rome wanted one of my sons—a son who would not be exchanged or freed until the debt is paid in full. I cannot send Seleucus. He is the heir to the throne—and I do not grow younger." The king pulled Antiochus to his feet and hugged him. "I am very sorry, my son."

"I serve the king!" the prince declared. "When are the hostages to leave?"

"Soon, my son. The hostages are to be taken to

43

Ephesus where Gnaeus Manlius, a general from Rome, will take charge."

"When, Father?" the prince persisted.

"Tomorrow, my son. Like you, Rome is young and impatient."

"All honor to Quintus Fabius!"

"Death to Hannibal!"

"Disgrace to Antioch!"

The shouts again captured the prince's attention. The plebeians were having their holiday and were enjoying it to its fullest. Young Antiochus had no idea how long he had ridden in his animal cage or how long it would be until they reached the Forum.

The memories had crowded in upon him. Farewells with father, brother, and servant. The absence of his stepmother. A quick glimpse of his sister, Laodice. He had left Antioch so quickly.

The rocking of the cart again began to feel like the rolling vessel on the Aegean and the Adriatic. The residual stench of the cage began to overwhelm him. The shouting deafened him.

No longer could he center his thoughts upon the past. The present imposed itself with noise and odor and pain. He felt sick. The prince surrendered to the spasms and cramps and heaved up whatever was left of his breakfast.

Unable to move and covered with his vomit, fearful that someone along this *Regium Viarum*—this "Queen of Roads"—would see his shame, young Antiochus buried his head on his folded arms and knees, struggled for air, and sobbed.

The torrent of tears subsided. The young prince

did not know how long he wept, but he felt drained and ashamed that he had so easily yielded to his emotion. Seleucids had to be strong, even cruel, and never weak. He was grateful, now, that the cage partially hid him from view. He vowed never again to give these Romans any opportunity to see his degradation.

But he would no longer deceive himself. The future was bleak. The defeat of his father's kingdom, although not total, was formidable. Rome's demands would impoverish Antioch for years to come, no matter how many temples his father might rob. And he was a hostage in Rome for one purpose only: to make certain that his father paid his debt, to the very last denarius.

He breathed a prayer to Apollo that his father, the king, would find enough temples. Then, realizing what he had asked, he laughed.

"No, Apollo," he murmured, "my father would not dare to rob one of your temples! Have no fear. There are so many other gods and so many other temples. Just help him to find enough of those—and he will probably build a new temple to you!"

It was healthy to laugh again.

He could spend the next dozen years in Rome brooding in melancholy and self-pity. Or he could keep his emotions under control, like a Spartan, wearing whatever mask was necessary, never allowing his captors to know what he really felt or thought. He would advance himself first and be strong. And never again would he shed a tear.

Let the people jeer and curse! He would show them a true prince of his realm.

Prince Antiochus raised his head as high as the cage would allow and once again, now more arrogantly, began to observe the Romans who were his captors.

Suddenly, he grabbed the bars at the side of the cage, began to shake them, and cried out as some wild animal. He saw that he shocked many and frightened a few.

Then he began to laugh, almost as though he were mad. He laughed so loudly and hysterically that for a moment he thought he again might cry.

3

The parade ended at the Forum. The sun had set, and soon it would be dark. Antiochus suddenly felt ravenous. Lucius, the centurion, released the prince from his cage, which had been placed near the Rostrum, the huge podium used by Roman orators.

"I'm hungry!" Antiochus murmured, struggling to his feet. "And stiff as a board."

"You should be, in both regards," Lucius responded. "You haven't eaten since this morning." He wrinkled his nose at the stench. "And you haven't been riding in the consul's *quadriga*. You need a bath. There is a public place nearby, and I have brought fresh clothes. We'll need to hurry."

"Why?" asked the prince.

"You are to dine at a senator's house tonight."

Antiochus exploded.

"The senate insults me by putting me in a cage, and now it will entertain me?" The prince was furious. "Or am I to perform some sort of animal act for the senator?"

"Pass judgment after you have met Publius Popilius Laenas. Things could have been worse for you today, were it not for him." Lucius led the prince through the retreating crowd. "That's the Curia over there," he pointed. "That's where the senate meets. The baths are behind the shops. The Forum was once a marketplace."

"Centurion, I am in no mood for conversation or facts about this city."

"Then be careful where you step."

The prince guffawed in spite of himself.

"I was referring to that stone," said Lucius. They stopped in front of a circular base, securely placed in the pavement.

"That is the *umbilicus urbis*," the centurion continued. "The 'navel of the city.' "

"That is what you call that stone?" asked the prince in amazement. The centurion nodded gravely. Antiochus shook his head, and they continued their walk to the baths in silence.

"You will have a good meal tonight," the centurion declared when they approached the senator's home. "Publius Popilius is known for providing good food and entertainment." Lucius extended his arm to Antiochus's shoulder. "Farewell, young prince."

"You will not accompany me inside?" Antiochus asked, with surprise.

"I have other orders, Antiochus. You are not my ward. You will have to make your own way."

"Will we meet again?"

"That depends upon the gods. It is possible, I suppose."

The door opened.

"Lucius!" the prince cried.

But the centurion had already begun his walk back to the city and did not look back.

A slave escorted the prince to Titus, the legate he had met only yesterday and whom he had seen with Lucius that morning before the parade.

"My presence surprises you, I see," said the legate. The prince again noted that the man rarely smiled. "The senator is my father. Come. He is expecting you."

Antiochus now understood in part why Lucius had not wished to remain. He did not think the legate and the centurion got on well with each other.

The senator was obviously a wealthy and important man. His villa, the well-made furniture, the opulence of statues and paintings, as well as the large number of slaves, all underscored his position and power.

"Welcome to my abode, Prince Antiochus!" said the senator, beaming with a pleasant smile. He was a handsome, older man whose hair was still full but white. He wore a white toga and sandals, symbols of his office. He truly looked to be a patrician.

The prince was introduced to Livia, the senator's elegant-looking wife, and Lucretia, the senator's daughter, as beautiful a creature as he had ever seen. He was warmly greeted by Gaius, the senator's youngest son. Titus remained silent and surly, and quickly disappeared after the meal.

That meal was rich and lengthy, filled with small

49

talk about travel and history. Antiochus felt he was in a dream. It did not seem possible that only a few hours before he had been caged and paraded as a human prize of war. The meal itself nearly made him ill. It was not unlike the banquets he had enjoyed in the palace in Antioch, but it had been many weeks since he had confronted so much food so richly prepared. He was served fish and pheasant, sausage and mutton. There were rice, lentils, and cabbage. There were peaches and cheese and several kinds of wine. The prince ate sparingly, having the good sense to know that his stomach had shrunk and remembering the aftermath of the morning's meal.

After the meal, the senator invited Antiochus to join him privately. He led him into a room he called a *meditatio*, a place for study and thought, as he described it.

"I want us to chat, just the two of us," he said.

The senator spoke in effortless Greek and motioned Antiochus to sit.

"How fortuitous that you already met my older son, Titus!" The senator seemed genuinely pleased. "One day Titus will succeed me as a senator. And I hope you will become friends with my younger son, Gaius. I think both of you are about the same age. How old are you, if I may ask?"

"I am twenty-two, Excellency."

"You must not call me 'Excellency!' That is not good form in Rome. I am merely a citizen of the republic and, by the grace of Jupiter, a senator."

Antiochus smiled in acknowledgement.

"Was it a difficult day for you?" the senator asked.

50

The prince chose not to answer.

"It was not my wish to have you caged like that," continued the senator. "You see, the senate voted to call this particular Day of Triumph 'de rege Antiocho.' I don't suppose you know enough Latin, yet, to know what that means. Today was a *triumph* 'over the king of Antioch.' That is why his prince had to be seen."

Antiochus nodded.

"Besides, the people were expecting to see Hannibal. It had been promised. Hannibal and Hasdrubal, the two brothers, the two Carthaginians, the two enemies of Rome. Hasdrubal is dead, but that is small satisfaction. Hannibal is the man Rome wanted to see, and we must satisfy the Romans, mustn't we?"

The prince did not think an answer was expected.

"But today is now history," the senator continued. "We must think of tomorrow and the days to come. The senate asked me to discuss that future with you."

Antiochus did not know what to make of the senator. He was smiling, and he appeared to be sincere. The senator's polite and pleasant formality did not square with the ridicule and insults the prince had experienced only a few hours before. Perhaps this was the way of Rome: an illogical shifting of moods.

"Are you familiar with the treaty we signed with your father?"

"I am, sir."

"According to the Treaty of Apamea, you are a hostage. You represent a guarantee, perhaps even a

51

kind of ransom, that your father will fulfill his obligations to the republic. You are a hostage and not a prisoner. You have committed no crime, and you will not be jailed. Instead, the senate has decided to place you under simple house arrest. That means you will enjoy some freedom within our city."

"I am grateful to the senate." The prince quickly recognized his good fortune.

"The senate will provide you with a small residence and a servant. This will be done at the senate's expense, of course."

Antiochus had seen much intrigue and duplicity in the palace at Antioch, but it was hard for him to visualize anything underhanded in this gentle patrician sitting before him.

"There is only one condition or restriction," said the senator. "You must remain within the boundaries of the city of Rome. But that is no sentence." He laughed. "Especially for a young prince such as yourself. Rome will be an education for you. It is no idle saying: all roads do lead to Rome, and they bring culture as well as commerce."

"I traveled one of your roads, senator, all the way from Brundisium."

"The Appian is our oldest and best—but there are other roads, and more will be built! These highways will link our allies in a chain of friendship."

The prince had always thought of chains as restrictive, not friendly. But he saw no reason to comment.

Meanwhile, the senator reached for a scroll from a cabinet beside him.

"Three hundred years ago, a treaty was made

between the Romans and the Latin cities." He opened the scroll. "This is a copy of that treaty, and I think you may be interested in these words:

> Let there be peace between the Romans and all the Latin cities so long as heaven and earth are still in the same place. Let them never make war on each other, but help each other with all their forces when attacked, and let each have an equal share of all the spoil and booty won in wars they fight together."

Publius Popilius carefully replaced the scroll in the cabinet.

"That principle of sharing has guided us for three hundred years," he said. "It is the basis of our republic. Perhaps, my young friend, it helps to explain why today you were 'shared' with our people—indeed, why you are in Rome."

"I am part of the spoil of war," said the prince with a half smile.

"Exactly," the senator replied without a smile. "My son Gaius will escort you to your new home. And you and I will speak together often."

As they left, the prince thought he saw Lucretia gazing at him from the shadows of the atrium.

Antiochus was installed in a comfortable house on the *Via Ardeatina*. His servant was an older man, selected from the senator's slaves. His name was Caleb, and he was a Judean.

The prince became good friends with Gaius. It was still the time of *Ludi*—seven days of games and revelry, following yesterday's "triumph"—and Gaius assumed the role of guide to Rome and instructor of its language and customs.

"Explain to me how it is that you name yourselves," asked the prince.

"My full name is Gaius Popilius Laenas," the senator's son replied. "*Gaius* is my *pronomen*, my 'familiar name,' my given name. *Popilius* is the name of my *gens*, of my family. *Laenas* is also a family name, a surname, which we call a *cognomen*. That last name can be changed by the individual. It depends upon one's occupation or appearance."

"Then does 'Laenas' have a special meaning?"

"It could mean 'coat-maker.' Perhaps we were once tailors!"

"Do all last names have special meanings?"

"Usually. Do you know the name *Scipio*?"

Antiochus laughed. "Indeed," he said. "Especially my father. The Scipio brothers defeated us in Asia."

"*Scipio* means 'staff.' Perhaps the generals' ancestors were shepherds."

"What should I call you?" asked the prince.

"Call me Gaius. That is what my friends call me, and you and I are going to be good friends!"

"Would I dare call your father Publius?"

"You might dare, but it would not be proper." Gaius laughed. "Addressing older persons by their first names is thought to show a lack of respect. Call my father *Publius Popilius*. Use both names. Or call him *senator*. I think he prefers that."

"What should I call your sister?"

"Aha, you *did* notice her!" Gaius teased. "She

54

wondered if you had. You made quite an impression."

"What do I call her?"

"We are of the same age. Call her Lucretia."

"Do I require your father's permission to see her?"

"It would be wise. My father is quite rigid and formal. He abides by the traditions, and Romans have great respect for their women."

"You speak with sarcasm, Gaius," Antiochus observed. "Your father seems to me to be a very wise man."

"Did he recite the Treaty of the Romans to you?"

"Yes."

"Expect a lecture on *gravitas* one of these days."

"What does that word mean?"

"Gravitas is the thing of which all patricians in Rome are most proud. It means 'dignity of character.' But you will learn its full meaning from my father. I have heard it many times already. So has my brother Titus. And so will you."

They discussed government and politics—the role of the senate, made up of property owners, who approved treaties. They talked about praetors and quaestors and aediles—governors, administrators, and tax collectors. Antiochus learned that Appius, the man who built the famous road, bore the title of *censor*, which meant he kept the census records and was also responsible for public works such as roads.

"But you have no kings?" asked the prince.

"We are a republic, Antiochus. We elect *consuls*."

"But are not consuls like kings? Have some not become dictators?"

"A consul may become a dictator only with sen-

55

ate approval, but only for a limited period of time. A dictator has full powers for only six months, unless the senate decides otherwise."

"The Greeks have dictators called *tyrannos*."

"Tyrants!" mused Gaius. "And they serve for life."

"A tyrant may be good or bad. He is merely a leader."

"So are our consuls, but we would never give one man power to rule for his entire lifetime. My father has strong convictions about that."

Antiochus was infatuated with systems of government. He knew that his father would not approve of any form of representative government, but the prince thought the Romans had improved upon the Greek experiments with democracy. Antiochus was convinced that one had to learn from one's neighbors; in order to survive, one had to adapt to new ideas and to new ways of carrying out those ideas. And the prince was determined to survive.

Antiochus was pleased with Caleb, his servant. He was an old man—approaching his fiftieth year—but he was quietly efficient. He made the necessary purchases, was a good cook, and kept the house and the prince's clothes spotlessly clean. There was a physical similarity to Benjamin, who had been his personal slave in Antioch.

"Were you born in Judea, Caleb?" asked the prince.

"No, sire. Do you know Judea, Excellency?"

"Judea is part of our kingdom. I have not been there, but my father has traveled through Judea. And Benjamin, my slave in Antioch, came from Judea. From a place called Mizpah, I think. Benjamin told me many things about the Jews. And about Adonai."

"The Lord of Hosts!" Caleb whispered, reverently.

"So you have not forgotten the name of your god."

"No, I have not," Caleb replied softly. "We are part of the *Diaspora*, Majesty."

"The Dispersion. We have heard of it. Your people were scattered by the Persians."

"There are Jews in Rome, sire."

"There are Jews wherever I go." Antiochus chuckled. "But where are you from? You haven't told me."

"I was born on the island of Cyprus. Phoenicians captured my family, and we were taken to Carthage. When Carthage was defeated, I was brought to Rome and sold as a slave. That was many years ago."

"Do the Jews in Rome worship this 'one God,' this Adonai?"

"Yes, Majesty."

"Then you still keep to your own particular ways. That isn't the simplest way to survive, Caleb."

"It is necessary to remain faithful to the Almighty."

"That is what Benjamin said also."

The prince thought about Benjamin that night as he tossed about in his bed. Benjamin was a modest man—a man who insisted upon wearing a loincloth when attending his master in the baths, a man whom the boys taunted and teased about his circumcision. The noble youths regularly exercised in the buff, in the manner of the Greeks in their sports events, but Benjamin seemed embarrassed even to watch.

Antiochus remembered the day of his thirteenth birthday, the day he felt he became a man, the day he defied his schoolmaster and insisted that Benjamin accompany him to the top of Mount Silpius. It was a long hike, and Benjamin had argued with him.

"Your father would not approve!" said the slave. "He would want you to attend the school."

"How will he know?" Antiochus asked with impertinence. His father was still fighting in the south.

"You probably want to go to the Iron Gate," protested the slave. "It is not safe."

"I am not afraid of 'donkey-drowners!'" That was the Chaldean word for the winter floods that could inundate the valley were it not for the iron sluice gate, built in the cleft of rocks in the upper reaches of Mount Silpius. "Besides, Benjamin, it's summer— not winter!" The prince pouted. "Why must you antagonize me, Benjamin, when you are my slave?"

"I am your slave, but I am also your *pedagogos*," Benjamin reminded him. "In Greece, a *pedagogos* is as strict as a father. We do more than escort our charges to and from classes. In the absence of the father, we are permitted to discipline a child!"

Antiochus roared with laughter.

"This is not Greece, Benjamin, and I am not a child."

And so they had climbed to the top of Mount Silpius and sat beside the rusting sluice barrier.

Antiochus knew, now, that he was homesick for his city. He remembered how Antioch had looked that day, nestled below them, with the plain of Amuk beyond it.

The Orontes River glistened in the sun. It was not a lengthy river, but it was powerful. It began in Syria, flowing northward. A few dozen miles below its source, another river, called the Jordan, flowed southward. The Orontes moved northward then curved to the west and south, passing through Antioch, before reaching the Mediterranean Sea. Huge ships fought the dozen miles of current to reach Antioch. Antiochus often visited the wharves and saw ships from Tyre, Patara, Alexandria, and Brundisium. Once he saw a ship from Syracuse, the Greek colony on the island of Sicily.

Antiochus breathed deeply, smelling the aroma of the eucalyptus trees growing below them. He enjoyed the pleasure of identifying different scents. He detected cedar and laurel, although those grew in greater profusion to the south, near Daphne. He smelled the oeanthe herb, from which a medicine was made. He noticed the odor of fermenting grapes and ripening olives drifting up the hillside as well as the pungency of dried, salted fish from the commercial *agora* or marketplace. Lilies were in bloom— the famous lilies of Antioch—from which a perfume called "Syrian Oil" was made and exported everywhere.

He and Benjamin talked about many things that afternoon.

That was where Antiochus first heard about Adonai, maker of heaven and earth, the god of the Hebrews, whose writings were now translated into Greek. He learned about Judea, where Benjamin had been captured.

59

They spoke about his brother Seleucus and what sort of king he might make when his father died.

They gossiped about Heliodorus, the son of Tryphon, the royal treasurer. Heliodorus was a classmate who thirsted to be a prince, and Antiochus did not trust him.

They talked about names.

"I must acquire another name!" the young prince declared. "I must have a name to distinguish me from my father."

"Others have done so," Benjamin allowed. "You could do so as well, I suppose."

"How about *Nicator*?"

"It means 'victor.' You should win a battle first, my noble prince!" Benjamin rarely laughed, but he did so now.

"I could call myself *Gryppus*!" the prince continued, joining in the laughter. The name meant "hooknosed," and there had been a Seleucid king by the name.

Growing serious, the young prince admitted to often dreaming that he was king, knowing that was impossible. And yet his mother had said that of all her sons, Antiochus had the Seleucid *demon*, the desire and the will to command and control the kingdom.

"What do you think of *Soter*?" Antiochus asked.

Benjamin did not answer immediately.

"It depends upon events, majesty," he said. The name meant "Savior," and the Jew devoutly believed that only his God should bear such a name.

"Have you heard the name *Epiphanes*?"

"Was there not an Egyptian king with that name?" Benjamin asked.

"Yes, but I like the sound of it. *Theos Epiphanes!* 'God Manifest!' "

Benjamin tried to disguise his shock.

"It would be so satisfying to be a god, to have supernatural power. You could do anything you wanted. You would always be honored. You could do no wrong. What do you think, Benjamin? Shouldn't that be possible?"

"My faith does not allow me to think so, Majesty."

"But you are only a Jew—an exiled Judean, Benjamin. What you believe doesn't really matter to me, you see." Antiochus was carried away with himself and his vision. "I should like very much to be a god and to have people bow down to me. I would even change the coins of the realm. No more elephants on coins but pictures of our gods and kings!"

Antiochus, still trying to find sleep in his new home in Rome, found it difficult to realize that the scene he had just conjured up had occurred nearly a decade before. The youth he had been was naive and restless, but the prince thought he was prologue to the man he had become.

Gaius and Antiochus often discussed the custom of slavery.

The prince had observed that the Roman economy depended upon its slaves. They provided the essential labor required in homes or on farms. Slaves were the muscles and the machines of the republic. Former slaves, those granted manumissions by their owners, or who had been able to purchase their own freedom, were the tradesmen of Rome. They were the merchants, the blacksmiths, the tinners, and the tailors. Because there were slaves and former slaves to do the work, Antiochus saw that the elite of Rome were free to study, to discuss issues, to legislate and govern, and to play. After the battle at Magnesia, some two thousand soldiers of his father's army had become slaves of Rome.

"Do you ever worry about having so many slaves in Rome?" Antiochus asked Gaius one day as they walked to the Circus.

"The world has always had slaves," said Gaius, avoiding the question. "Who would do the work if we did not have slaves?"

The answer seemed obvious enough to the prince, but he did not reply.

"If people are foolish enough to be captured, they deserve to become slaves," Gaius said with finality.

"What if people have no choice?" Antiochus asked. "Sometimes they are captured against their will, you know." The prince accepted slavery as a necessity of life just as much as Gaius, but he was not fully comfortable with it. He hoped, for example, that his old slave, Benjamin, had been given his freedom.

"If those people are soldiers," said Gaius, "and if the battle goes badly and they see there is possibility of being captured, they should commit suicide. If they are civilians, they should escape, somewhere, before they are attacked. Or they should hire soldiers to protect them or arm themselves and fight.

No one should ever allow himself to be made a prisoner and thus a slave."

Antiochus was not yet convinced.

"What if you are captured by pirates, unexpectedly, in raids that are never anticipated? We both know that there is such commerce in slaves."

"People must also be prepared for that eventuality. Why do you trouble me with this talk about slaves, Antiochus?" Gaius was angry. "People must arm themselves, defend themselves. To be captured is always a sign of weakness. That is why I have no sympathy for slaves."

"What would you do, Gaius, if Rome were attacked?

"Rome will never be attacked."

"Hannibal almost achieved that feat. But suppose Rome were attacked and you were in danger of being captured?"

"I would kill myself first. I would never willingly become a slave."

Antiochus decided not to continue the discussion. He knew that he, too, would not wish to be captured. And yet, as he sighed, he wondered if any person had ever willingly become a slave.

The young men arrived at the Circus, the large arena built by the senate to provide free entertainment for the plebeians, the ordinary, lower-class Romans. These were the people who expected holidays and free entertainment, in addition to doles of food, as a reward for their support of Rome. Thus, the senate provided "bread and circuses."

Patricians were also allowed to attend the specta-

63

cles, of course, and they and their families were provided with reserved seats in the most select area.

The Circus offered exhibitions of horsemanship and human prowess, including fights and swordsmanship. Men fought wild beasts in an attempt to bring the African jungle to Rome. Recently, a new feature had been added which attracted much comment and was responsible for the capacity attendance.

"We arrived none too soon, Antiochus!" Gaius was eager for the amusement to begin.

When a patrician died, it was believed that he required slaves to attend to his needs and wants in the "other world." Thus, it had been customary to kill slaves so an adequate number of servants might accompany the relative who had died.

Someone, one day, thought of a new sporting event that would make use of this patrician funereal need and custom.

Slaves would fight each other, to the death. Some of them would be killed anyway to serve their deceased masters. The plebeians enjoyed swordsmanship. Why not see the *gladius*—the sword—used with real effect and authentic danger? Death could be entertaining. The *bustiarii*, as they were first called, eventually became known as *gladiators*.

Antiochus was curious about the event, not yet having witnessed swordfighting to the death. Gaius, however, was already a veteran spectator.

"What's exciting about it, Antiochus, is that you know that someone—not an animal, but a person! —is going to be killed." The glazed eyes of Gaius did not move from the arena.

The prince was no stranger to sporting events. They were common wherever Greek colonies were established, including his own city of Antioch. He enjoyed wrestling. He, himself, was good in field events, especially throwing the discus and javelin.

But human fight-to-the-death was different. Below him, two slaves were probing and slicing each other with their swords. They were inexperienced fighters, and both were already bleeding profusely.

"Isn't this much more exciting than watching slaves fight wild beasts?" Gaius exclaimed.

Antiochus was about to respond when he realized, with a shock of recognition, that he, too, like Gaius, was hypnotized by the activity in the sand below them. He was in a kind of stupor. He realized that he was enjoying the spectacle of movements of the slaves, the initial parrying of blades, the feinting and thrust of sword. With a taste of salt in his own mouth, the prince felt almost erotic satisfaction at the sight of human blood. This was not play-acting; it was real, and he cheered loudly with the rest of the crowd. The fighting became a frenetic dance of death. Within a few moments someone would indeed be killed before this strange game had ended.

Antiochus now understood why Gaius came every week to see these combats. He knew that he, too, would return.

"Well, it's as I told you!" Gaius laughed as they prepared to leave. "What do you think of it?" He nudged the ribs of the prince.

"Fascinating!" Antiochus exclaimed.

And the prince shook his head in amusement, suddenly remembering that he was using a Latin word that meant "bewitched!"

The first year in Rome passed quickly for Antiochus, and he was a frequent visitor in the home of Publius Popilius.

He had been summoned late in the evening to the villa, and the senator was not smiling.

"The Senate has received an important communication from your homeland, Excellency, which must be shared with you." The prince was pleased but surprised to be called "Excellency." The senator was unusually formal, but he was now the leader of the senate assembly and would be the first to receive official documents of state. He took his position of leadership seriously.

"Your father is dead, my son."

Antiochus had expected to hear such news some day, but he felt unprepared. There was a stab in his chest and a sudden clouding of his eyes.

"My father was no longer a young man," said the prince, after a moment of silence, willing himself to be strong. "He enjoyed a long reign.

"It was the longest reign of any Seleucid king, I am told," said the senator.

"How did he die? And where?"

"He died in Elymais." This was in Elam, near Babylon in the east.

"There is a famous temple there," Antiochus observed. "The temple of Bel."

66

"We are informed that he was attempting to re-trieve certain treasures from the temple."

"You put it politely, senator. My father was with-out doubt robbing the temple and most certainly was doing that to secure gold for Rome."

Publius Popilius started to reply, but decided to remain silent. Spirited young men would speak bit-ter things in their grief, and Antiochus, as he had learned many times already, was a young man of unusual and unpredictable spirit.

"When did my father die?" the prince inquired.

"Ten weeks ago." The senator sighed, regretting the slowness of communication. "Your brother Seleucus is now the king."

"He is the fourth Seleucus of our dynasty to reign." Antiochus was brother to a king. Seleucus the Fourth! "Has he taken any other name?"

"The document mentions the name of Philopater."

"Which is Greek for 'lover of his father.' The name is apt, senator. Seleucus had great respect and love for my father. Perhaps more than I."

"I doubt that, Your Majesty," said the senator. "You have shown love and loyalty for your father. Few sons would so willingly have served him as a hostage."

"My life, sire, has had very few challenges."

"But that will change." The senator drew himself closer to the prince. "I have called you 'Excellency' and 'Majesty' today. You should know me well enough by now to know that I do not use words carelessly. You, sir, are heir apparent to the throne."

"You are misinformed, senator. My brother has a son."

"I am not misinformed, young prince," said the senator sternly. "I know about this son of Seleucus and Laodice. She is your sister, is she not?"

The prince nodded.

"Young sons can die of disease or intrigue. You are an heir, and we intend to protect you if that seems necessary."

Antiochus was unsettled by the senator's tone.

"Someone may consider you to be a threat."

The prince had not pondered that possibility.

"You are useful to us, Antiochus. Your status has not changed, as you must surely realize. The indemnity must be paid in full, and its payment is now the responsibility of your brother. You will remain in Rome so that your brother does not forget."

For a moment Antiochus wondered if his brother cared that much about him to risk a default of payment. The senator must have read his thoughts.

"If Seleucus delays payment or, worse, refuses payment, there are other measures we can take. We are aware of Demetrius, his son." Antiochus winced at the senator's words. "We know his name, and we know how he is cared for in the palace," the senator continued. "And you, my son, are here—perhaps as a king-in-waiting?"

Antiochus now understood. The treachery and plotting of Rome equaled that of Antioch.

"We are sending your brother our greetings and good wishes," said the senator, once again smiling

68

with innocence and good will. "The message will be sent on behalf of the senate and the republic."

Antiochus nodded in appreciation and decided that with his own message of condolences he ought to include a word of warning.

4

In Jerusalem, Mattathias had brought his two oldest sons to the Temple. As was their custom, they often discussed the Sacred Writings at mealtimes, and Mattathias most recently had dwelt long upon the mysteries of Daniel the seer. He wanted John and Simon to see and read from the scroll itself.

He would bring his other three sons at some other time. The boys were frequent visitors to the Temple, but Mattathias surmised that Onias, the high priest, did not greatly appreciate having five young boys running about and being underfoot. Not that the boys were a nuisance. Mattathias took pride in them. They were well-mannered and well-behaved lads. One had to remember that Onias was growing old, was easily angered, and could be overbearing.

The priest was pleased that the Temple was beginning to look like its old self. Mattathias chuckled at the thought. A building was not a person, yet the Temple did have a special meaning and even a personality.

Antiochus the Great had kept his word. After the destruction of the city and the damage to the Temple, he had promised materials and money for the holy place. Of course, the king had died, and it was not yet known what sort of ruler his son Seleucus would be. Nevertheless, workmen were still in evidence, doing the more delicate work of replacing broken or charred decorative carvings of wood and stone. The art, of course, was merely ornamental. The Jewish law did not allow for any imagery of the human form. The people of Adonai were not to live and worship as the heathen.

The priest rejoiced that worship of the Most High had once again resumed in the holy Temple.

Mattathias took John and Simon into the room set aside for reading the ancient scrolls. Only priests and scholars normally came to this room, but Mattathias knew of no specific prohibition for sons of priests of Adonai.

The priest commanded his sons not to move and

to be quiet while he removed the scroll from its place of safekeeping. He knew they would behave.

When he returned, the boys were eager to begin.

"I wish Judah Maccabee were here," said Simon.

"I wish you would call him Judah and nothing else," reprimanded his father. "Maccabee" was a nickname Judah had acquired. It was not his fault that his forehead was smooth and flat. But the children one day began to call him "Hammerhead," or *Maccabee*, and the name had stuck.

"Why should Judah be here?" asked the priest.

"Because Judah likes to pretend he is Daniel in the lions' den," Simon replied. "And we are to read about Daniel."

"There will be another time for Judah to see the scroll," Mattathias said. "Besides, today we read not the stories of Daniel but his prophecies." Those prophecies occupied the priest's mind constantly.

He unrolled the scroll onto the table, as his sons watched in wide-eyed, silent awe. This was a sacred book, and they were properly reverent.

Mattathias found the place he was seeking and began to read.

"In the third year of the reign of Belshazzar the king a vision appeared to me, Daniel, subsequent to the one which appeared to me previously. And I looked in the vision, and it came about while I was looking, that I was in the citadel of Susa, which is in the province of Elam; and I looked in the vision, and I myself was beside the Ulai Canal.

Then I lifted my gaze and looked, and behold, a ram which had two horns was standing in front of the canal. Now the two horns were long, but one was longer than the other, with the longer one coming up last.

I saw the ram butting westward, northward, and southward, and no other beasts could stand before him, nor was there anyone to rescue from his power; but he did as he pleased and magnified himself.

While I was observing, behold, a male goat was coming from the west over the surface of the whole earth without touching the ground; and the goat had a conspicuous horn between his eyes.

And he came up to the ram that had the two horns, which I had seen standing in front of the canal, and rushed at him in his mighty wrath.

And I saw him come beside the ram, and he was enraged at him; and he struck the ram and shattered his two horns, and the ram had no strength to withstand him. So he hurled him to the ground and trampled on him, and there was none to rescue the ram from his power.

Then the male goat magnified himself exceedingly. But as soon as he was mighty, the large horn was broken; and in its place there came up four conspicuous horns toward the four winds of heaven.''*

"Father, what does it mean?" asked John. His brother Simon also looked perplexed.

*Daniel 8:1-8.

"The ram of Persia," said Mattathias. "For two hundred years, ever since Cyrus defeated the Babylonians, the Persian ram magnified himself. The Medes are the small horn of the ram. The he-goat, who overcomes the ram, was Alexander."

"Alexander the Great?" asked Simon. "The conqueror from Macedon?"

"The same."

"Now I do wish Judah were here," said Simon. "Alexander is another of his heroes."

It was true. Judah had an insatiable interest in anything to do with battles and conquests. Mattathias had seen the younger boys playing in the dirt outside their home, with Judah arranging and rearranging his troops of sticks and stones in mock battles.

"Alexander was indeed this male goat who came out of the west," the priest continued. "You remember how swift was his conquest? There was no one who could rescue the ram! But do you also remember how quickly he came to his end? 'As soon as he was mighty,' says Daniel. The large horn is broken and four horns take its place."

"The *Diadochi*!" Simon shouted. "The four generals who took Alexander's place when he died!"

"Not too loudly, my son!" Mattathias cautioned. "But you are correct. Of course. Just as it was prophecied!"

"Now I begin to understand!" said John, his oldest son.

The priest was turning the scroll forward, looking for another passage.

"Did you know that Alexander was once in Jerusalem? That he visited the Temple?" he asked. "That he may have been in this very room?"

The boys were struck silent as they thought of the famous Greek general standing in the room where they now sat.

"It is said that the prophecy I just read to you was read to Alexander. It is said that he understood the meaning and that he bowed his knee to Adonai, to our God, for the wonder of His Word and this place. Alexander never harmed our people or our place of worship."

Mattathias had found the selection for which he had been looking.

"We spoke last night at supper about a prophecy regarding Antiochus the Great, who just died. I have found the portion of Daniel's writing that I wanted to recall. Listen!" commanded the priest.

"Now in those times many will rise up against the king of the South; the violent ones among your people will also lift themselves up in order to fulfill the vision, but they will fall down.

Then the king of the North will come, cast up a siege mound, and capture a well-fortified city; and the forces of the South will not stand their ground, not even their choicest troops, for there will be no strength to make a stand.

But he who comes against him will do as he pleases, and no one will be able to withstand him; he will also stay for a time in the Beautiful Land, with destruction in his hand.

And he will set his face to come with the power of his whole kingdom, bringing with him a proposal of peace which he will put into effect; he will also give him the daughter of women to ruin it. But she will not take a stand for him or be on his side.

Then he will turn his face to the coastlands and capture many. But a commander will put a stop to his scorn against him; moreover, he will repay him for his scorn."

Mattathias looked up from the scroll.
"Now listen very carefully, my sons:

So he will turn his face toward the fortresses of his own land, but he will stumble and fall and be found no more."*

The two boys were deeply moved, although they did not fully comprehend what they had heard.
"Antiochus did wage war with Egypt. He did give his daughter to be queen. He did occupy our land, and he did make war against Pergamum and won the wrath of Rome. A stop was put to his actions, and he has stumbled and has fallen."
"The writing frightens me," said John.
"There is more written here that should cause fear in the hearts of our people," said the priest. "It is foretold here that there will be other kings and other kingdoms and that this holy Temple will again be attacked and the people of Adonai abused."
"But, Father, the Temple has just been repaired!" said Simon.

*Daniel 11:14-19.

"Nevertheless, it is written, my son." Mattathias closed the scroll. "It is written clearly in this holy writing. But we have spent enough time here today. We will read the scroll again. And, next time, I promise you, I will bring Judah as well!"

At that precise and inopportune moment, Onias, the high priest, accompanied by Abijah, another priest, entered the room.

Onias said nothing. He merely stood in the doorway and glared at Mattathias.

Mattathias whispered to his sons to return to their home as quickly as they could and to be respectful to the high priest as they left. Both left immediately, bowing to the high priest. Mattathias could hear their running feet on the stones in the covered corridor.

"Excellency, I wanted my sons to hear the prophecy of Daniel." Mattathias felt that an immediate explanation was essential. "We have discussed the sacred writings at home, but I wanted my sons to see and hear the scroll itself!"

"Abijah, return the scroll to its proper place!" the high priest commanded.

"My sons may be priests one day, sire," Mattathias persisted. "At least one of my five sons will probably serve Adonai as a priest. It is not too early to begin to teach them His Word!"

"It's all right, Mattathias!" declared the high priest. "I haven't complained, have I? As long as the boys don't run about, I'll be patient."

"I merely wanted you to understand."

"Enough of your explanations!" Onias sighed deeply. "We have more important matters to discuss. Follow me."

As Mattathias followed Onias to the high priest's private chambers, he hoped he had not offended the old man. Aside from the problems associated with the growing infirmities and irascibility of Onias there were also constant tensions growing out of the political factions within the Temple itself. Those who followed Onias were conservatives and were called Oniads. Those who followed Simon, the administrator of the Temple, cared less for conserving the old and relished the new. Since Simon was the son of Tobias, followers of this party were called Tobiads.

Mattathias mostly aligned himself with Onias. He certainly had little use for the worldly Tobiads, who were so impressed by everything that was Greek. When Judea was occupied by Egypt, the Tobiads favored Egypt. Now that Antioch ruled Jerusalem, they were loyal to Syria. These Hellenizers, in Mattathias's view, were people who thought first of their own welfare and comfort and only afterward about serving Adonai.

When they had entered the apartment of the high priest, Onias closed the door.

"Will Abijah join us?" asked Mattathias.

"I wish to speak with you alone," Onias replied. "We are in danger. Heliodorus approaches Jerusalem."

"There is no question of this?"

"I have it on the best of authority," said the high priest. "From the governor himself."

Mattathias had heard of this Heliodorus. He was

the royal tax collector but was now also an aide to the king himself. Doubtless he would come as representative of the new king, Seleucus.

"Does he come in peace?" asked Mattathias.

"The tax collector comes to collect taxes."

"But Antiochus the Great promised exemption from taxes."

"And Antiochus the Great is dead." The high priest shook his head. "But this Heliodorus comes to do worse mischief, I fear. I believe he will attempt to rob the Temple."

"Is it to be another *Tisha B'Av*?" Mattathias felt the pain of fear in his chest. *Tisha B'Av* was a date good Jews wanted to forget. The Temple had been devastated twice already, the first time on the ninth day of the month of Av.

"May it please the Holy One of Israel to spare His Temple."

"Perhaps Your Excellency worries without cause."

"Mattathias, not only are the Seleucid kings well known for their competent temple-robbing, but the governor also has warned me about the intentions of this Heliodorus."

It seemed incredible to Mattathias that the Seleucid governor would have such concern for the Temple.

"You wonder about the governor?" asked the high priest. "He is no friend of our Simon, the Temple administrator. And Simon has been to Antioch."

Mattathias was astounded by this news.

"To ingratiate himself with this new king, Simon has turned informer. He has said there is vast treasure in the Temple."

"Why would Simon do this?"

"Because he knows that the new king needs money."

"But why, Excellency?"

"You ask questions like a child, Mattathias! Why do kings wish to be kings or to live as kings?" Mattathias recognized the point being made. "Besides," Onias continued, "Seleucus still has a heavy debt to be paid to Rome. He needs much gold."

"Simon does know about our treasury. He is the administrator."

"But such a small treasury, Mattathias! It consists mostly of the savings of widows and others who trust us to keep their treasure available and safe. The Temple itself has very little. A few golden vessels and candlesticks. A very few precious stones."

"There is the treasure of Hyrcanus," said Mattathias.

"What do you know about that?" asked Onias guardedly.

"There has been talk."

"Merely rumors, Mattathias!"

"It is known, sire, that Hyrcanus took very little with him when he fled to the Ammonites. It is said that a very large treasure was given to the Temple for safekeeping."

"You must not speak of this."

"Simon has never forgiven his kinsman for becoming so rich—for retaining so large a portion of the taxes due Egypt. I think he would tell the new king about that treasure."

"May the Lord preserve us!"

"If Simon cannot secure the wealth for himself, he would gladly allow another to take it."

"You may be right." The high priest placed his

hands in an attitude of prayer. "What would you do, Mattathias? About the treasure, I mean?"

"I would hide it, sire, as quickly as I could!" The priest answered without hesitation. "We are responsible for the widows and orphans. And as for the treasure of Hyrcanus, assuming that it exists," he said with a slight smile, "I would rather it be kept for our people rather than given to the Seleucids. Renegade though he be, Hyrcanus was a Jew, and his treasure should be preserved for the Jews."

"Well spoken!" said the high priest. "I knew I could count on your loyalty, Mattathias."

"What do you wish me to do?"

"Secure the treasure in a safe place, perhaps in one of the underground passageways. It must be done quickly and quietly. It must be done secretly, Mattathias. The less people know, the less they are involved, the better off we shall be."

"I will attend to it, Excellency."

"When this is over—once Heliodorus has come and gone—two things must be done. First, Simon must give an accounting of his actions."

Mattathias nodded his fervent agreement.

"Then I must go to Antioch myself."

"Would that be wise, sire?" asked the priest.

"I must see this new king, this Seleucus, and explain to him how his father promised our Temple his special protection." The high priest placed a hand on Mattathias's shoulder. "I know how much you love the Temple and how zealous you are for the law. I am grateful for your service, Mattathias. I will not forget it."

The younger priest was deeply moved.

"And before anything further is done," Onias continued, "we must offer our prayers. Surely Adonai will not allow the heathen to again desecrate His holy Temple."

5

Prince Antiochus received word about the Temple robbery, and took great delight in telling Gaius about it.

"The Judean version is quite a story," he said as they walked toward the Circus Maximus. "The Jews make it sound as though their God himself intervened to protect their treasure and their Temple. In fact, it sounds very much as though no robbery occurred!"

"What did happen?" Gaius asked.

"Heliodorus arrived with great ceremony and simply demanded the treasure, which he assumed to be considerable," Antiochus said. "I've told you about Heliodorus, haven't I?" Gaius nodded. "He was my classmate, and he always thought he served beneath his ability."

"We have many such public servants in Rome." Gaius laughed.

"There probably was considerable treasure in the Temple, but Heliodorus expected those miserable Jerusalemites to surrender and simply hand over their wealth."

"Which, of course, they wouldn't do."

"I wouldn't! Would you? Anyway, Heliodorus then threatened everyone that he would enter the Temple. The high priest pled with him not to desecrate their holy place."

"Who is this high priest?"

"I do not know his name, but his position is that of the person you call *Pontifex Maximus*."

Gaius was only half-listening to Antiochus. He wanted to get to the circus as quickly as possible. The funeral of Publius Licinius would be celebrated today with more than two hundred and fifty *bustiarii*. Much blood would be shed.

"There is a special room in the Temple called the Holy of Holies. Heliodorus was certain that the treasure was hidden in that room."

"How is it that you know so much about the Jews?" Gaius asked suddenly.

"Because the gods have blessed me—or cursed me, depending upon your viewpoint—with two slaves who were Jews. My slave in Antioch, Benjamin, came from Judea itself. Caleb, the slave given to me by your father, comes from Cyprus. If you give these Jews a raised eyebrow of encouragement, you will soon learn their entire religion!"

Gaius had heard that Jews persisted in many strange practices.

"I am an expert on Judeans," Antiochus declared as they continued their walk. "The sign of being a

86

Jew is to have a piece of your penis cut off."

"A barbarian custom!" Gaius said, with a shudder.

"They call it circumcision. We are the heathen, of course. And we are called, by them, the uncircumcised."

"Absolutely vulgar," Gaius declared.

"But you see, Gaius, no uncircumcised person is allowed to enter the Temple."

"Do they hold an inspection upon entry?" Gaius roared with laughter. Antiochus shared his hilarity and then continued his story.

"They couldn't keep Heliodorus from trying to enter. He had his mind set on seeing that room called the Holy of Holies, and he would not be deterred. It really is a holy place, Gaius. As I heard of it, only the high priest is allowed to enter, and then to enter it only once every year. Lesser priests may not enter."

"Did Heliodorus enter?"

"Eventually. He had to climb over or walk over the high priest and the rest of the Temple priests. They had prostrated themselves in front of the entrance. They again pled with the emissary of my brother—weeping and carrying on as only Judeans can—begging him not to enter. But he did."

"And I hope he found the treasure!"

"He found nothing. The room was empty. Absolutely devoid of anything."

"The treasure was hidden elsewhere."

"Perhaps. But listen to the rest of the story. This place called the Holy of Holies was very dark, although Heliodorus could see that it was empty. Suddenly he saw bright flashes of light. He heard loud, screaming voices. And strangest of all, he thought he saw horses rising up as if to attack him."

"Heliodorus must have been drunk."

"Then why was he content merely to leave, empty-handed?"

"Antiochus, now you are embellishing the story!"

"The person who wrote to me was there! Heliodorus ran out of the Temple with blood on his face and arms. There were deep gashes on his scalp and forehead, and bruises all over his arms and chest."

"Do you believe the story?"

"I do," said the prince. "For a very good reason: I know Heliodorus. He did not remain to find the treasure, even though he knew it was hidden elsewhere. Like most of the royal tax collectors, Heliodorus has been known to have sticky fingers. He desperately wanted that treasure—for himself as well as for my brother—but he didn't stay because he was thoroughly frightened."

"How do you explain what happened? There must be an explanation," said Gaius, now preoccupied with the strange event.

"If Xeniphon were living, I would have wagered that a few of his well-trained horses had appeared. You've seen the posture in heroic statues—where the horse balances on his haunches, forelegs outstretched to flail the enemy! We try to train our horses that way, but some of the secrets must have died with Xeniphon. But a standing, leaping horse in front of you can inspire fear in the best of soldiers. And I think that some kind of beast attacked Heliodorus."

"You've spoiled my day, Antiochus," Gaius protested. "I shall not be able to watch the gladiators because of this riddle you have given me. It had to be a trick."

"I suppose the priests are capable of tricks in Jerusalem as well as in Rome. But there are witnesses to the fact that the high priest and his helpers were lying on the ground in front of the Temple when Heliodorus entered. There may have been other priests or other helpers inside to create the disturbance. But I am not satisfied with that explanation. Where did the lightning come from? These Judeans are not known for their warfare. Whence came the horses and the warriors? Our own army has few horses trained to inflict wounds. And how you do get such huge animals inside a small room which is inside another building?"

"You have created a mystery. What do these Jews say? How do they explain the occurrence?"

"The Jews speak of their god as 'the God of *Hosts*.' They would tell you that the armies—the hosts of heaven—came to protect the Temple of Adonai."

"But, of course, you don't believe this."

"I claim not to believe it. But, Gaius, I swear to you that I do not understand it."

"So your brother did not find the treasure he expected. How will he make payment to Rome?"

"That is the problem of Seleucus," said the prince.

"It is your problem also, Antiochus," said Gaius solemnly. "Your life may depend upon those payments."

Antiochus laughed.

"Is laughter proper respect for your benefactors?" Gaius only appeared to be angry. "You are a hostage, sir. We are on our way, at this very moment, to watch brave men die in an arena. Do you think that the senate would hesitate for a single moment from exacting your life if your brother does not fulfill the demands of the treaty?"

Antiochus looked at his friend in amazement. And then Gaius broke into laughter, doubling up in mirth, pleased at how cleverly and successfully he had duped the prince.

"You should become an actor, Gaius," Antiochus said.

"But I am an actor, Antiochus!" Gaius said as he threw back his head and again laughed at his friend. They were at the entrance of the Circus. "Come. We must take our places," said the Roman. Jerusalem was now forgotten.

Gaius appeared to be intrigued with the preliminary activities, but Antiochus could not focus his attention upon them. A few Greek musicians were playing. He would wait for the main event to begin— when two hundred fifty brave and strong gladiators would fight each other to the death.

The prince reflected upon what his friend had said in jest.

He did not think he would forfeit his life if Seleucus did not pay his debt to Rome. The senator, Gaius's father, had suggested some future role for him. Antiochus knew he was well-liked, that he was popular, that he had the freedom of the city with entry to the best of homes where he had been invited for meals and entertainment. He enjoyed the companionship of beautiful women and wise men. One day, Antiochus had pretended that he himself was a Roman senator; he had worn the white toga and walked throughout the city. Even when apprehended, his little escapade had been thought to be nothing more than a rather clever joke. Antiochus knew that he was not an ordinary prisoner-of-war, that Rome was paying for his upkeep, and that he was still something of a novelty in a city where few princes lived.

And yet he was a hostage.

He could not leave the city, and he had seen how its citizens could be fickle and cruel. Antiochus was learning to emulate his hosts.

There was much about Rome that he liked. But, he had decided long ago to survive, and that meant to carefully accomodate himself to the given moment, never completely revealing everything that he thought or felt. He had to be cautious if he were to survive.

He knew that he had matured. Physically, he was in his prime, and captive Greek sculptors in Rome often convinced him to pose for their work.

Intellectually, he no longer pretended to be Spartan or Stoic. He now followed the teachings of Epicurus. It did not deny the need to think and discuss, to use one's mind; but neither did it deny one's need for pleasure and comfort.

Antiochus knew that he was a more calculating person today than when he had arrived in Rome. He was harder. He thought he was more clever and a much better schemer.

He once again thought of Heliodorus attempting to rob the Temple in Jerusalem.

He knew that his father would have found the

treasure. He was an expert when it came to robbing temples, an example any son could imitate. He would not have been stopped by an exhibition of lightning and hoofbeats.

His brother Seleucus had emerged as a weakling. He had refused to go to Jerusalem himself, and Heliodorus, the conniver he had sent, had botched the job.

Had he himself been there, he knew the outcome would have been different and the treasury in Antioch much richer.

"Antiochus, the fights have begun!" Gaius awakened him from his reverie.

With the sound of swords and the first sight of blood the prince was transfixed. He wondered how it felt to kill someone. It was the one emotion he had not yet experienced. Not even in the battle at Magnesia had he killed anyone. He set aside the thought because the first killing had just occurred, in front of him: real death in real life.

One hundred twenty men were slaughtered that day and thus accompanied their master, Publius Licinius, to the netherworld. It would become an event of much discussion and public record. Antiochus felt drained and overpowered, sweaty and stuffed as though he had overeaten.

The hour was late as Gaius and Antiochus made their way toward their homes. The city was, of course, still very much alive. Because of the laws governing noise during the daytime hours, deliveries had to be made in the late afternoon and after twilight. The streets of Rome were clogged with carts transporting merchandise and making deliveries.

"That is the fourth wine wagon we've seen to-night!" said Gaius. "There must be a drought in Rome." The wagon carried a huge, suspended container made of leather, in the shape of a wineskin. It was said that the contraption allowed the wine to "travel" without damage. Antiochus thought the phrase to be typically Roman.

After the games and the fights in the circus, the two men decided they were hungry after all. They would have supper together and then seek other diversion, involving, it was hoped, a female or two. They chose a public tavern. Both were hungry and thirsty. An afternoon in the open air had that effect.

"You were very quiet this afternoon," said Gaius. "Especially before the main event began."

"What did I miss?" Antiochus asked.

"A few Greek musicians."

"I've heard Greek musicians before."

"Ah, but our good Roman plebeians did not wish to hear music. They wanted to see action. The musicians could not leave until they threw their instruments and themselves at each other."

"That is what I missed?"

"Indeed."

"Then I am glad I retreated into my own thoughts, Gaius."

The wine began to take its effect, and Gaius turned to a recital of family matters that would never have been mentioned had he been sober.

"Did you know that my father is twice as rich today as he was yesterday?" Gaius asked.

Antiochus shook his head.

"My father signed a contract with the censor!"

Antiochus knew that censors did more than maintain census lists. They were builders and sought contractors.

"The work is only repair work in several buildings. Nothing difficult, and enough time to do it. It will pay a goodly sum."

"Your father is a senator, Gaius. I thought such contracts were illegal."

"They are illegal," said Gaius with a laugh. "But always there are ways to circumvent the legalities." He gave Antiochus a wink. "There are means to encourage cooperation. Ask my father, the senator, about it when he discusses *gravitas* with you."

"It isn't any of my business, Gaius."

"We shall be very rich!"

"Good," declared the prince. "You can pay for this meal."

They laughed and slapped each other on their shoulders. Their waiter was standing to one side, and the other guests appeared to be amused by their antics. One learned to be tolerant of patricians and their sons.

"Now to some important decisions!" Gaius said with mock seriousness. He motioned the waiter to pour more wine. "Where should we go from here?"

Antiochus suggested a part of Rome already well-known to both men, where abundant companionship was available for a fee.

"You can squander more of your father's new fortune," said Antiochus. The waiter left to serve another table.

"I have a much better idea," said Gaius with a grin.

"What?"

"Lucretia!"

Antiochus frowned. "Lucretia is your sister," he said.

"And my sister has been begging me to arrange a private meeting with you."

Antiochus was quite aware of Lucretia. She intrigued him each time he had visited the senator's home. She was an exceedingly beautiful woman, but he had kept his distance. He did not dare risk breaking the patronage of the senator or the friendship of his son.

"Antiochus, let me bring her to you tonight."

"That is not possible. I won't have it."

"I know my sister. It is possible."

Antiochus wondered if both of them were so drunk they had lost their reason.

"Just tell me you will see her," Gaius pleaded.

Antiochus finally agreed.

"There is one condition, however," said Gaius.

"You always have conditions, my friend," said the prince.

"I must remain. I must be present."

Antiochus nodded. "If this is a formal visit, your presence would be quite proper."

"You misunderstand," said Gaius. "I must be present, but I will not be seen. I must not be seen!"

Antiochus could not believe his ears.

"Why do you do this, Gaius?"

"Because it gives me pleasure," he smiled. "As an Epicurean, you should be able to understand."

"You are quite serious," Antiochus said. "If you assure me that she is willing," he said finally, "then I accept your condition."

And so it came to pass.

Gaius brought his sister, remained, sequestered behind a curtain, and after a suitable time had passed, presented himself to escort Lucretia to their home.

Before they left, Gaius pulled Antiochus to one side, out of the hearing of his sister.

Antiochus was speechless. He managed to say a quiet "Thank you, friend."

"My pleasure," said Gaius, with no apparent loss for words. "As I told you, it was all for pleasure."

Antiochus sat in the nearest chair to ponder the strange evening, wondering if Gaius was more interested in him as a man. It was an aspect of his friend's personality that was new and might prove useful to the prince in the future.

He thought of Lucretia, who was genuinely happy to see him and had accepted him without questioning. It was obvious that Lucretia was not an inexperienced lover.

Antiochus closed his eyes, smiling at the memory of this evening and in hope of its recurrence.

Suddenly he heard a rustle of drapes and sat upright, his heart pounding. Someone else was in the room.

He stood and walked quickly to a writing table on which he kept a sharpened dirk. He then walked toward the drapes, where he thought he had seen movement. He listened for steps and thought he heard breathing.

Gaius had left with his sister, but he wondered, now, if Gaius had arranged for one of his friends to witness the evening's proceedings. These Romans were constantly looking for new forms of excitement, and nothing would surprise the prince, not after tonight.

The drapes moved once more, and Antiochus now heard footsteps. He gauged his distance, took three quick steps, and plunged the short, straight dagger through the drapes. He heard a cry as he struck something solid. He then twisted the dirk in an upward motion. There was another cry, and he heard a body fall.

He pulled back the drapes.

The body was that of Caleb, his servant, the senator's slave. He had wounded him in the abdomen. He was bleeding profusely, but he was still alive.

"I saw nothing, master," Caleb whispered. "I heard, but I did not see."

"But you did not serve me well by even being in this room, Caleb," Antiochus said. "By being here, you have pronounced sentence upon yourself." He then fell to his knees beside his servant and plunged the dagger a second time. Caleb, the Jew who became a slave in Carthage, was dead.

Antiochus returned with the dirk to the chair where he had been sitting.

His head was spinning, but he thought it was still from the wine and the physical exertions of the evening.

He had killed a man for the first time in his life.

He remembered, suddenly, that earlier on this very day, he had wondered how it would feel to kill another human being.

The blood on his blade was still warm when he touched it, and he found that to be strange. The sight of blood did not sicken him. He had seen blood shed on battlefield and in the Roman arena and had never felt nauseated. But he had wondered how he would feel when he himself shed blood.

It was not difficult to kill. One merely had to have enough strength and do the job quickly. Beyond that, life was very much a transient thing.

He was sorry, to a degree, about Caleb. He was an old man, but he was a slave without a family. He might have to repay the senator for his financial loss. Caleb should not have been in the room. Caleb. He had said his name meant a "faithful dog." It was a pity that he had to be killed.

Antiochus should have been weary after the many events of this day. Instead, he felt more alive and awake than he had in years. He smiled to himself, realizing that he had enjoyed killing Caleb as much as he had enjoyed Lucretia.

6

Publius Popilius Laenas, senator and patrician of
Rome, asked Antiochus to be seated. They were
alone, just the two of them, in the senator's study.

The Seleucid prince felt his age as he settled
himself in the comfortable chair. It was his thirteenth year in Rome as a hostage. He would soon be
thirty-five. No longer was he the trim, muscular
youth sought by Greek sculptors as a model.

"You seem to be melancholy today, Antiochus,"
said the senator, who seemed to be ageless.

"I mourn the loss of my youth," said the prince.

"You have not yet reached middle life. You've
acquired a few lines on your forehead, that's all."

"I've acquired a proper Roman paunch as well,
sire," Antiochus jested. No one would call him fat,
but the prince was sensitive about his growing girth.

"As long as it is proper and dignified it will be
truly Roman," said the senator with a smile. "In all

of your years here in Rome I don't think I have ever lectured you on the subject of *gravitas*."

Antiochus broke into a broad grin.

"What is so amusing?" asked the patrician.

"Your son Gaius gave me fair warning about the lecture many years ago. I wondered if I would ever hear it."

"My son makes light of dignity and character?" Publius Popilius shook his head. "It will be the tragedy of Rome."

"Your son admires you greatly, sir, have no fear."

"I shall not give you that lecture, Antiochus. If you have lived thirteen years in Rome and not seen evidence of the highest and best qualities of our nation, then we have failed, not you." He leaned forward, his body rigid with intensity. "*Gravitas* is not merely being grave or somber. It is a matter of character, of principle, of authority that grows out of respect. I do consider it, still, to be the mark of the true Roman and our civilization."

Antiochus nodded in agreement, and then thought he might risk another jest.

"We seemed to begin by discussing my paunch. I was afraid that *gravitas* might refer to an appearance of being *gravida*!"

"Your Latin is now of such excellence that you make jokes in it." The senator chuckled. "No, you are not pregnant, despite the appearance. You haven't the Roman *constitution* for it!"

Antiochus visibly groaned at the Latin pun.

He knew he was fortunate in his relationship with this family. He continued to see Lucretia frequently, although she was now married. His friendship with

Gaius had grown stronger. Titus even spoke with him from time to time. And the senator had been a counselor, almost a father to him. Not even the killing of his slave Caleb had broken their friendship.

"We must get to business, Antiochus," said the senator. "We can visit another time." The tone of his voice suddenly became more formal. Antiochus became immediately wary and apprehensive.

"Hannibal is dead."

"Was he captured?"

"He was to have been turned over to our forces in Bithynia. But he committed suicide."

"He was a worthy enemy, sire," said the prince.

"We shall never see his like again. I wonder how Rome will manage without having the challenge of pursuing the old scoundrel." The senator scratched his balding head. "Of course, Cato will demand, now, that we teach the Carthaginians a final lesson. Since we didn't capture Hannibal and put him on display, let's burn Carthage to the ground. Even though Carthage is the commercial jewel of the republic!"

Antiochus had heard Cato, and admired his skill as an orator. "You and Cato agree on very little, is it not so?" he asked.

"Cato has four themes. Carthage I have mentioned. He also says that slaves should feel the lash, that women should be kept in their place, and that Hellenism is an infection which must be rooted out." The senator shook his head and hand. "But enough of Roman problems. We must talk about yours."

At last the senator had come to his point. Antiochus

wondered what problems had arisen for him.

"The indemnity payment has not been made. Your brother, Seleucus, has defaulted."

The prince quickly perceived a problem. He was a hostage, still, to insure that payment be made promptly and on schedule.

"Only one payment remained, is that not true?" he asked.

"Correct. Only one payment of one thousand talents. And it fell due three months ago."

"Sir, I have no idea why there has been this delay," the prince protested. "I do not receive many communications from Antioch these days."

"We are aware of that, Antiochus." The prince caught the implication that his private life was observed to a greater degree than he had suspected.

"Your brother has written the senate, however. He avoided the matter of the gold, but he did make a request, which affects you."

Antiochus bit his lip and kept silent.

"He requests that his son, Demetrius, be sent to Rome. In your place."

This was strange news, indeed.

"My brother has two sons. Why should he choose Demetrius?"

"Because one of your nephews is a mere infant, sir!" the senator exclaimed. "Demetrius is now twelve years old. And the senate is willing to make the exchange."

"Exchange?" Antiochus did not immediately comprehend.

"Antiochus, once Demetrius is here you will be

free to return to Antioch!"

The thought of leaving Rome was suddenly over-whelming.

"Why does my brother wish to make the exchange at this time?" he asked.

"He hints at some kind of palace intrigue. Perhaps that is why you have not been hearing from your friends."

Antiochus knew it was possible.

"Your brother thinks Rome would be a safer place for your adolescent nephew. Perhaps he fears Demetrius would be murdered in Antioch."

"I'm sure Seleucus is best able to judge," said the prince. "You say that the senate has approved the exchange?"

"As I said, you will be free to leave as soon as young Demetrius arrives."

Antiochus shook his head slowly.

"It will be difficult for you to leave Rome, won't it?" suggested the senator.

"Thirteen years is a long time, sire."

"Your official status would cease upon the arrival of your nephew. You could remain in Rome, of course, if you abdicated your princely privileges and prerogatives."

"With all due respect, senator, I should not wish to do that."

"I think I can understand," said the senator. "Let me ask you something, Antiochus, out of mere curiosity. You wish now to remain a prince. We once spoke of this many years ago. Would you ever want to be king?"

"There is no possibility of that, senator."

"That is not what I asked. Besides, almost everything in life is possible, given the precise configuration of the stars and the appropriate human constellations."

That was well put, thought the prince.

"Yes, senator," he said, "I will be honest with you. I have often considered being king."

"I will be honest with you, too. I have often thought of you as a possible Seleucid monarch. I've tried to imagine how you would govern. Do you know what I decided? I would much rather have you as a friend than as an enemy."

"We will never be enemies, Publius Popilius!" Antiochus declared.

"Never?" The senator sighed and did not speak for a moment. "Antiochus, *never* is an extravagant word and should be used with great care."

The mood and manner of the Roman patrician had taken a subtle change.

"I will speak plainly to you, young prince," he continued. "You have been a frequent guest, and you have become a friend of this house. You and my children have grown up together. And I have observed you—from a distance to be sure—as I would one of my own sons. So you will forgive me if I now speak as a Roman *paterfamilias*. You know the term?"

Antiochus nodded. The word meant "father of the family" but represented much more. The *paterfamilias* literally had the power of life and death where his immediate family was concerned. A Roman father could kill his son if he felt death were warranted, and not be prosecuted. But so could a Seleucid father, the prince reflected.

"You are a man of many contradictions, Antiochus. You prefer to be thought of as a Greek, but you have adapted well to our Roman ways, perhaps too well."

"What do you mean, sir?" Antiochus asked quietly.

"You would make an excellent Roman politician. You are a person who plans well. In other words, you are a good schemer."

"I'm not sure how to take that, senator."

"Accept it as the evaluation of an old man who will soon leave this world to his sons, who are also schemers, perhaps less competent in that regard than yourself." Publius smiled sadly. "But you are neither Greek or Roman entirely. You are also an Asiatic. There must also be Persian and Syrian blood in your veins. So with all of your love for Greek aesthetics and Roman administration, you are, I think, pulled by a desire for Oriental absolutism. Antiochus, my son," the senator placed his hand on the prince's knee, "you are capable of much mischief. I neither want you as my enemy, nor do I wish this for Rome."

Antiochus felt as though he had been struck with a blow in some gladiatorial combat.

"I have a request of personal privilege, Antiochus," Publius continued. "You will be leaving Rome when your nephew arrives. Under no circumstances is Lucretia to accompany you."

"Sir!" Antiochus protested.

"I may be growing senile," the senator interrupted, "but I am not blind. I have known what has transpired between my daughter and you—as well as my son and you. I have known this for many years. That I said nothing, that I did nothing, is a judgment upon myself. I will not judge others in matters where I myself might also be judged." The senator's jaw had tightened. "I believe you understand my meaning."

Antiochus was stunned. His assumptions about living a life as he wished, thinking he involved only himself and his consenting companions, had evaporated as a morning mist.

"I was speaking about my daughter," said the senator. "I know of her affection for you. I fear that she might do anything you would ask, and that might include her agreement to leave Rome. That must not happen, Antiochus. You must promise me that. I am not powerless, as you well know, and if my daughter were to go with you to Syria, life would not be comfortable for either of you."

The threat was clear and real.

"Lucretia is married," Publius continued. "She does not love her husband—but many wives do not love their husbands here in Rome, and *vice versa*. The marriage was arranged, and its union is politically expedient to me and to my party. She must remain in Rome. Will you allow this?"

Antiochus quickly weighed his choices.

"I accede to your request, senator," he said.

"Good. That is wise. And you will demonstrate more wisdom if you will cease to see my daugther, even before you leave. It will be best for everyone."

7

It was in Athens that Antiochus learned that Seleucus, his brother, had been murdered.

Titus Popilius Laenas brought the news. He still served as the legate, the official messenger of the Roman senate, but he would, himself, soon become a senator.

"We believe Heliodorus was the assassin."

It was strange that he used the Arabic word. *Hashashin*. The smoker of hemp and the user of hashish. It was a word that now also meant murderer.

"Heliodorus was an ambitious man, but have you proof?" asked the prince.

"We have sufficient evidence of his complicity, Your Highness."

That, too, was strange usage, especially for Titus.

"I am not a king, Titus," Antiochus said.

"You are the brother of Seleucus."

"And my brother has a son who is his heir. In

107

fact, my brother has two sons. Either one has precedence over me."

Titus smiled. "Demetrius is still a mere child, and he could not govern, not in his own right. The senate wishes him to remain in Rome as hostage, until the final payment of gold is made."

"That has not yet been done?"

"No."

"What does the senate wish of me?"

"That you return to Antioch," said Titus, "that you assume the throne."

"There is an Antiochus in Antioch already. My other nephew."

"A child of less than two years?" Titus laughed. "Perhaps Heliodorus plans to be regent for your nephew. Is that what you wish?"

"Titus, I have no following in Antioch! I have lived in Rome for fourteen years. I have stayed here in Athens for half a year. No one has kept me informed about the affairs of my country. I have been an exile!"

"The senate urges you to return."

"That requires more explanation."

"It is a matter of security. Rome's security." Antiochus raised his eyebrows. "The senate has no faith whatsoever in Heliodorus," Titus continued.

"Neither do I," said the prince. "I grew up with him, and I think I know him, despite my not seeing him these many years."

"The senate wants the final payment of a thousand talents of gold to be made. It wants stability in Asia. The senate wants a known friend of Rome to govern the kingdom of the Seleucids. Is it clear to you now, Antiochus?"

"Rome's desire is clear. How this is to come about is not!" declared the prince.

"There is a way," said Titus. "Pergamum will help you if you will see Eumenes."

"He was the enemy of my father! Because of him, Rome entered the battle and defeated my father. Because of Eumenes I was a hostage in Rome for fourteen years."

"Would you agree to see him?" asked Titus.

"Why should he see me?" Antiochus countered.

"Because I have just returned from Pergamum and have discussed this entire matter with the king." Titus enjoyed springing this surprise upon the prince.

"The senate must indeed be concerned about our affairs," Antiochus responded with sarcasm.

"Eumenes also fears Heliodorus. He has greater reason than Rome to be certain that the kingdom of Antioch remains on the other side of the Taurus mountains. He assumes that your long residence in Rome must count for some friendship and confidence. We have assured him that it does." Titus suddenly grinned. "Besides, Eumenes is in no position to quarrel with the senate. He owes us a small obligation."

The prince was in a quandry. The early antipathy Titus had shown toward him had long since disappeared. They had become friends. Antiochus believed he could trust this legate of the Roman senate.

"Will you see Eumenes and talk to him?" urged Titus. "The senate has taken the initiative. I have laid the groundwork. At least, give each other the

109

opportunity to discuss the matter?"

"I would like to think about it," said the prince.

"Of course," Titus responded. "But you will need to make a decision soon."

"I will," said Antiochus. "How is your father?"

"He grows older, but he continues to have a sharp tongue. He sends you his greetings."

"And Gaius?"

"He has become a soldier. Publius felt the experience would be good for him." Titus looked at the prince, expecting another question. "You do not ask about Lucretia."

"I was instructed to forget her," said the prince. "It was your father's command."

"Lucretia sends her love to you," said Titus. "Those are her words. She said to tell you that she has not forgotten you, that she thinks of you every day.

Titus said he would remain in Athens until Antiochus made his decision. He said he had to report that decision to the senate.

Antiochus struggled with the dilemma. Apparently, he was being offered a crown, although he would have to work for it in some way. Without an army or a following, it would be difficult. On the other hand, he enjoyed his life of leisure in Athens, where he had no responsibilities or decisions to make regarding affairs of state.

He had lived six months in Athens. Originally, he had intended only to pass through the famous city, on his return to Antioch, after his release from Rome. However, he soon realized that while he had enjoyed Rome, he adored Athens.

He took great pride in the city. He felt he had discovered his roots, that he now knew what it meant to be Greek.

The Greek way of thinking, debating, and planning had made its impact upon the entire world. Greek art, Greek music, and Greek drama expressed to everyone the Greek sense of order and beauty. Civilized people around the Mediterranean knew and discussed Greek philosophy and political science—and they discussed it in Greek, the international language of civilized people. Rome was strong and getting stronger, but Rome was indebted to Greece for its own culture and style. All others were barbarians, outlanders, foreigners.

Antiochus loved Greece and Athens and its spirit of Hellenism. He felt more and more that it was that spirit, that *ethos*, that could truly unify the world. He believed that the *polis*—the Greek understanding of community—could truly progress to *metropolis* and even *cosmopolis*. That was the way toward a world community.

He really did not want to leave. In fact, he had been made a citizen of Athens, with all of the rights and privileges. He could vote. He could even be elected to office. Being a prince opened a few doors, but it was more important to be an Athenian.

From every part of the city one could look up and see the Acropolis, for the Greeks always built their major temples on the highest hills.

The agora had become a favorite place to visit. This was where men learned the latest news or debated philosophies, old and new.

111

There was still so much that Antiochus wanted to do for his adopted city. He had used some of his wealth to strike a few coins, which he distributed to friends and passers-by. He had ordered the coinmaker to use the symbol of the elephant, the symbol of the Seleucids.

He was distressed that the temple to Zeus, begun so many years before by Pisistratus, was not yet finished. Athens had many temples and many deities—and Antiochus had visited all of them, had made sacrifices in all of them—but he vowed that if he ever became a man of wealth, he would himself complete the temple of Zeus. He would do it not only to the glory of the supreme deity of the Greeks but as a gift to the people of this city who had done more than merely tolerate or indulge him.

He gave his answer to Titus the following day.

"First, I have a question," he began. "If I return to Antioch, what will be the status of Demetrius in Rome?"

"What do you have in mind for your nephew?" asked Titus.

"For instance, once the indemnity is paid," Antiochus said, "once that final one thousand talents of gold has been sent to Rome, will you return Demetrius to Antioch?"

"I do not know, Your Highness," Titus replied. "It would be something for the senate to decide. But several possibilities occur to me."

Antiochus asked that Titus elaborate.

"Obviously, you would not wish to have a rival to the throne close by," said Titus. "The senate might

112

agree to keep Demetrius in Rome until you requested his return. Or, the senate might consider arranging for his disappearance."

The prince did not comment but stared steadily at Titus.

"We could not execute the young prince and retain our honor," said the Roman. "But there might be other ways of achieving the same purpose. I can discuss the matter when I return to Rome."

"Do so," Antiochus urged.

"Will you go to Pergamum and see Eumenes?" Titus asked.

"I will," the prince affirmed. "Perhaps it is fate, perhaps it is mere curiosity, but I will go."

Both men clasped arms and hands in the Roman manner.

8

Mattathias was privately studying the scroll when Onias, the high priest, entered the reading room in the Jerusalem Temple.

"Have you no work to do?" Onias asked the priest.

"I have completed my tasks for this day, Excellency," Mattathias declared.

"And so you read."

"I cherish God's Word."

The high priest glanced at the scroll and saw that it was the sacred writing of Daniel.

"You are obsessed with sheep and goats and horns and little horns!" Onias liked his young assistant but thought he should read more widely. He sat down beside his subordinate. "Show me where you are reading."

Mattathias pointed to the place.

Onias glanced at the passage. "At least there is no mention of horns in this part of the writing," he grunted and then began to read. " 'Then he will turn his face to the coastlands and capture many. But a commander will put a stop to his scorn against him; moreover, he will repay him for his scorn.

" 'So he will turn his face toward the fortresses of his own land, but he will stumble and fall and be found no more.' "

"This speaks of the Seleucids and their wars with Egypt and with Rome," said Onias.

"That is my view also, Excellency," said Mattathias. "But what think you of this next passage? 'Then in his place one will arise who will send an oppressor through the Jewel of his kingdom; yet within a few days he will be shattered, though neither in anger nor in battle.' "*

"It is a strange word, my son," said the high priest. "If the preceding passage refers to Antiochus the Great and his defeat by Rome, then this passage must speak of his son Seleucus."

"He did send an oppressor, a tax collector, an exactor!"

"You speak of Heliodorus who came to rob the Temple."

"Indeed."

"You may be correct. But the passage suggests, then, that this new king will die. Seleucus Philopater lives."

"Death will come to all men," said Mattathias.

"But I trust it has not yet visited Seleucus," said Onias, "for I go to see him."

"Must you go to Antioch?" Mattathias exclaimed.

*Daniel 11:18-20.

115

"Perhaps I have delayed my journey too long already."

"Could not someone else go in your place, Excellency?"

"I must go myself, Mattathias," the high priest continued. "I must see this Seleucid king and explain to him why I could not allow this Heliodorus to enter the Temple. He may not know that his father, Antiochus the Great, decreed that our sanctuary would never be defiled by the Syrians."

"Will you explain the beating this Heliororus experienced?"

"I will try to do so. This worries me greatly, my son. I do not know what this Heliodorus may have reported to the king, and I am sure that Seleucus is angry that his tax collector did not return with any treasure. I must talk with the king. It is for the peace of the Temple."

"And who will govern the Temple in your absence, Excellency? Mattathias asked.

"Simon will manage the market and only the market. I have made that clear to him. As for the Temple, my brother, Yeshua, will be in charge. You will assist him, of course."

Mattathias nodded. "A safe journey, Excellency," he said.

"If I require anything in Antioch, Mattathias, I will send for you. Is that understood?"

Mattathias beamed at the prospect of being of special service to the high priest.

"Be prepared to travel, my son."

The high priest stood to leave.

"The blessing of the Almighty remain with you,"
he said.

Mattathias remained to read and to think.

He had misgivings about both Simon and Yeshua.
Simon, the Tobiad, had already caused trouble in
Antioch. Yeshua, or Joshua, was of course a member
of the Zadukim. He was the brother of Onias,
but everyone in the Temple hierarchy knew that
Joshua constantly sought greater authority.

The scroll was still open, and the eyes of Mattathias
were drawn to the passage he and Onias had just
read. The very next sentence shocked him into rigid
attention.

"And in his place a despicable person will
arise, on whom the honor of kingship has not
been conferred, but he will come in a time of
tranquility and seize the kingdom by intrigue."*

Every muscle of his huge frame was taut. If, indeed,
this prophecy was concerned with the present
kingdom and age, if Seleucus was mentioned and
would die, his successor, according to Daniel, would
bring greater harm to Judea.

He wondered who this despicable person might
be.

It was a day for godly men to plead for mercy. He
wanted to be such a godly man. A *chasid*. Suddenly
the priest was overcome by emotion and prostrated
himself upon the floor, pouring out his heart in
praise and prayer.

*Daniel 20:21.

117

"The LORD is my light and my salvation;
Whom shall I fear?
The LORD is the defense of my life;
Whom shall I dread?
When evildoers came upon me to devour my
     flesh,
My adversaries and my enemies, they stumbled
     and fell.
Though a host encamp against me,
My heart will not fear;
Though war arise against me,
In spite of this I shall be confident.

"One thing I have asked from the LORD, that I
     shall seek:
That I may dwell in the house of the LORD all
     the days of my life,
To behold the beauty of the LORD,
And to meditate in His temple.
For in the day of trouble He will conceal me in
His tabernacle;
In the secret place of His tent He will hide me;
He will lift me up on a rock!"*

Tzur olomim!
The Rock of Ages would be his security and his
strength!
Mattathias arose, clasped the scroll to his bosom,
and kissed it before returning it to its sacred place.

*Psalm 27: 1-5.

118

9

Antiochus thought that Pergamum was the most distinctively beautiful city he had ever seen. Of course, it was not as large as Rome or even Athens. But although he had great affection for both of those cities—as well as for his native Antioch—Pergamum in the fertile Caicus Valley was a jewel in its own right.

His voyage across the Aegean had been good and swift.

He had seen the island of Lesbos at dawn. It was not yet high noon when he reached Pergamum, first seeing the crescent ridge above the city, dominated by its temple to Zeus.

He was met by Attalus, the brother of the king. Pergamum was the capital of the Attalids, who with the Seleucids and the Ptolemies of Egypt had carved up the Asian kingdom of Alexander.

Pergamum was not laid out in the gridiron pattern of Greek cities. It literally climbed the hill, with simple, less expensive homes at its base and more affluent homes and public buildings built in stages and steps as one progressed up the hillside. On its crest were several temples and massive buildings, one of which Antiochus surmised would be the palace. The streets seemed to wander at will.

It felt strange to be among the Pergamenes, the traditional enemies of the Seleucids. Antiochus was not fearful but merely uncomfortable. He had come because Rome had requested it. He felt that gave him some protection. Besides, he had no kingdom to offer or to lose. Visiting one's enemies should, at least, be interesting, and he would try to make the most of it.

Eumenes greeted Antiochus at the palace. He was considerably older than the prince—perhaps in his fifties—but looked tanned and healthy and eager for their meeting.

He escorted Antiochus along the balustrade lining the porch of the palace. The view of the river and valley was magnificent and breathtaking. The sea could be seen on the distant horizon.

"That is our museum, Antiochus," said Eumenes, pointing to the building just below the palace. "It is truly a temple to the muses, and it is there that you will find our famous library. We think that it rivals the one in Alexandria. Pergamenes—the citizens of Pergamum—are lovers of books. And they are books, not scrolls. You must see them before you leave."

120

"I saw books while in Rome, Your Highness," said Antiochus. "They were small volumes, intended for travelers, to be placed easily in pocket or bag."

"Our city gets its name from the word *parchment*, you see. Our books are copied on this material, cut, and then bound."

Antiochus was interested in the tour and the information, but wondered when Eumenes would introduce the topic for his coming.

"Below us, to your left, are the sports arenas. We have three gymnasiums."

Antiochus doubted whether Antioch had added to the single gymnasion it had had when he left.

"You must have many athletes," Antiochus said, to continue the conversation.

"I give you fair warning. Pergamum will gladly accept the challenge to any game you care to name or play!" Eumenes grabbed the prince's arm. "But before we return to the palace and the discussion of our business together, I must show you our temple."

Actually, there were several temples. Antiochus identified two of the smaller ones, dedicated to the honor of Athena and Hermes. However, the structure that caught everyone's eye, even from a distance, was the altar to *Zeus Soter*—Zeus the Savior.

Its sheer size strained credulity. It was built against the hill in the shape of a U. Its Ionic columns supported a roof in the style of the Parthenon in Athens.

An esplanade of steps led to the altar. "How many steps are there, Your Highness?" Antiochus asked.

"Sixty-five," Eumenes answered.

121

Bigger-than-life-size statues adorned the roof. However, the chief wonder of the edifice was a carving that surrounded the U-shaped base. It was seven feet high and extended for four hundred feet.

"It depicts the battle of the gods with the giants," said Eumenes. "There is a similar work in Athens."

Antiochus was truly impressed. "I have seen the carving in Athens," he said. "This one is far superior. It's magnificent!"

The king was pleased and led the prince to one of the corners. "You'll notice that the marble is lighter here. This is a recent addition. Look closely. You may notice something you recognize."

Antiochus was astounded. The face of one of the "giants" was that of his father.

"How is this possible?" he asked.

"It is the way I chose to remember the battle at Magnesia," said Eumenes.

Both men remained silent. Antiochus fought to swallow his rising anger at this affront to the house of the Seleucids.

"This may be the place to discuss the reason for your coming," said Eumenes.

"I would prefer some other spot, Your Grace," said the prince coldly. "I do not need to be reminded that we are former enemies."

"Then let us sit on yonder bench, beneath the trees," said Eumenes, appearing not to have noticed that he had offended his guest. "We are alone. Not even my brother will be present. We can speak openly and freely, man to man." When they had seated themselves in the shade, the king continued. "We should begin by forgetting the past."

"How can I when it is carved in stone?" the prince remonstrated.

"We should never have fought, your father and I. And perhaps I should never have ordered the carving. All of this took place fifteen years ago, Antiochus. Today we face new problems, and we can be helpful to each other."

"You are aware that the Roman senate wishes me to return to Antioch," said the prince, determined to control his emotions.

"And I concur," said Eumenes. "You must return to claim the throne."

Antiochus gazed at the far horizon.

"I don't have an army," he said finally.

"We will provide you with one. And with money."

Antiochus believed there was sufficient wealth in Pergamum to finance the venture, but he could not yet understand why a former and a formidable enemy would be willing to do this.

"Why do you choose to be my sponsor?" he inquired.

"That is a reasonable question," Eumenes replied. "I want my eastern borders to be secure."

"My brother, Seleucus, had no designs upon Pergamum. I know that he adhered to every provision of the treaty."

"Except for payment of gold to Rome."

"I am sure that Seleucus had his reasons, but it really does not concern Pergamum, Your Grace," Antiochus said quietly, controlling his rage.

"You make your point well," Eumenes said with a smile. "Titus Popilius told me you were a good diplomat. Very well. My controversy was not with

Seleucus. He did keep the treaty, and he is now dead. My concern is Heliodorus. I do not trust him. He is ambitious, and he will want to test his new power. That makes him very dangerous."

"You say you don't trust Heliodorus," said the prince. "Do you trust me?"

"Up to a point," Eumenes replied bluntly. Antiochus burst into laughter. He would remain alert but was no longer angry.

"Perhaps we do understand each other," said the prince.

"Of course we do," Eumenes agreed. "Royal blood will tell. Heliodorus is merely a common adventurer. I know that you and I can strike a bargain."

"I am here to listen, Eumenes."

"From what I have heard of you, you enjoy the good life. You don't want anyone to upset it."

"I'll concede—for purposes of debate!" The prince smiled broadly.

"I also enjoy the good life. I am older than you, and I am weary of warfare. I have fought two wars since Magnesia."

"Perhaps you did not wisely choose your ally," Antiochus teased. "Let us be honest with each other, Eumenes. You and I are speaking together here, today, because we were instructed to do so by Rome."

Eumenes did not immediately reply.

"Neither of us wishes to offend the Roman senate," Antiochus continued.

"Very well," Eumenes agreed. "Rome brings us together, but we can build an understanding between us that goes beyond the wishes of Rome. We both

124

want peace. I am content with my borders. I think you can be content with yours, especially since yours are so much larger than mine, extending nearly to distant India!"

"I am prepared to abide by the provisions of the treaty of Apamea, as were my father and my brother."

"You have lived in Rome long enough to appreciate its politics and its objectives. You know that Rome is our ally," Eumenes smiled, "for better or for worse. You will not risk offending Rome. That is why I can trust you when I have not one whit of confidence in Heliodorus."

"Then I think we are close to an understanding," said the prince.

"I think the idea of being a king grows within you," declared Eumenes. "As recently as a week ago, you had little hope of ever becoming a king. Today you have the chance, and I am able to offer it to you. Despite all of the past battles and animosities, I believe you will remember the fact that it was Pergamum that gave you your crown."

"I will remember," Antiochus said calmly.

"Then we have an arrangement?" asked the king with equal calm.

"We do!" declared the prince.

They laughed and embraced.

"We must share the good news with my brother Attalus," said the king as they reentered the palace.

As they walked, Antiochus noticed a statue in an adjacent room he had not noticed before.

He pointed to it. "May I have a look?" he asked.

Eumenes led him into the anteroom. "That is one of our great treasures," he said. "The sculptor is

125

unknown, but the statue was carved more than a hundred years ago. The work is known as 'The Dying Gaul.'"

Antiochus was overwhelmed. The statue was that of a fallen warrior—a Gaul or Celt, Eumenes had said—wounded, holding himself up with his right hand. The prince was a lover of fine art and had an eye for detail. The face was long and angular, truly a Gaul, perhaps from Galatia. The intricate carving of mustache, hair, and a finely-tooled band around the soldier's neck was masterful. Antiochus then saw the wound, carved in marble, but so real and painful that he expected to feel warm red blood if he dared to touch the spot. This Gaul was truly dying. One could read the pain in his face and flexed muscles. The prince knew he was seeing the reality, albeit in stone, of approaching death.

"It is a great treasure," he said.

"May it remain in your memory," said Eumenes. "We possess the statue, but we were the ones who defeated the Gauls. Let us be friends and allies, never again enemies!"

Again they embraced.

"Titus Popilius asked me to send him word about your decision regarding Demetrius," said the king as they resumed their walk toward the dining room. Antiochus looked surprised. "I speak of your nephew in Rome. Shall he continue to live in exile? Or shall he die?"

"Let him live," said Antiochus. "At least for the present."

He hoped he would not regret his decision.

10

Mattathias the priest was once again reading the
sacred book of Daniel. He had found an older copy,
in which the seer had written Adonai's message in
both Hebrew and Chaldean. The priest was bothered by more than curiosity since he now knew the
book quite well. He felt that somehow he had missed
an important fact or an allusion or a statement, and
so, again, he returned to the latter part of the prophecy. Daniel had resumed his writing in Hebrew.

And in his place a despicable person will
arise, on whom the honor of kingship has not
been conferred, but he will come in a time of
tranquility and seize the kingdom by intrigue.
And the overflowing forces will be flooded
away before him and shattered, and also the
prince of the covenant.
And after an alliance is made with him he

will practice deception, and he will go up and gain power with a small force of people.

In a time of tranquility he will enter the richest parts of the realm, and he will accomplish what his fathers never did, nor his ancestors; he will distribute plunder, booty, and possessions among them, and he will devise his schemes against strongholds, but only for a time.

And he will stir up his strength and courage against the king of the South with a large army; so the king of the South will mobilize an extremely large and mighty army for war; but he will not stand, for schemes will be devised agianst him.

And those who eat his choice food will destroy him, and his army will overflow, but many will fall down slain.

As for both kings, their hearts will be intent on evil, and they will speak lies to each other at the same table; but it will not succeed, for the end is still to come at the appointed time.

Then he shall return to his land with much plunder; but his heart will be set against the holy covenant, and he will take action and then return to his own land.*

There was a light knock on the door, which was ajar, and Abijah, another of the Temple priests, entered.

"Peace be with you, Mattathias," he said in greeting.

*Daniel 11:21-28.

"*Shalom*, Abijah."

"I know that you did not wish to be interrupted," said Abijah, "but a merchant stopped and left a sealed message addressed to you. It was given to him in Antioch. I thought you should see it at once."

"You did well, Abijah. Thank you," said Mattathias.

The message was probably from Onias, the high priest. He had been in Antioch, for more than a month. As everyone in Jerusalem now knew, Onias did not arrive in time to see Seleucus. The king was dead, and it was said that he had been poisoned by his prime minister, Heliodorus. A new king was to be crowned, the brother of Seleucus. Very little was known about this Antiochus, who had lived most of his life as a hostage in Rome and who was returning, it was rumored, with the knowledge and support of this new power of the West. Perhaps Onias was remaining in Antioch in order to have an audience with the new king.

Mattathias broke the seal carefully and unrolled the scroll.

The message was indeed from Onias, and it was brief.

"Come quickly. Yeshua is also here."

He handed the message to Abijah.

"That is all our high priest says?" asked Abijah. "Is this Yeshua our high priest's brother, Joshua?"

"It must be he. I have not seen Joshua for several days."

"I had heard he was ill."

"That was the word I also received. Apparently he also journeyed to Antioch."

"Why, Mattathias? Why would he do such a thing?

129

He was left here to take the place of his brother, the high priest!"

"I do not know the reason, Abijah. Perhaps I will learn that reason when I see Onias. He commands me to join him."

Reluctantly, Mattathias rolled up the scroll. Although he knew the words that followed, he had wanted again to read them, to ponder them. There was prophecy of still another war with the king of the South and of the rage of this new king against the holy covenant. There was even a prediction of something Daniel recorded as "the abomination of desolation."

The priest closed his eyes from weariness and fear. The sacred writing of Daniel spoke so clearly about Antiochus the Great and Seleucus. Did he also speak of this new king, this new Antiochus?

He opened his eyes so that he might look toward the heavens and make his petition to the Almighty.

Mattathias found Onias, the high priest, in the house of Eleazar, the aged teacher and rabbi of the Jewish community in Antioch.

The city was in celebration, welcoming its new monarch, and Onias had seen the new king from afar.

"Prince Antiochus rode in a chariot, preceded by his troops from Pergamum. Although he wore a crown, he was dressed as a Roman," the high priest reported. "And he threw coins to the people—coins bearing the symbol of the Seleucid elephant."

"How did he appear to you—this new king?" Mattathias inquired.

"I saw him only from a distance, my son. He laughs and jests and throws out his arms in greeting. He was loudly cheered." Onias was somber. "But somehow, Mattathias, I think there is something sinister about the man. I will stay on to see him. I must see him—and you must remain until I do!"

"Your message said that Joshua was here," Mattathias reminded his superior.

"My brother is here, but we have not spoken. I understand that he also wishes to see this new Antiochus." The high priest was extremely weary, it seemed to Mattathias. "Many strange things are happening, my son. That is why I wanted someone I could trust to attend me. I am suspicious of my own brother, may Adonai forgive me. It may be necessary to carry word back to Jerusalem. I may have to remain here in Antioch for a time. Do you understand, Mattathias? I need you, my son."

The young priest nodded in agreement.

"Was there fighting—any bloodshed—with the coming of this new king?" he asked.

"None whatsoever," Onias declared. "That is something strange as well. The former king, Seleucus, was poisoned by Heliodorus, it is said. And Heliodorus has fled. The people of Antioch did not support him, and, thus, there was no battle. The people appear to be satisfied with this new Antiochus. He has come in a 'time of tranquility.'"

"Your Excellency has used a phrase from the prophetic writing!" Mattathias whispered in wonder.

"The very words of Daniel, my son!" Onias smiled wanly. "Perhaps your obsession has now become mine."

11

Now that he was away from the crowds, Antiochus looked as weary as he felt. He did not try to hide his fatigue as he climbed the stairs to the second level of the palace.

He had marched steadily for ten days, and the triumphal parade had been arranged immediately upon his arrival at Antioch's gates. He had had less than four hours' sleep.

He was grateful that there had been no battle at any point along his journey from Pergamum. It was not that he was fearful of fighting; he knew that he was not a coward. He was grateful because he had never tested his troops. They were few in number, and they were borrowed. They were mercenaries, and Antiochus was certain that their loyalty would be short-lived, lasting as long as food and money came their way. In time, he would build and train his own armies and be sure of their loyalty. But that would lie in the future. For the present, he was numb with exhaustion.

He had barely noticed the city in which he had been born, which he had not seen for a decade and a half. He had a faint recollection of seeing the two statues as he entered the city—one of the sacred eagle that had first discovered the site for the royal capital, and the other of Amphion, the priest of mystery who had also played a part in the founding of Antioch. There would be time another day to retrace his steps, to renew his memories, to see how his city had changed since his youth.

His city. He smiled at the thought as he trudged down the corridor toward his private chamber. Antioch was indeed his capital. He was the king. He would have to get accustomed to that idea, but that would not be difficult.

A door opened as he continued to walk. His sister, Laodice, gestured for him to join her.

"I was hoping you would stop by," she said.

"It has been a long day, my sister," he replied. "I am weary to the very marrow of my bones, and I would truly like to rest."

"There is much that we must discuss."

"But surely it can wait until tomorrow?"

"Why do you avoid me, Antiochus!" Laodice bristled.

"My dear sister, I only returned to this city late yesterday and have been on display all day!"

"I saw the parade, and I saw you," she said. "Come inside and sit. We can talk for a while. If you have time for your rituals and your formalities, you can grant me some time as well."

Antiochus shrugged his shoulders and entered the queen's bedroom. Although Laodice was older than he, she had retained a stately figure. Her height gave her a severe, regal appearance. And yet, as Antiochus saw his own reflection on the mirrored wall and then again observed his sister, he admitted that neither of them would now qualify as raving beauties. Both of them had aged and were showing it.

"What is it that cannot wait until tomorrow?" he asked.

"First, there is the matter of Heliodorus."

"What about Heliodorus?" Antiochus stifled a yawn.

"He must be captured and made to pay for his crime!"

"I will issue orders tomorrow, Laodice."

"You could have issued them today, my brother!" she shouted. "Heliodorus has escaped. It will be difficult to apprehend him."

"He escaped more than a week ago, my lady. My orders will make little difference."

"You do not wish to apprehend him."

"Laodice, if Heliodorus returns to Antioch, he knows he is sentenced to death. If he can be found without waging a major war, we will find him and make him pay for his crime against my brother. But I will not ape the Romans as they pursued Hannibal around the Mediterranean! Heliodorus is simply not that important to me."

Antiochus began to rise.

"Stay!" commanded the queen. "You too easily forget my husband and his heirs." Laodice was furious, and the blood had drained from her face.

Antiochus kept his seat, leaned forward, and glared at his sister.

"You speak of Seleucus, your former husband," he said with equal heat. "I am now your husband."

Laodice bit her lip before responding.

"Have you already made the decree?" she asked, pleading with her eyes. "Must it be so, Antiochus?"

"It is expected, my sister. It is the law."

"You could take another wife."

"I do not choose to do so," Antiochus said slowly.

"Then I shall end my days by being sister and wife to three of my brothers," she said with a catch in her voice.

"Be grateful then that I am the youngest and there will be no other brother to marry."

"I have had enough of marriage, Antiochus!" Laodice now began to sob, quietly but steadily. Antiochus made no move to comfort her. "Marriage for me began so long ago."

"That was no marriage, my sister. My namesake was a mere boy, and you were a little girl. It was a charade, a game. You were a tiny girl married to a boy prince."

"He died before we could have children."

"He was murdered, Laodice," said the new king. "The first Antiochus was killed by our father."

"You should not speak of our father that way!"

"It is the truth, my sister. Our family is not blessed but cursed. Face the truth!" he commanded. "Seleucus, your second husband, was also murdered."

Laodice remained silent for a moment. "What do you want of me?" she asked, as she dried her tears.

136

"I do not understand your question," Antiochus responded.

"The question is clear. What will you want of me? What will you demand of me? We have not seen each other for years and years, Antiochus. We were never close as we grew up. I was always the older sister. I think we have no great affection for each other."

"Perhaps that could change."

"You don't believe that any more than I do. I ask you again: what do you want of me?"

"I shall want a son."

They looked steadily and coldly at each other.

"I must have a legitimate heir," said Antiochus.

"There already is an heir, Antiochus," said his sister. "In fact, there are two heirs."

"They are not my sons!" murmured the king.

"They are your nephews. They are your responsibility."

"I accept the responsibility, Laodice, but my nephews are not my heirs."

"One of them should be named co-ruler with you."

Laodice stood in anger, challenging Antiochus. The new king gripped her arm violently and pushed her back to her couch.

"Listen to me, sister or wife, whichever you prefer" —Antiochus fumed with his own rage—"Demetrius remains in Rome, at my request, and will be the ward of Rome. As for your infant son, my namesake, he is now a half-orphan who will be cared for as a half-orphan. Nothing more!"

"He is a prince! His mother is a queen!" she exclaimed.

"Indeed?" Antiochus glowered. "You are a queen for as long as I wish you to be queen. Your sons, my lady, are sons by Seleucus, your late and departed husband, and they are not my heirs. You are not regent. You are merely queen by the will of your king. And I will have my own heir." He had begun to pace the floor and then turned to his sister. "I assume you are still capable of providing me with an heir?"

"If you ask whether I am still able to conceive, the answer is yes."

"Then provide me with a son, and we shall have little else to do with each other. An heir will satisfy our customs and our people, and the kingdom will prevail."

"And will that arrangement satisfy you, Antiochus?" his sister asked.

"No," the king replied. "You yourself said we have no great affection for each other. I intend to take a concubine."

Laodice sighed. "Very well. It is better that we understand each other about these matters."

Antiochus walked to the door.

"We can talk more on the morrow. I will leave you for tonight."

His sister could not resist a final barb. "You leave to search the market for merchandise?" she said with a sneer.

Antiochus took a step toward his sister and stopped.

"Take care, my sister." He spoke deliberately and firmly. "Take great care. I am not a boy-king like your first husband. I am not the submissive Seleucus

138

whom you next married. I am Antiochus, and I am
now the king. Play none of your courtly games with
me, my lady!" He turned and paused. "I am tired
and weary, not only from my journey but also of
this conversation."

Antiochus slammed the door as he left.

The next day, the king summoned two men to
his quarters.

Andronicus was a general who had served his
brother, the son of Zeuxis, who had served his father. Andronicus had the reputation of being shrewd
and efficient, reluctant to show his face at public
functions.

Appolonius was a civil servant, an able administrator by all accounts, who had assisted Heliodorus.
Appolonius was several years younger than Andronicus.

Antiochus believed that both men would serve as
excellent advisers, especially if he were certain of
Appolonius's loyalty.

"There is no need for ceremony," said the king.
"Please be seated."

"I prefer to stand," said Andronicus, the general.

"As you wish." Antiochus smiled. The king sat
upon a couch. Appolonius found a footstool.

"Is the city at peace?" asked the king.

"The city rejoices in the return of Your Majesty,"
the general replied. "I know of no restlessness."

"That is good," Antiochus declared. "What is the
talk concerning Heliodorus?" He looked toward
Appolonius for an answer.

"Only that he should pay for his treachery, Majes-

139

ty," said the young man without hesitation.

"Will Heliodorus be sought out?" asked Andronicus, the general.

"And where might we find him now?" asked the king, with a smile.

"There are rumors that he is in Greece," said Appolonius.

"I have heard he has taken refuge on the island of Miletus," said the general.

"We would not be welcomed or even tolerated in either place," said the king. "We must be very careful in our relations with the nations of the West. In particular, I have an understanding with Eumenes of Pergamum. At least for the present, I have no desire to antagonize any country beyond the Taurus mountains. If Heliodorus is truly in the West, he has found his haven."

"He will not be punished?" inquired the general.

"Only if he appears within our kingdom. You can proclaim word of our displeasure and intent, of course." Antiochus looked at both men carefully. "I have long disliked and mistrusted Heliodorus. I would quickly sentence him to death if he were in our hands. I merely feel that we have more important things to do, presently, than pursue this exile."

Both men appeared to agree.

"Are any of the soldiers loyal to Heliodorus?" asked the king.

"The armies are loyal to the king!" Andronicus declared. "I will see to it, sir." The king was sure that he would.

"And you, Appolonius?" Antiochus decided to

ask the question without preamble. "You worked under Heliodorus. What say you?"

"I serve the king," he replied. "Gladly and loyally."

"Of course, Heliodorus was an able man." Antiochus decided to probe more deeply for the truth.

"When he carried out the king's commands, he had the support of myself and the others who served him, Majesty," Appolonius replied. "That support ended with his treachery."

"He was an ambitious man, Your Highness," said the general.

"He was proud and ambitious," the king agreed. "Remember that I knew him from my youth." Antiochus stared at his fingers and nails, which had been artfully manicured by a delightful companion of the previous night. He smiled at the memory. "Pride is acceptable only insofar as it serves the king."

"Your majesty will be served," said Andronicus. He said it plainly, in a matter-of-fact way, without a trace of fawning.

"Both of you will have ample opportunity to demonstrate your devotion to the crown," said the king. "I have many dreams and plans for both Antioch and the empire." Antiochus walked to the window and pulled the drapes. "This is a beautiful city, but it will be made more beautiful. Perhaps we can transform it into another Athens. If that cannot be, then at least it can become another Pergamum or Alexandria."

The men remained silent, preoccupied with their own thoughts. The king continued to gaze across the Orontes River toward the fertile fields beyond.

"Our ancestors chose well, and Xenarius built well. But we shall do better!" said the king, returning to his couch.

The general was beaming. "Your Majesty was away for so long a time, and yet he has such a feeling for the city!"

"It is not a feeling, Andronicus. It is an affection," said the king. "There is much that I learned in Rome and in Athens. There is much that I admire in both cities. But this is my home. You are my people." He paused a moment. "But let us turn to matters of the kingdom, of the empire."

The two men waited for the king to continue.

"My father was not called 'The Great' for naught. His memory will always remain with me, and it is my wish that the kingdom be restored to the glory and grandeur of which he dreamed. I know we cannot regain the glory of Nicator. I mentioned, moments ago, that we must not look westward. But we can look eastward and southward and rebuild the kingdom."

Andronicus asked to speak.

"Sire, is it not true that Rome encroaches upon us?" he inquired.

"Rome is powerful and ambitious, but there are limits to what she is able to do," the king replied. "We have heard about the threat of Rome since my childhood. My father believed it. Hannibal encouraged it. And having myself been sacrificed for fourteen years to Rome, I have few illusions about the objectives of Rome. However, for the time being, I truly believe we are safe."

"Would Your Majesty explain?" prodded the general.

"Rome must govern Spain in the far west. She fights enemies along her northern borders. She is involved in Macedonia. The senate encouraged me to return to Antioch, with the help of a former enemy, Eumenes, in order to provide stability. I interpret that to mean security for Rome."

"Are we then to serve Rome, Your Highness?" the general persisted.

"No. If our common interests fit together, well and good. I do not propose to antagonize the Romans. I do propose to strengthen ourselves in every way we can so that when Rome does in fact threaten us, we will be prepared. We can begin by building new alliances. Perhaps we can even go beyond formal alliances." Antiochus saw that the men were bewildered.

"For example, Seleucia and Egypt must unite," he continued.

Andronicus whistled slowly through his teeth.

"Would Rome countenance such an alliance, Excellency?" he asked.

"It would if its attention is directed elsewhere. The Seleucids and the Ptolemies have had alliances before. My sister is queen of Egypt."

"And our two kingdoms have fought before, Majesty."

"Did I say that we would not fight?" asked the king. "I don't recall saying that. Why did I ask you to be present, general?"

The mood relaxed into laughter.

"The Ptolemy to whom Cleopatra is now married

143

is a mere lad. He is weak. The government is weak. I think my sister might listen to reason. She will if we control Coeli-Syria."

"We do control it, sir," said Appolonius. "We occupy the entire Basin, including Judea."

"Judea is still a weak link in our chain. The reason is clear. Judea is made up of Judeans—of the people called *Jews*—and never have I met such a proud and stubborn people. They have defied every conqueror. But I have a plan, and you are to be part of it, Appolonius."

Appolonius nodded.

"What single thing has thus far united our kingdom?" asked the king.

"The dynasty?" answered Andronicus.

"Our history?" asked Appolonius.

"It goes beyond history and dynasty. Our *heritage* holds us together. We are Greek—or we ought to be more thoroughly Greek. That is what binds us. This is why Antioch and Alexandria can work together. Both dynasties are Greek. In between and stretching all the way to Persia are Greek colonies that are part of our empire. If we speak Greek and think Greek, we will have a strong kingdom that can hold its own against any enemy, including Rome."

"You have given this much thought, Excellency," said Andronicus.

"Everywhere we will insist that the Greek language be used. We will build Greek gymnasiums and schools and sports arenas. We will build more temples and encourage worship of the Greek Pantheon. We will extend the Greek *polis*—the Greek *city*—with its special forms and traditions. Do this

144

in Judea, for example, and we will have a Seleucid province that will always be subservient and loyal."

"You would make Hellenization a primary policy of your government, Excellency?" asked Appolonius.

"Exactly," said the king. "And I am appointing you, Appolonius, to be the new governor of Judea to begin to put this policy into practice."

Appolonius murmured his thanks.

"Antioch will create a new universe of Greek cities in Asia, throughout our inhabited world." The king moistened his lips with some wine.

"You, Andronicus, must begin to rebuild our army and navy. If Phillipus is still alive, he's the one to purchase and train the elephants."

"He is alive, although he is an old man, Excellency. But the Treaty of Apamea does not allow us to own elephants."

"There are two aspects of that treaty that I now reject," said the king. "I will not threaten Eumenes and the West. I will make that final payment of one thousand talents to Rome; somehow we will find the money, perhaps in the Temple of Jerusalem since Heliodorus didn't retrieve it. But I will have an army, and an army requires elephants. We are forbidden to have a navy, but we must have ships, precisely because Egypt has a strong naval force. Find Phillipus. And locate a new admiral who will supervise the construction of a new fleet. Find more soldiers. Train them. We must again become strong. We can do so without telling Rome!"

Andronicus broke into applause. "I have long waited to hear such words, sire! It will be done as you command."

"Do you wish me to secure treasure from the Temple in Jerusalem?" asked Appolonius. "There is strong belief that the Jerusalem Temple has special divine protection."

"I do not believe that story." Antiochus snorted. "I think Heliodorus was bloodied and fooled. There are no heavenly hosts to defend Jews or anyone else. I have never seen them. Have you? Which only makes Heliodorus a fool—and us, simpletons for believing his story for so long." Antiochus wiped his forehead; the afternoon had grown warm. "Yes, Appolonius, I want you to find treasure for me in Jerusalem!"

Antiochus stood.

"Appolonius, I will dismiss you for now since I have one other matter to discuss with Andronicus. I trust your good judgment in keeping confidence about what we have discussed today."

Appolonius saluted the king and retired from the room.

"You will not be seated?" asked the king.

"I do prefer to stand, Excellency," the general replied.

"Then we shall both stand," said Antiochus.

"Andronicus, I shall have to test your loyalty."

"If it is necessary, Highness, I am prepared," said the aging warrior.

"Will you kill for the king?"

Andronicus realized that this was no idle, rhetorical question. He did not move an eyelid.

"A soldier always does what is required by his king," the general replied.

"That is well said!" Antiochus emphasized his

pleasure with a firm embrace that surprised his general.

"My young nephew, my namesake, must be killed."

"You speak of young Antiochus."

"The son of my recently departed brother."

"Demetrius is to remain in Rome, sire?"

"At my request, he is not to be harmed. He is the firstborn, he is a hostage, and the senate has no intention of returning him to Antioch."

Andronicus sighed deeply. "I trust the king's wisdom," he said.

"As long as Demetrius remains in Rome, he is no threat to the crown. On the other hand, young Antiochus, my nephew, despite his tender years, lives in Antioch, and some might be tempted to use him against me."

"That is a possibility, sire," Andronicus agreed.

"So the infant must be eliminated. It must be done by someone other than me. No one must ever have any cause to say that I had anything to do with this killing. Do you understand, general?"

"Precisely, sire."

"I leave the means and method to you."

"It will be done, Majesty. Have no fear."

"Long live the kingdom!" said Antiochus.

"Long live the king!" Andronicus replied.

12

The Jew named Joshua had been waiting patiently to see the king.

Antiochus surveyed him carefully through a parting of the drapes. The man had come from Jerusalem, had requested an audience, and seemed to have much urgency about his mission. Antiochus had summoned Appolonius, his new governor for Judea, to be present at their interview.

Antiochus and Appolonius entered the room together. Joshua stood and bowed. The king gestured that they should be seated.

"Identify yourself, sir," commanded Appolonius.

"I am Yeshua, or Joshua—but I also go by the name of Jason."

"Jason is a Greek name," said the king. "But you are a Judean."

"Many Judeans now adopt Greek names, Your Majesty," said Joshua, again bowing before the king.

"Tell the king what you do," urged Appolonius.

"First, I am a Jerusalemite. And I serve in the Temple."

"Are you a priest?" asked the king.

"Yes." Joshua dropped his eyes momentarily.

"Appolonius is my new governor for Judea," said the king.

"I have heard the news," Joshua replied. "My congratulations, Excellency." Again he bowed. Antiochus wondered if the man had some kind of device in his neck that made his head fall and rise at will.

"State your business with the king," ordered the new governor of Judea.

"It is a rather delicate matter, sire," said Joshua.

"State it then!" demanded the king. "We have many other things to accomplish today."

"I come regarding the position of high priest in our Temple." Joshua swallowed nervously.

"*Pontifex Maximus.*"

"Sir?" Joshua asked.

"That is Latin for 'high priest' or 'chief priest,' if you will." Antiochus scowled. "You Jews are not the only ones who have high priests."

"The high priest is Onias, Excellency," Appolonius coached his monarch.

"Yes. The one who kept Heliodorus from the Temple treasury," said the king. "I remember the name of Onias. Tell me, Joshua—or Jason—were there divine horsemen in the Temple?"

"Many of us believe that Heliodorus and Onias made some sort of arrangement."

"What do you mean? What kind of an arrangement?"

"To withhold the treasures until Heliodorus would be king."

"I suppose it is possible that Heliodorus had already begun to plan his treachery," mused the king. "Appolonius, what do you know about this Onias? He interests me."

"He has been high priest for many years, since the days of your father's reign. He pays an annual tribute to the treasury."

"I was not aware of that," said the king.

"He is a friend of Egypt, Majesty!" Joshua interjected.

"Is this true, Appolonius?" asked the king.

"Judea was once a province of Egypt, sire," said the governor. "I suppose that this Onias may have journeyed to Alexandria from time to time. There is a large community of Jews there."

"There are Jews everywhere, Appolonius," said the king. "It is amazing. I have seen them in every place I have lived."

"Onias is a friend of the Ptolemies!" Joshua declared.

"You do not seem to like this Onias, *Jason*," the king observed. "Do you know him personally? But you must, since you said you were a priest in the Temple."

"I know Onias quite well, Majesty. He is my brother."

For a moment, the king was speechless.

"I expect such intrigue within palaces. I did not know it existed in temples," he said to Appolonius.

151

"There are at least two rival political groups in Jerusalem, Excellency," said the governor. "There are conservatives, who hold to the old ways. And there are the more liberal—many of whom favor our Greek ways."

"Well, Jason, you must be a Hellenist since you have adopted a Greek name," said the king.

"I belong to both parties!" Joshua declared. "I support both the law of Moses and the laws of Antioch."

"It is difficult to straddle a fence, Jason. I speak from experience," said the king. "I am sure you have come with a proposal."

Joshua pretended surprise.

"Come, now, you haven't traveled this distance merely to see the inside of the palace. Let us hear what you have to say. And do it quickly."

"I do not wish to speak against my brother, the high priest."

"Of course not," said the king sardonically.

"However, it is felt, by many in Jerusalem, that he should be replaced."

"Is that not a matter for you Jews?"

"The position is hereditary, but it must be confirmed by the king."

"It would be foolish for me to go against custom."

"I am the brother of Onias. I have the same heritage."

Finally Joshua had stated his real reason for coming to Antioch.

"You believe, then, that you would be a suitable high priest?"

"Yes, Your Majesty. In all humility."

"Indeed." The king spoke seriously. "I have noted a large measure of that quality in what you have said today." Antiochus doubted that this Jason, this Joshua, even caught the subtlety of his comment since he was obviously so intent upon obtaining a higher position for himself. "Give me reasons why I should appoint you."

"First, it will be good for Jerusalem. Our city grows but must grow still larger. My brother would be content for Jerusalem to remain a small caravansary."

"So it would be good for commerce."

"And the merchants—the Tobiads—fully support this action. In fact, I am here with their knowledge and the assurance of their support." Joshua swallowed quickly and continued. "The Tobiads are my cousins. We understand each other."

"Very well," said the king. "You have stated a benefit for Jerusalem. What benefit would there be for Antioch?"

"Oh, Your Highness, there would be many benefits!" Joshua declared. "Many of us are greatly attracted to the Hellenic way of life, but my brother, the high priest, is not sufficiently accomodating to our wishes."

"Explain yourself," commanded the king.

"We would like to issue our own coins, for example."

"You must become a Greek *polis*, you must organize and administer yourselves in the Greek manner, to secure that right."

"We request that right, Excellency! We already have a council of elders. It could serve as the

Gerousia, which is required. We would establish a *Boule* as well, a council of the people. We wish permission to set up *ephebeioi*—the youth societies— in order for our young men to improve their knowledge of Greek and its ways."

"That would mean establishing an academy for sports and education, a *gymnasion*. Are you prepared to build one, at your expense?"

"Our merchants have already agreed to do so. In fact, Excellency, we truly wish to become known as Antioch-in-Jerusalem!" Joshua smiled broadly.

"You flatter us with these requests," said the king.

"They are spoken with sincerity and urgency," said Joshua.

Antiochus placed a hand over his mouth, deep in thought.

"Appolonius, what do you think?"

"The stars appear to be in conjunction," Appolonius replied.

"I ask you not as an astronomer but as a governor," the king said sharply.

"If our presence is sufficiently visible and strong in Jerusalem, I believe these changes would prove to be truly beneficial," said the governor.

"Would your people allow Antioch to build a citadel, to house our troops, within the city itself?" the king asked Joshua.

"We would expect the king to do so."

"And so we return to you, Jason," said the king. "How can I appoint you high priest, despite your tribal connections, without upsetting your people? Jerusalemites are capable of much mischief."

"We will control our own people," Joshua declared firmly.

"Let us hope that you can." Antiochus paused to emphasize his concern. "You said that the high priest pays a tribute—an annual tribute—to the king. What are you prepared to do?"

"I have with me, today, three hundred and sixty talents of silver which I will leave for Your Majesty's coffers, should the king appoint me high priest."

Antiochus raised his eyebrows with surprise and pleasure.

"My friends will make an additional gift of eighty talents."

"Of silver?" asked the king.

"Of silver," Joshua confirmed. "This tribute would be made yearly. One thing more, Excellency: if we are permitted to make Jerusalem a Greek city with all of the privileges enjoyed by citizens of Antioch or Tyre, my friends will provide Your Majesty with an additional one hundred fifty talents, in silver."

"Appolonius, what is the sum?" asked the king.

"Five hundred and ninety talents, Excellency," the governor replied.

Antiochus pondered the unexpected treasure. A talent was equivalent to seventy-five pounds of silver—or six thousand drachmas. Thus Jason was offering nearly forty-five thousand pounds of silver, not an insignificant amount, especially now when he needed money to pay Rome and rebuild his armies. It was clearly a bribe, but Antiochus could receive as well as give bribes.

"What has this Onias paid as tribute?" the king asked his governor.

"One hundred talents a year," Appolonius responded.

The king sighed.

"How shall we deal with this Onias—in the event that we decide to appoint you high priest?" Antiochus asked Joshua.

"My brother is presently in Antioch."

"He is here—and not in Jerusalem?"

"He hopes, still, to see Your Majesty. If he does, he will tell you about a compact made between him and your father."

"I see," said the king. "It is good to be forewarned." The king was ready to recess the meeting and stood.

"Jason, I believe I should like to visit your city. I should like to see this Jerusalem for myself."

"Your Majesty, you would be welcomed with great honor!" said Joshua.

"Then I shall come," said the king, smiling, "when you have built your gymnasium." The king looked at Appolonius and winked.

Joshua desperately wanted clarification but did not dare question the king directly.

"Set your mind at ease, Jason," said the king. "I appoint you high priest of the Temple in Jerusalem.

Joshua's face radiated joy.

"Wait for the governor outside. He will do whatever is necessary, and the talents you have brought can be delivered to him."

"Thank you, Excellency!" Joshua whispered.

When he had left, the king turned to Appolonius.

"A strange morning, Appolonius," said the king.

"Do you trust this Jason, Excellency?"

"No," replied the king immediately. "I don't fully

trust anyone who deals in intrigue. I know how the game is played, you see!" The king chuckled. "But I trust that the talents he has brought are truly made of silver. Furthermore, what this fool has requested for his Jerusalem is precisely what we would have arranged. Jerusalem will be Hellenized, and Judea will be the buffer we need in our dealings with Egypt."

"Remarkable!" said Appolonius.

"Remarkable indeed!" agreed the king. "The gods deal kindly with us today. Deal with this Jason as you see fit. Put the understandings into writing. That always helps."

Antiochus escorted his governor to the door.

"One thing more, Appolonius," said the king. "Find Andronicus and send him to me. I want to talk to him about this Onias."

13

Three months had passed since Joshua had seen the king.

Mattathias had returned to Jerusalem but had again been summoned to Antioch to see Onias.

The high priest was still living with Eleazar, the teacher of Hebrew, but kept himself in seclusion. He was overjoyed to see Mattathias.

"How are your sons?" he asked. "Are they well?"

"They grow like reeds in Lake Galilee!" Mattathias replied.

"How I would like to see them!" Onias smiled. "You do not believe me, the way I used to scold them for running about in the Temple. Mattathias, I thirst to see them and all the children. I hunger for Jerusalem and the Temple." The old man was close to tears. "Tell me about Jerusalem. Everything," he commanded.

"There have been changes, Excellency."

"Do not spare me. This is why I asked you to come."

"A garrison is being built, on the Akra, within sight of the Temple."

"Then there are foreign soldiers within the city."

"There is a battalion of Syrians. We are told they are in Jerusalem to protect the city, now that it is a Greek *polis*."

"Simon must rejoice," said the high priest.

"Simon is dead, Excellency. His nephew Menelaus has taken his place."

"I know him. He is as staunch a Hellenist as his uncle." Onias sighed. "Do the Greeks prevail among our people?"

"Some of our young men wear the *petasos*, the Greek brimmed hat. Many seem to wish to appear to be Greek and forget the ways of our fathers."

"Why must it be so? Why must our people depart from the holy covenant?"

"The academy is nearly finished, and it is said that we may expect a visit from King Antiochus himself when it is completed."

"If there is to be a *gymnasion* in Jerusalem, then there will be public sports events, in which the young men will cavort naked before God and men."

"And sometimes even before women, sire," Mattathias added.

"A disgrace!" Onias declared, fingering the white curls of hair at his ears. "And how fares my brother?"

"Joshua supervises the building of the Greek academy. He is frequently seen with Appolonius, the new governor. And he has been seen wearing the *petasos*."

"So he has joined the enemy. Does he perform any of his duties at the Temple?"

"Occasionally, sire," Mattathias replied with caution.

"He is now the high priest, my son. He purchased the office from the king. But I am sure that you know that."

"To us, Excellency, your brother is not the high priest. The office does not pass from brother to brother but from father to son."

"Antiochus has decreed it!" cried the high priest.

"Antiochus is not Adonai, Excellency," said Mattathias, "and the priests of Jerusalem do not accept the king's appointment."

"How can you continue to serve as a priest of Adonai?"

"I cannot, Excellency. Perhaps I should tell you now. I cannot serve Adonai in His Temple when an usurper makes a mockery of the law."

"Then what will you do?"

"I will return to my birthplace, to the village of Modein. I will go with my wife and my five sons, and we will worship Adonai as He has decreed. We will be faithful to Him as godly ones, as *chasidim*."

"Perhaps there is no other way for you."

"And you, Excellency, what will you do?" asked Mattathias.

"I should like to return to Jerusalem, but I cannot. I thought I might be able to risk going to Egypt—to Alexandria, where so many of our people live, but I am an old man and the distance is great." Onias frowned. "I shall remain in Antioch for the time being, Mattathias. I would still like to see this Antiochus, and persuade him that he has been duped and that he goes against his own father's wishes."

"What are the prospects?"

"I have been in Antioch for nearly twenty weeks, Mattathias. The closest I have come to the king is to meet a man named Andronicus. He is a general, and he appears to be friendly. He says he will arrange for me to see Antiochus—but those may be only empty words."

"Be careful, Excellency. Do not trust these men of Antioch."

"My trust is in Adonai, Mattathias! Keep your trust only in Him," Onias admonished. "When you return to Jerusalem, give my blessing to the faithful. And if you truly return to your birthplace, take copies with you of the holy Scriptures. They must be preserved at all costs. And they must be taught to our children's children! Will you promise me that?"

"I will, Excellency, I will!" Mattathias affirmed fervently.

"If we do not meet again, Mattathias, remember that Adonai is the Avenger, that He will not forget the cry of the humble, He will judge the nations, He will crush evil, and Adonai will triumph!" Tears poured down the faces of both the high priest and his assistant.

"Amen!" Mattathias cried softly and fervently.

Painstakingly but swiftly, Mattathias copied the Torah, the psalms, the proclamations of the prophets, and the sacred writings. He knew he did not have much time, but the task had taken weeks instead of days.

The words of the prophets seemed to be written for his own day. He could not understand how a people so blessed of the Almighty, living in covenant with the Lord of the universe, could so easily and so quickly depart from doing justice and living righteously. As had happened so many times before, his people had turned to their own way, had abused themselves and their neighbors, and worshiped idols instead of the one true God.

He often wept as he wrote.

Joshua should truly be called Jason, for he was now more Greek than Jew. Although the gymnasium was not yet finished, classes had begun, and Jason was one of the teachers. He was certainly no priest of Adonai; to call him high priest would be a lie. His cousin Menelaus was also an evil man, both by reputation and practice—and yet he was even allowed to perform certain duties as a priest in the Temple, something that was strictly forbidden for one of his character and tribe.

Mattathias would not dare enter the unfinished academy of sports, but he had heard what was planned. Rooms were designed for wrestling, tumbling, and swimming. The corridors were covered tracks for running. There were to be a few classrooms where literature, philosophy, and mathematics would be taught, all in Greek. In classes devoted to sports, none of the young men wore clothing, not even loincloths. Many Jewish boys had been recruited, and Mattathias had heard that a few of them, ashamed of their pubic appearance, had found surgeons to remove the evidence of their circumcision.

The priest had heard of more sordid deeds—of men who made love to men, something said to occur frequently in Greece in the *ephebeion* societies but a perversion clearly denounced by Moses and forbidden by Adonai.

The evil was great, and it was condoned by the renegade high priest—this self-appointed high priest —himself. Jason, he had heard, was planning to send a group of Jewish athletes to the Olympic games to be held in Tyre the following year. Their training had begun. And it was well known that the games were dedicated to the honor and glory of Hercules. A sacrifice would be made to the Greek deity. It was idolatry. Mattathias knew it in his heart.

He was completing a copy of Daniel's book. He read what he had copied to be sure he had made no mistakes.

At the appointed time he will return and come into the South, but this last time it will not turn out the way it did before.

For ships of Kittim will come against him; therefore he will be disheartened, and will return and become enraged at the holy covenant and take action; so he will come back and show regard for those who forsake the holy covenant.

And forces from him will arise, desecrate the sanctuary fortress, and do away with the regular sacrifice. And they will set up the abomination of desolation.

And by smooth words he will turn to god-lessness those who act wickedly toward the covenant, but the people who know their God will display strength and take action.

And those who have insight among the people will give understanding to the many; yet they will fall by sword and by flame, by captivity and by plunder, for many days.

Now when they fall they will be granted a little help, and many will join with them in hypocrisy.

And some of those who have insight will fall, in order to refine, purge, and make them pure, until the end time; because it is still to come at the appointed time.

Then the king will do as he pleases, and he will exalt and magnify himself above every god, and will speak monstrous things against the God of gods; and he will prosper until the indignation is finished, for that which is decreed will be done.

And he will show no regard for the gods of his fathers or for the desire of women, nor will he show regard for any other god; for he will magnify himself above them all.

But instead he will honor a god of fortresses, a god whom his fathers did not know; he will honor him with gold, silver, costly stones, and treasures.

And he will take action against the strongest of fortresses with the help of a foreign god; he will give great honor to those who acknowledge him, and he will cause them to rule over the many, and will parcel out land for a price.

And at the end time the king of the South will collide with him, and the king of the North will storm against him with chariots, with horsemen, and with many ships; and he will enter countries, overflow them, and pass through.

He will also enter the Beautiful Land, and many countries will fall; but these will be rescued out of his hand: Edom, Moab and the foremost of the sons of Ammon.

Then he will stretch out his hand against other countries, and the land of Egypt will not escape. But he will gain control over the hidden treasures of gold and silver, and over all the precious things of Egypt; and Libyans and Ethiopians will follow at his heels.

But rumors from the East and from the North will disturb him, and he will go forth with great wrath to destroy and annihilate many.

And he will pitch the tents of his royal pavilion between the seas and the beautiful Holy Mountain; yet he will come to his end, and no one will help him.*

Mattathias trembled as he again read the prophecy. He truly believed these words were spoken about the very times in which he lived.

Adonai would judge His people, and this Antiochus might be the instrument of God's holy vengeance. Surely, as in times past, there would remain a loyal remnant. Not everyone would be destroyed.

*Daniel 11:29-45.

Mattathias knew of many in Jerusalem itself who already prayed for the day of deliverance, who would not bow the knee to any new Baal the Syrians of Antioch might bring. He knew that he and his sons would honor the God of Israel. Woe to Jerusalem, he pondered, wealthy and worldly, who, like King Saul of old, did not know when God's own Spirit had departed.

On the day, a fortnight later, when Mattathias was packed and prepared to leave Jerusalem for his home village of Modein, Abijah, his friend and fellow priest, brought him the tragic news.

Onias, the true high priest, was dead.

He had been killed, and Mattathias suspected treachery. Somehow, Onias had been lured to Daphne, the resort town south of Antioch, perhaps, Mattathias surmised, because he had been promised an audience with the king.

Instead, he had met Andronicus, the general of the army of Antiochus. In meeting him the old and weary servant of the Almighty met his end.

14

Queen Laodice was seriously ill, along with most of the citizens of Antioch.

She was in her sixth month of pregnancy, but she was well past the time of morning nausea. The symptoms of the disease that seemed to grip the city were severe stomach cramps, vomiting, and fever. Many had already died, and Antioch was stricken with fear.

Laodice had lost much weight, and Antiochus was fearful as well, both for her and the child she carried.

"Is there anything I can get for you?" he asked.

Holding her abdomen and wincing with pain, she said, "You have given me more than I can manage!"

"Perhaps I can find another physician," said the king.

"Leave me to die!" the queen cried out. "You do not really care for me—only for this possible heir of yours!"

"You are my wife and my sister," Antiochus declared. "Of course I care about your welfare."

"I am merely one of your objects, Antiochus," she scoffed. "Not even one of your subjects, noble king, merely an object."

"I will make allowances for your pain, but take care in what you say," Antiochus warned.

"Then leave me in my misery!" The eyes of Laodice were filled not only with pain but with hot anger.

"I must do something!" Antiochus shouted. "Not only for you but for the entire city!"

"Then consult with the gods," replied his sister. "Visit the seer. Go to the mountaintop and seek the advice of the oracle. That is something you can do!"

"It is, indeed," Antiochus agreed.

He rushed out of the queen's chamber. They neither embraced nor kissed. The time for even such amenities had long since passed.

Antiochus was actually grateful for the suggestion of Laodice. He had heard of the hermit who lived in a cave beyond Mount Staurin, who was said to be some sort of prophet, but he had not given any though to seeing him in this time of plague.

Something had to be found, something had to be done. The streets of Antioch were deserted. So many people were sick, and far too many had already died from this strange malady that constricted stomach and bowels. He had sought the best physicians for help, without success. He could lose nothing by seeking out a seer.

170

He had dismissed his guard and walked alone. He anticipated no danger. It was pleasant to be by himself, without pose or pomp, to think and reflect as he walked.

He recognized the road. It was the path he had taken with Benjamin, his slave, so many years before. He saw that the Iron Gate still stood, high in the cleft of Mount Silpius. He turned toward the north and Mount Staurin.

He had been king for nearly a year. So much had happened, nothing had stood still. He wondered if the great Alexander had felt this way—that too much was happening too quickly. It was said that Alexander had died at the age of thirty-three because there were no more worlds for him to conquer. Antiochus surmised that the true reason for his death might be more earthly and common. At any rate, *he* was well past the age of thirty-three, and he had many worlds still to conquer.

Nevertheless, the final payment of gold had been made to Rome, and Demetrius, his nephew, would continue to be the ward of the senate. Andronicus had taken care of his other young rival, and now Laodice was pregnant and would doubtless provide him with his own, legitimate heir. *She will if she lives*, he thought, and quickened his step.

Andronicus had been extremely useful in the matter of his nephew. *Parricida*, the Romans would call it—the murder of a close relative. Andronicus had also been of assistance in the business with Onias. Antiochus had not wanted to get enmeshed with the squabbles of the Jews; he certainly did not care who was high priest in Jerusalem. But this Onias had become bothersome with his constant requests for an audience. A bargain had been made with Jason, and there was no purpose to review the arrangement and certainly for him, the king, no need to explain it. Onias was doubtless a good man, and he would be missed by a few of the Jews; but he was an old man and would soon be forgotten.

Onias had been enticed to go to the temple of Zeus in Daphne. He wondered how the devout Jew, believing in his one true God, had felt about entering a pagan temple—even though it was believed by everyone that temples were sacred sanctuaries and offered safety and asylum to anyone within their walls. Andronicus had led Onias to believe that the king would meet him there—in the temple, in Daphne, away from Antioch where they would not be seen and could speak honestly and privately with each other. It had been a good deception.

Andronicus was also an old man, the king mused. He certainly was loyal, competent, and clever. The day might come when Antiochus would have to sacrifice Andronicus. He, too, would be missed, but he was also an old man and would soon be forgotten. The king had someone readily at hand who could be blamed.

The cave was in sight. A wisp of smoke circled casually upward from its entrance.

Antiochus did not know what to expect, but he was excited. He was a mature man who now knew what he wanted in life and from the kingdom, and nothing would deter him from realizing his ambitions. At the same time, he felt like a little boy, running up a hill, not knowing yet what would be seen on the other side. Perhaps it was a valley or a lake. Perhaps a frightening beast or a playful rabbit. Perhaps one would not see anything beyond the crest except more rocks that would have to be climbed. It was a strange feeling of anticipating some new wonder, some new adventure.

The seer was seated before a small open fire against a blackened wall. The air was chilly, and Antiochus shivered. The cave seemed to extend far into the recesses of the mountain, but it was so dark that the king could not be certain. The seer appeared to be very old. His white hair and stringy beard were soiled and may never have been washed. The odor of the place was sour but not repugnant.

"You are the king!" said the seer. His voice was remarkably deep and steady for one who seemed to be so old.

Antiochus did not yet speak but nodded in response.

"I have expected you for many days," continued the old man.

Antiochus pretended amazement but thought it was a trick. He decided to test the man.

"And by what name am I called?" he asked. It was generally believed that this hermit had not left his mountain retreat for many years.

"You are called by the name of your father. You are the fourth monarch to be named Antiochus, and you are the eighth of the Seleucid house to sit upon the throne."

"Your Reverence knows me well," said the king. 'It is reported that you do not leave this place, so

173

your knowledge of me is truly remarkable."

"I know everything that transpires below," said the seer.

"You refer to the city, to Antioch, of course?"

"As I said, I know everything that transpires below."

His voice was as cold as the air coming from inside the mountain.

"You are here because of the plague that has come to your city," the old man continued, gazing intently into the eyes of Antiochus. "Dozens have already died, but hundreds more will die. The queen will die, and so will the child she carries."

"Have the gods decreed this? Is there no remedy?" asked the king.

"There is always a remedy, if you are prepared to take it."

Antiochus felt fear for the first time.

"Do you have a name, ancient one?" he asked.

"My name is Amphion. Some call me Leios, but my name is Amphion!"

"That was the name of the priest who attended the first Seleucus."

"I remember Seleucus well," said the seer calmly. "I gave him the sacred meat that was carried by the eagle to mark the site of the city below you."

It was impossible. The event had occurred more than a century before. The man before him would have to be a hundred and fifty years old, perhaps even older. Antiochus knew that Amphion had always been a man of mystery, a priest of unknown alliances, but surely this man was not that Amphion.

"You must not doubt me, King Antiochus. You

174

are in need of my help. It was ordained that you come to me. I have been waiting for you."

The king did not know what to believe or accept. He was only aware of a more rapid beating of his heart and a strange pulsating hammering in his head.

"What must be done to save the city and my queen?" he finally asked.

"There are three things. Mark them well."

"Speak, O Man of Wisdom. I listen," said the king.

"First, it is decreed that you make an image of stone. I will give you the outline of the image, which you will take to the architect who now works to enlarge your city. The image contains two faces, two personages, and the final design will be revealed to you at the appointed time."

"There must be an image," Antiochus agreed. "Where must it be placed? Should I construct a special temple?"

"The image requires no temple. It is to be carved from the stone of this very mountain. The image must face the western sun, to be seen by all of the people of your city. At the close of each day, with the setting of the sun, your people must be commanded to bow down and honor the image. You yourself must give special homage to this being. The plague that afflicts Antioch will disappear on the day the image is completed. You will do this?"

Antiochus wondered if it were a question or a command.

"I will do whatever your gods decree," he answered.

"I serve no gods, Antiochus!" said the seer, raising his voice.

175

"Whom do you serve?" whispered the king, amazed and frightened. "If you are Amphion, you are a priest. You serve some god!"

"The lord whom I serve is one you will come to know. He is a lord who is powerful and wishes you well."

"How am I to know that this lord wishes me well?" The king struggled with his voice. His throat was dry. His breath seemed weak.

"The illness will depart your city. Your queen will live, and you will have your heir."

"But how am I to know that this lord wishes me well?" Antiochus repeated his question.

"I mentioned three things you must do. Hear now the second." The old man struggled with his garment and brought forth a shimmering medallion, hung upon a bright silver chain. "Place this around your neck," he said.

Antiochus looked at the necklace first. It felt warm, but it had been next to the body of the old man. It looked new, which seemed strange in the presence of the ancient seer who had given him the medallion. It appeared to be made of silver, but the weight did not seem right. It was, in fact, made of a metal Antiochus had never seen before. He stared at the oval amulet. The characters seemed familiar, but he could not read them.

"Put it around your neck, Antiochus!" commanded the seer. "It will bring you all of the things you desire. It will insure an heir to your throne. It will guarantee a kingdom to compare with that of your father. You will enjoy victory in battle and wealth and pleasure in your palace."

Antiochus did not move.

"Wear it! It is a talisman of good fortune!"

Antiochus again fondled the piece of metal and then, quickly, placed the necklace around his neck. The warmth he had felt in his hand became warmer and penetrated into his chest. It was not an unpleasant feeling.

"How am I to know that all of these good things will happen to me?" asked the king.

"The lord whom I serve will see to it." The seer pointed a thin, bony finger toward Antiochus. "He is the lord whom you will now serve!"

"I serve many gods, great Amphion," said the king. "We Greeks worship a Pantheon, a large assemblage of gods."

"You will serve my lord and him alone," declared the old man. He said it with a quiet, determined voice, and Antiochus felt both the burning warmth of the amulet and a chill rising up his spine. "You will honor my lord each evening when you bow to the *charonion*, the image you will build. You will honor him each time you touch the talisman. My lord will come to you when you call. He will tell you what to do. He has done so to me for many long years."

"How can this be?" said the king, struggling to retain a sense of reality.

"You will soon see how it can be. You will learn, Antiochus, that through evil will come good."

" 'Through evil will come good'? " Antiochus shuddered as he repeated the words. "Your lord will come whenever I touch this amulet?"

"He will come whenever you call!"

"And there is nothing more I must do?" the king asked.

"I mentioned *three* things."

Antiochus nodded.

"Proof of your devotion to my lord must be exacted. A blood covenant must be made."

"You speak of a sacrifice, perhaps?"

"I speak of the shedding of blood. Andronicus must be killed."

"He is an old man, a good general. He has served me well!"

"And did you not think, on your way to meet me, that Andronicus might have to be sacrificed for the good of the kingdom?"

Antiochus was petrified, realizing that this man had somehow read his thoughts.

"And did you not once test the loyalty of your general by asking him if he would kill for his king?" the seer continued.

The king was stunned. The knowledge of this man was incredible.

"The test of your loyalty is the same. Will you kill for your lord?"

"I can have him killed," the king hedged.

"You are to kill Andronicus yourself. The shedding of his blood by you will be the seal of our covenant."

"Who is this lord of yours?" cried the king.

"He will reveal himself to you. He is our lord, Antiochus, yours and mine."

"I cannot do the thing you require."

"You accepted the amulet."

"I will return it."

"Try to do so."

Antiochus could not remove the necklace. He pulled and tugged, but the chain seemed to be glued to his body.

"Antiochus, you must now do this deed," said the seer calmly. "We have spoken of wealth and pleasure—and health for your people. We have not spoken of power. Great power. Unimagined power. Touch the talisman again."

Antiochus did so. The warmth was still there, but his fear dissolved. He seemed to be standing on a precipice, carefree and vibrant, gazing at all of the kingdoms of the world. As he looked he realized that they were his; he was viewing his realm, and it encompassed the entire world. The vision was glorious.

"I will do what is asked," the king replied. He did so without fear or reservation.

The seer who called himself Amphion handed to Antiochus a small piece of parchment on which two figures had been drawn.

"Take this to Cossutius, your architect. Set aside all other projects. The image must be carved at once."

179

"It will be done," said Antiochus without hesitation.

"Then go and do all that our lord commands."

Six months had passed, and Antiochus sat on the balcony of his island palace bedroom, facing the east. He felt a slight breeze moving from the south, from the coast, up the Orontes River. It had been a hot and humid day, and the coolness was welcome.

The sun was setting behind him.

The city was again prosperous and healthy. Antiochus had his son and heir. Mother and son had survived the dread disease. It was now the second year of his reign.

Antioch was growing in size and wealth. The city now had two agoras—one for commerce and another for affairs of government. A new community of homes had been built. It was located to his right, toward the south, just north of the Jewish Quarter. It was not yet named, but Antiochus had a name in mind. A new temple had been built, this one to honor Jupiter Capitolinus, intended to satisfy both Greeks, who preferred the name Zeus, and the Romans, who paid homage to Jupiter.

His architect, Cossutius, had been busy.

His greatest achievement faced him on the mountainside. The image had been carved—a large face, partially covered with a veil, and a smaller figure, which stood upon the shoulder of the other. It had been carved from the stone of the mountain as the hermit had commanded. It would last for as long as the mountain would stand. The promise had been kept on both sides. The plague was gone, and the *charonion*, as everyone now called it, was visible to and honored by all. Antiochus held the amulet in his hand and bowed to the image.

Cossutius had been astounded with the sketch the king had given him, the one the seer had provided.

The architect thought the large face was that of the woman Persephone, the wife of Hades, the king of the underworld, the god the Romans called Orcus.

Antiochus smiled at the memory of his meeting with the architect that day. He knew without a doubt whom he served. The lord of the talisman and the image, revealed to him by the seer, had spoken to him. His instructions were wise. His promises were true.

The king again bowed to the image. He had no need for a Pantheon, but would pretend to support and sustain the gods. It was wise to do so, and his lord understood.

Antiochus felt good. There were times when he looked into a glass and knew that he was not looking at Antiochus. He was bigger than life, larger than this body that was merely a vessel, more powerful and wise than any mere mortal.

He had grown beyond mortality. The implication was clear: if he were no longer a man, then he himself had become a god.

His lord had told him so.

And Antiochus knew that his lord would not lie.

15

The time for the month-long Olympic games in Tyre had arrived, and literally thousands of persons had flocked to the ancient Phoenician city on the Mediterranean coast. Among the thousands were participants in the games, families, visitors, merchants and hucksters, and King Antiochus and his retinue.

The king was relaxing before his official duties would commence.

"And are you happy in Tyre, my lovely Berenice?" he asked his paramount and favorite concubine, pulling her to his side.

"I think I prefer Tarsus!" she said with a laugh. "After all, you gave it to me, and here I am only a visitor."

"I gave you Tarsus?" Antiochus guffawed. "I must have been in a drunken stupor."

"You were, Your Majesty," Berenice teased. "Nevertheless, I have witnesses. Including Laodice."

"Was my wife indeed present?" asked the king. "I must have been magnificently drunk."

"She was—and you were."

"Did she protest? Did she say anything?"

"She said not a word. She merely stared at you through those eyes of hers that seem so full of pain."

"That describes Laodice. She must have been there."

"She is so thin and gaunt, Antiochus," said his concubine. "I worry about her."

"Worry for yourself, my dear," said the king. "If you become thin and gaunt like Laodice, you may also become as silent as she." They embraced. "Did I really promise to give you Tarsus?"

"I accept your gift with deepest appreciation," she said.

"Just remember that you have nothing in writing, my dear Berenice," Antiochus said. "But I may keep the possibility in mind. However, giving an entire city to one's mistress does seem a bit grand, don't you think?"

"Not at all, Your Excellency," Berenice replied demurely. "I believe I am worth every street of it."

Antiochus roared with laughter. "Your choice of words is most apt, dear lady."

His empire was growing, and he had many cities, perhaps enough, now, to give to friends and companions. Tyre was one of his jewels, and he enjoyed coming here. It had been captured by Alexander many years before in a maneuver that generals still discussed. He decided to tell Berenice about it.

184

"I am not interested in a man named Alexander!" she protested.

"It wouldn't hurt you to learn a few things, Berenice," Antiochus said. "You could improve your mind."

"And then we would spend our evenings discussing history," she teased. "Is that what you would like?"

The king ignored her.

"Tyre was once an island, you know. And the great Alexander built a half-mile-long causeway from the mainland over which to move his troops and war machines. He built tremendous siege towers, more than a hundred feet high, which he moved, on wheels, along this causeway he had built. The city soon surrendered."

"That is a very interesting story." She yawned.

"I thought so," said the king.

They were interrupted by a knock at the door.

"Enter!" the king commanded.

A servant approached nervously.

"Your Majesty, there is a man named Jason who wishes an immediate audience with you."

"We hold audiences in the afternoon, never in the mornings," the king said angrily. "I gave orders that I was not to be disturbed."

"This is what we told this Jason," said the servant. "I apologize, Excellency. The man was insistent. He said it was an affair of state that could not wait."

"Who is this Jason?" asked the king.

"He says he is from Jerusalem."

"Oh, that Jason," the king murmured. "Send him

185

in," he added with a sigh. "Stay with me, Berenice. You might find this amusing. This Jason is a priest. A high priest."

Jason entered, dressed as a Greek with tunic and skirt and wearing the *petasos* hat, which he did not remove. Antiochus thought he looked rather ridiculous, especially for a man of his age.

"All hail, Your Majesty!" Jason greeted the king.

Antiochus nodded.

"I have brought a contingent of Judean youth with me, Excellency," said the priest. "We will enter the games. I have even added my name to the list."

"*You* will be a participant, Jason?" demanded Antiochus. The thought of it was absurd.

"I have entered the pentathlon!" Jason said proudly.

"Five events will tax your energy, Jason," the king commented. "And you will get cold. You won't be wearing the tunic and skirt, you know."

Jason glanced at Berenice, who was covering a laugh with her hand. The priest blushed.

"But surely you have not come here to tell me about your team of Jewish athletes," said the king.

"I have brought the gift for Hercules," said Jason.

"Excellent. But there is a treasurer assigned to receive the silver." Antiochus was irritated. "You must not bother the king with such matters."

"Excellency, it is precisely about the gift that we must speak, before I see the treasurer, before I take my young men to the arena."

"The rules are quite clear," said the king.

Jason shifted his stance and showed his nervousness.

186

"With your special indulgence, Majesty, I request your intervention for our Judean contingent."

"You said you have the money."

"We do."

"Then what is the problem?" demanded the king.

"We feel—all of us who come from Jerusalem—that our gift must not be given to Hercules."

"Then why did you come to Tyre?" exploded the king. "The only way to participate in these games is to bring a gift to Hercules."

"But that is a problem for Jews, Excellency," Jason sighed. "Hercules is a god, a god of the Greeks."

"And you knew that before you agreed to come!" the king exclaimed. "Hercules is a god among many gods. He is the patron of sporting events. If you wish to be a Greek—as you say you do—then you must also honor Hercules."

"It is forbidden to Jews to honor other gods. It is called idolatry. We are to worship and honor the only true God."

"Yes, your Adonai," snorted the king. "I know all about him. Hercules serves Zeus. Perhaps he also serves your Adonai. Make your gift and be gone!"

"If it is known in Jerusalem that we have done this thing, there will be trouble."

"What do you mean by that, Jason?" asked the king.

"There will be a riot."

"I thought you and Appolonius had made Jerusalem into a Greek city! Antioch-in-Jerusalem you said you wanted it to be! I have planned to see this new Greek city of yours after I leave Tyre. What has transpired?"

"Not every Jew agrees with what is being done. As I said, we are to have no other gods. It is our law, and many of our people feel strongly about this. We dare not make a sacrifice to Hercules. There would truly be an uprising in Jerusalem, and the king would not wish that to happen."

"Then return to your Jerusalem. I am weary of Jews and their law and their Adonai!"

"I have an alternative to suggest to the king."

"Jason, leave!" commanded the king. "I am tired, and I should not have been disturbed."

"Please hear me out, Majesty!"

"I will give you half a minute and no more!" shouted the king.

"We have the proper amount of silver. Could we give it directly to Your Majesty, for some special purpose, and not present it as a sacrifice to your Greek deity?"

Antiochus pondered the possibility.

"I suppose that could be done," he said. "I am building a new navy. The ships are being constructed here in Tyre. The money could be used for that purpose."

"Then we will contribute the silver to the king, who will build ships with it. If I can report this in Jerusalem, there will be no difficulty."

"Then do so, Jason," said the king.

"I may leave the silver here?"

"You may take your silver to the treasurer and tell him that I have accepted it for building our ships."

"Thank you, Your Majesty!"

"You may leave, Jason. Good fortune in the games.

And we shall probably next meet in Jerusalem."

Jason nearly tripped over his sandals as he left. Berenice broke into hysterical laughter, and Antiochus quickly joined her.

"These are the Jews you worry about so much?" she asked.

"It is silly, isn't it?" Antiochus agreed.

"Can you imagine that man, stark naked, in the games?" Berenice hooted.

"I would rather not imagine it, my dear. No more than myself. Why do you think I did not enter the games this year?" He smiled. "Kings should be kingly, and priests should be priestly," he continued pompously.

"I suppose you would add that mistresses should be mistressly?"

"Why not?" asked the king without laughter.

The games had gone well in Tyre—they were as good as any held in Greece itself. Participants and spectators all enjoyed the festival, and Antiochus was particularly pleased that his favored new event was well received.

He had introduced a single gladiatorial fight, choosing fifty muscular slaves. At first the observers sat in shock, realizing that the swords and the blood they drew were real. However, before the afternoon had ended, they screamed for death as loudly as Romans, displeased that only one event of gladiators in combat had been scheduled.

Antiochus had hoped that the new sport would be accepted. He himself enjoyed watching the death-defying and death-dealing dance. With its success in Tyre, he could complete building the huge Circus arena in Antioch and would train gladiators as was done in Rome.

But first he had to journey to Jerusalem.

Antiochus and Appolonius, his governor, discussed the complexities of Judea. The governor had learned of Jason's visit with the king in Tyre, of course. In fact, he had made a joke of it, saying that it was typical of a man who had been elevated to a position of power that was beyond his competence.

The king felt there might be more to it than that. He was not concerned about the silver or the sacrifice. He did need money for his ships, and he intended to use money offered to Hercules for that purpose anyway. He had to have his ships if he were to launch his offensive against Egypt, despite Rome's prohibition of a navy. And if he were to attack Egypt, Judea had to be safely under control. He now seriously questioned whether this Jason was a strong enough agent and ally.

Jason, at any rate, provided a notable reception for the king.

It seemed that the entire city was there to welcome him. His own soldiers marched, but they were outnumbered by the Judeans whom Jason had got to march with displays of treasure or who danced in the streets. There were dozens of trumpeters who hailed Antiochus with fanfares throughout the waning afternoon into evening. When darkness fell, the streets suddenly became alive with candles and torches. It was a tremendous exhibition, and Antiochus was flattered and pleased.

The king met the leaders of the city and was

reassured of their loyalty. The party known as the Tobiads were obviously in favor of the policy of Hellenization and promoted it.

Antiochus visited the *gymnasion* and offered a few words of dedication for the completed academy. He ate a meal with his troops in the Citadel. And he was given a brief tour of the Temple. He took note of the silver and gold that was much in evidence on walls and in ornaments. He was impressed with the fine tapestries and wood carvings. Jason did not take him everywhere in the Temple—he would not show the king the library nor that room called the Holy of Holies—but Antiochus did see the sanctuary and its high altar. Jason told him that this was a special privilege.

"I know, Jason" the king surprised Jason—"I am uncircumcised and am not to be allowed in your sanctuary."

"You know this, Excellency?" Jason said fearfully.

"I know more about your beliefs than you would think possible," the king replied cryptically. He would not tell this high priest how much he had learned from Benjamin and Caleb. He had even found a copy in Antioch of the Pentateuch, the Torah, in Greek, and he had read most of it. But, as he fingered his amulet, he thought of his other mentor, who seemed to know everything about every religion in the world but who seemed to take particular pleasure in humiliating any belief in Adonai.

There was a disturbance as he left the Temple. A bearded man led the shouting, but Jason said the men were rabble from nearby villages and the king should not worry. Antiochus did worry. Jerusalem had to be kept secure. Confrontation with Egypt was at hand.

He had a visitor before he left for Antioch.

"My name is Menelaus," he said. "I am a cousin of Jason, the high priest."

"Menelaus is a Greek name. How are you called in Hebrew?" asked the king.

"My Judean name is Onias."

The king was visibly perplexed. "Were you related to the high priest who was killed?" he asked.

"No, Your Highness," said Menelaus. "I belong to the house of Tobias. I am not a Levite, which is to say I do not belong to the priestly caste."

The man spoke well and easily. He was confident and at ease. Antiochus was impressed as he noticed Menelaus staring at his necklace.

"Are you interested in seeing this?" asked the king, holding out the amulet but not removing the necklace.

"If it would not be an impertinence," said Menelaus.

The Jew stared at the talisman for several seconds.

"Does it interest you?" inquired Antiochus.

"I simply wonder why your majesty wears a medallion with Hebrew characters."

"Is that what they are?" the king exclaimed. "Do they mean anything?"

Menelaus shook his head. "Not these three letters. They do not form any word that I know."

"Might the letters stand for something?"

Menelaus again studied the amulet.

"There might be this meaning: we do not have numerals in Hebrew, but we give a numerical value to certain letters. This letter is repeated three times. The letter *vav* has the numerical value of six."

"Three sixes, then?" Antiochus smiled. "Just three sixes."

"It is possible that the letters stand for six hundred sixty-six," said Menelaus. "This amulet has a strange warmth to it, Your Majesty."

"So you feel it, too," the king murmured quietly. "Tell me why you came to see me."

"I am not sure whether I am a Jerusalemite or an Antiochite."

"Speak plainly, Menelaus."

"Jerusalem is not the Antioch some of us hoped to see."

"From what I have seen, its Hellenization has progressed to a substantial degree," said the king.

"You have seen only what the Temple authorities wished you to see. There is much danger to Your Majesty in this city."

"My governor does not think so. He is pleased with the implementation of our policy."

"With all due respect, Majesty, Appolonius also sees what the Temple authorities wish him to see."

"And what is your occupation in Jerusalem, Menelaus, if I may inquire?" asked the king.

"I am one of the Temple authorities. I am the Temple administrator, a traditional position for a Tobiad. As I said, I am the cousin of Jason."

Antiochus was dumbfounded. "Then you indict yourself, Menelaus, as one of the Temple authorities. What is your true purpose in seeing me?"

"I seek the position of high priest."

The effrontery of the man was astounding.

"It could not be done," said the king. "My understanding is that a Tobiad could never be high priest."

"The high priest, Your Majesty, can be anyone you name."

"You state your business clearly," Antiochus said with a smile as he shook his head.

"The times require it, Your Majesty."

"Why should you be appointed high priest?" asked the king.

"First of all, because I will serve you better than my cousin, Jason."

"Are you not supposed to serve your Adonai first of all?" Antiochus probed.

"I serve myself first of all, Excellency. In that respect, I believe we are much alike." The man had audacity, but the king did not become angry. "I admit to ambition, and I care very little for our law or our tradition. I can serve you better than Jason because I do not have his inhibitions. Jason tries to be both Jew and Greek. In these times, one cannot be both."

Antiochus recalled that he had once said almost the identical thing to Jason.

"You require a high priest, Excellency," Menelaus continued, "who will be always loyal to you and who will truly make of Judea a province of Antioch. I know that I can achieve this objective for you."

"Is there another reason that I should consider?" asked the king.

"Yes," said Menelaus. "There is the matter of tribute. My family and I are prepared to pay three hundred talents more each year than Jason now pays Your Majesty as tribute for the office of high priest."

"You hide behind neither bushes nor words," said the king. "I think I like that." And he also enjoyed contemplating the additional revenue. The king wondered why the Temple position was worth so much to this man. Before he could voice the question, Menelaus provided him with an answer.

"My family owns most of Jerusalem," Menelaus said. "It is in our interest to protect our properties and our markets."

"Obviously, you are not a religious man. How can I appoint you a priest?"

"I am no less religious than Your Majesty," Menelaus replied.

"Some would consider you shameless and arrogant."

"That is for the king to decide."

"How might this thing be accomplished, assuming that we agreed to proceed?" asked the king.

"Jason is to make his yearly payment of tribute within a few weeks. I can convince him that I should carry this treasure to Antioch. I will bring my own tribute, in advance, and you will be that much richer, Excellency." Menelaus smiled unabashedly. "While I am in Antioch, you can issue the proper decree, through the governor, and Jason will be deposed."

"It is a clever plan," Antiochus concurred. "It might be wise to again have a high priest named Onias."

"I will not go by that name, Excellency. My name is Menelaus."

Antiochus wrestled with his thoughts, not wanting to make a hasty decision. He knew that Jason was weak and vacillating whereas this Menelaus would surely be strong and decisive. He had been disturbed about the security of Jerusalem and Judea—and perhaps an ambitious and openly cynical high priest might be the person to better control these Jews. In many ways, this Menelaus and he were much like. He wondered if their allegiances might possibly be the same. Perhaps they were like two sides of the same coin. Thinking of a coin gave the king an idea.

He reached into a pocket.

"You asked, earlier, to see the amulet," said the king. "Let me show you something else. Fewer than a dozen people have seen it, but soon it will be the coin of the realm." He handed a coin to Menelaus.

"It is newly minted and beautifully made, Your Majesty."

"Observe it well. You see the image?"

"The style is that of Zeus, but the face is that of the king."

Antiochus smiled. "Read the inscription!" he commanded.

"ANTIOCHUS THEOS EPIPHANES," Menelaus read. "Is this to be your new title, Majesty?"

Antiochus nodded affirmatively. "Of course, you know the meaning?" he asked.

" 'Theos Epiphanes'—God Manifest!" Menelaus stared at the coin, for the moment lost in his private thoughts.

"You may keep the coin if you like," said the king.

"I thank Your Majesty," Menelaus replied and paused. "Do we have an understanding, sire?"

Antiochus now knew that he would have to give an answer. Menelaus was cunning, ambitious, and would have to be watched carefully. But there was no question that he could help the kingdom far better than Jason. The Jews would have to be contained and controlled. A conniving but dutiful Jew might accomplish that.

"I will expect you and the tribute in Antioch," said the king. "We can make commerce together."

16

It was to be the climax of the feast honoring
Dionysius.

Several hundred persons crowded into the Grand
Hall of the palace in Antioch, and the king was
pleased that so many of his friends had come.

Some of the faces were those of old stalwarts.
Phillipus, master of the elephants was there, a strik-
ingly handsome man even in his eightieth year.
Appolonius, governor of Judea, had come. Berenice
was at his side. Laodice was in her chamber fighting
a high fever; Antiochus knew that she suffered from
sickness of mind as well as body.

There were new faces as well. Gorgias was his
new general, a Macedonian who directed his armies. Unlike Andronicus, whom the king still remembered especially during the sleepless moments
of night, Gorgias enjoyed public display and speech-
making.

Lysias was a newcomer, but the king knew he would one day find his way into the highest councils of his realm. Lysias was a brilliant administrator and would be a cautious diplomat. The king intended that Lysias would have a major hand in the education of his son the young prince. Lysias was a true prize, thought Antiochus, and a pleasant companion.

The long evening of eating was ending. Wine, of all kinds and ages had flowed like the Orontes; whether in tribute to the Greek Dionysius or the Roman Bacchus, it did not matter. The room was far from silent. People conversed and musicians played their instruments, but the cacophony seemed to be more subdued, less strident. Perhaps the wine was lulling everyone into a stupor that for many would become sleep.

The king clapped his hands to gain attention, and the spectators seemed to awaken.

"It is time for gifts!" shouted the king, trying to control the slurring of his speech. He himself had selected and wrapped these gifts, and it was an event that gave him great pleasure.

He reached into a pocket and threw out a handful of golden coins. He laughed as dozens of people fought over them.

"For you, my delightful Berenice!" Antiochus shouted as he handed her an unwrapped cedar chest. "Open it," he commanded. Berenice lifted a delicately carved figure of Diana. It was made of ivory, and the people who saw it cheered.

"Phillipus!" Antiochus held up an object that had been wrapped with papyrus. "For you, my friend!"

He beamed. The old man graciously undid the parcel and then stared.

"What is it?" he asked incredulously as he held it up for all to see. It gleamed brightly but had no recognizable shape. Suddenly, Phillipus recognized it for what it was and burst into laughter.

"It is a silver-plated elephant turd!" he shouted, wiping the tears from his eyes. The people stamped their feet and shouted laughing derision.

Thus it continued for the remainder of the evening. Gifts were distributed to friend and courtier with no discrimination. One received a ruby, another received a common pebble. Another found an expensive silver dish, while someone else unwrapped a foul-smelling knucklebone. It was intended to be a gigantic joke, and the king hoped that his subjects would talk about it for years to come.

Later that night he walked, alone, into the city.

He had escaped both the palace and his guards, wearing a simple peasant gown and tarboosh. He walked toward the commercial agora, where a few shops would still be open and, perhaps, a place where he could purchase more wine.

It felt good to be alone. Antiochus had no fear, only exhilaration. He was sure that no one would recognize him, and, if he avoided street brawls, he would be safe. So often he felt torn between the obligations of royalty and a need to mingle with common people. He often thought that the patricians of Rome had found the ideal way of combining aristocracy and democracy. He wished it were possible to achieve that in Antioch. Tonight he would try his best to do so.

He purchased a pear from a roving vendor. He savored its flavor and was pleased that his disguise was effective.

A silversmith's shop was still open, which he entered.

"Are you here to look or to buy?" asked the owner.

"I wish to look," Antiochus said. "Perhaps I will buy," he added, amused that the owner thought he might be too poor to purchase anything.

"Yes, your royal highness!" the owner said.

Antiochus was shaken, but then he saw the man's sneer and realized that the owner was being sarcastic.

"Are you the silversmith as well as the owner?" the king asked.

The man nodded.

"You do beautiful work. The links of this chain are quite delicate. How do you do it?"

"With flame and a glass."

"What do you mean—flame and glass?" the king inquired.

"The hot flame keeps the metal workable. The glass enlarges my vision so that I can see fine detail."

"I see that you make medallions."

"A few."

"You pour hot metal into molds?"

"No!" said the silversmith. "I make them as coins are made. They are struck between heavy dies." The man looked at his customer curiously. "You ask strange questions for a peasant."

"Have you ever struck coins for the realm?"

"No. But I am capable of doing so."

"We have a king who delights in making coins," Antiochus said slyly.

The silversmith snorted. "We have a king who delights in much extravagance."

Antiochus laughed at the reply but marked the man for some future task. He did like the quality of his workmanship.

"Well, sir, have you seen anything you like?" asked the owner.

"I have seen much that I like," said the king, "but I will return another day to buy."

"I thought that our negotiation would end this way," said the artisan with irritation and anger.

Antiochus chuckled as he left and found a place where he could drink wine and watch those who passed by. He was amazed that there was this much movement and traffic at such a late hour. Of course, the children and their matron mothers were at home, but there were still many people about. It was pleasant to gaze at them, to dream as he continued to assuage his thirst.

Lysias and two palace guards discovered the king slumped over his table, snoring loudly.

"Wake up, Majesty!" said Lysias, shaking the king gently.

Antiochus wakened quickly. "Quiet, Lysias!" he said, "no one must know who I am." He was drunk, but not as drunk as Lysias thought.

"We will escort you home then," said Lysias.

"No!" said the king. "We have much yet to do this night. Perhaps it is good that you came when you did."

Lysias looked at the two guards and shrugged his shoulders.

"How much money do you have with you, Lysias?" asked the king.

"I have the two gold pieces you gave me at the banquet."

"Good. That should be enough. And when we need more money, one of the guards can get it from the palace!" Antiochus grinned broadly.

"Do you wish to buy more wine, Excellency? Lysias asked.

"Do not call me 'Excellency!' " Antiochus whispered dramatically. "Not in this place!"

"You wish more wine, sire?" Lysias repeated, more quietly.

"Much more wine, Lysias!" said the king.

"Forgive me, sire, but perhaps you have drunk enough for one evening?"

"The wine is not for me, Lysias. It is for my people! All of them!" Antiochus in extending his arms knocked a glass off the table.

Lysias felt helpless.

"Find a wine wagon!" commanded the king.

"Sir, it is late."

"Find a wagon with wine, Lysias! You must obey your king!" he shouted and then, realizing what he had said, covered his mouth with his hand in embarrassment.

The tavernkeeper had been watching and motioned to Lysias.

"If the king wants to purchase a wagon full of wine, there is such a wagon in back of my shop. We have not yet poured the wine into jars."

203

"You heard him call himself king. He is drunk, he only pretends," said Lysias, trying to protect his master.

"I knew he was the king the moment he entered," said the tavernkeeper. "It is his face upon the coin, is it not? And do you think this is the first time he has been here? Antiochus may pretend that he is a commoner, but he cannot pretend that he is a king, for that is who he is."

Lysias nodded in agreement.

"Do you want the wine or not?"

"I have only two gold pieces."

"That is more than enough. I will have some change for you."

"You are an honest man."

"I wish to remain a tavernkeeper," he said. "Your master has a good memory, according to some of my friends. The cart is in back. Return it when you are through."

Lysias reported to the king that the wine had been found.

"Good!" said Antiochus. "We will go up the mountain."

Lysias marveled at the king's capacity for wine but thought it best to humor his sovereign.

"You wish to return to the palace, do you not, Excellency?" he asked.

"No!" declared the king. "We go to Mount Silpius. I will tell you what should be done with the wine when we are there."

The four men found the cart. The king sat in the teamster's seat and promptly went to sleep. Lysias told one of the guards to hold the reins, and he and the other guard marched alongside the cart.

The roadway was steep, and the night was dark. With much difficulty they managed to travel halfway up the mountain when Antiochus wakened and directed them to turn southward to the aqueduct.

They heard the rushing water before they saw it.

"Now find a place where we can empty the cart into the water!" said the king.

The guards looked at Lysias in disbelief.

"You would waste good wine, Majesty?" asked Lysias.

"I will repay you in the morning, Lysias. These guards are my witnesses."

"I do not worry about repayment, sire. I do worry about wasting wine."

"Then drink of it before you dump it." Antiochus began to laugh. "I want all of Antioch to have a taste of wine in the morning."

Lysias finally understood the trick the king intended to play. A trace of wine would indeed be in water tanks of most of the homes of Antioch by morning. He explained this to the guards, and all of them began to laugh, pouring themselves a flagon each, and then began searching the darkness along Cossutius's aqueduct to find a place to easily relieve the wine wagon of its contents.

They watched the wine mix with the water and even in the half-darkness saw the water change color. Each man continued to drink—with flagon and cup and even cupped hand—and king and subjects were soon thoroughly and noisily drunk. They laughed and sang and hung to each other in a comradeship

205

that would not have been possible had they been sober.

"And now we must go to the baths!" Antiochus declared.

"Sir, we should return to the palace," Lysias remonstrated.

"The baths are still open?"

"They remain open all night, Majesty."

"Then we must go and clean up. All of you will be my guests," the king said grandly and unsteadily.

They went immediately to the room of hot waters, and the king absorbed its warmth and movement with pleasure. The guards beat his back with clusters of reeds to increase the circulation of the royal blood. Lysias found a scraper and used the few coins he had left to purchase a fragrant ointment for the king. Antiochus invited all of them to join him in the waters.

Then someone shouted, "The king is here!" Antiochus stood up to see who had called out, and soon recognition swept loudly around the room.

"I walk the streets of Antioch all evening in peasant clothes and no one recognizes me," Antiochus said, red-faced with anger and not from the heat of the room. "Here, where I am bare as a mountain goat, the whole world knows who I am."

Lysias could not keep himself from laughing since the king was still standing. "Sire," he said, "a mountain goat is covered more than you are at this moment!"

They all laughed.

Another voice was heard in the room.

"How elegant to be rich and enjoy ointments and slaves!"

The man was also obviously inebriated—but most people who came to the baths at this early morning hour came because they wished to rid themselves of their superfluity of wine.

"Who said that?" asked Antiochus who was still standing.

"I see the man, Excellency," said Lysias. "Do you wish him arrested for his impertinence?"

"No," said the king with a smile. "But do not allow him to leave this room. And bring me more ointment."

"I can bring another vial, sire."

"I require more than a vial. Find an urn of perfumed oil. Better still, a firkin of ointment!"

"It would cost a fortune, Excellency!"

"Find the manager of this place and tell him I command that he provide a firkin of ointment. He will be paid!" shouted the king. "And I want the oil brought here without delay. To this very spot!"

As Lysias left to do the king's bidding, Antiochus shouted: "Everyone is to remain in his place. No one is to leave." He then ordered his guards to post themselves at the door. They grabbed towels and swords as they went.

Lysias returned a few minutes later with the manager of the baths and two of his helpers. They struggled with a small wooden tub, filled with a mixture of fragrant ointments and oils. The manager was obviously irritated but seemed determined to say nothing, wanting only to be paid for his wares and trouble.

207

"What are your wishes now, Excellency?" asked Lysias.

"Bring the man who ridiculed the king," he said.

The man was brought forward. He was now shaking with fright.

"You are a brave man to address the king as you did," said Antiochus in a mock rage. "Why do you shake, now, like a willow tree? You should see yourself in a glass, spindly-legs!" The king no longer pretended to be angry and burst into laughter. "Pour out the ointment," he commanded.

"Here, Excellency?" asked the manager of the baths.

"Right here," said the king, pointing to the tiled floor beside him. The ointment was poured.

King Antiochus then gave the drunken man who had ridiculed him a massive shove. He slipped and fell into the spreading pool of aromatic oil.

"You wish to know the pleasures of the rich? Enjoy yourself!" the king declared.

Antiochus then lay down upon the floor himself and began to roll and frolic in the oil. As the ointment spread, other bathers followed suit, until the tiled floor was full of every bather in the room. Word spread throughout the establishment, and bathers from the room of cold waters joined them. The room of hot waters became a screaming, wrestling scuffle, with men dousing each other with the expensive oil, skidding about, rubbing themselves and their unknown neighbors. Everyone seemed oblivious to the spectacle of which they were a part, and the king gamboled and skipped with all of them.

Lysias stood to one side, silent, unsure of what he should do.

The manager came to him, gesturing to the enormous mess that had been created.

"That is Epiphanes?" he muttered. "*God Manifest*? Better to call him *Epimanes*!" And he stalked off in anger.

Lysias decided he would not report the words of the manager to the king. The poor man had been grossly provoked, and it would take hours to clean up the place. Probably the baths would have to be closed for a day.

"Antiochus Epimanes," he pondered.

Antiochus, *the Mad Man*.

17

A dozen men were gathered in the home of Mattathias the priest, in Modein.

"You say, Mattathias, that you saw Joshua escort the heathen king into the Temple itself?" The man who spoke was Japheth, an elder in the village of Emmaus, which was close by.

"I saw it with these very eyes," cried the priest. "And so did these my five sons, who were with me."

"How long was this Antiochus inside the Temple?" asked Japheth.

"He was inside for at least two hours," Judah, who was also known as Maccabee, replied.

"Then the king has seen everything," said another of the villagers.

"The Temple was desecrated by one of our own people, by a priest, by a so-called high priest," Mattathias sobbed.

"He is a renegade," said Japheth.

"A traitor!" shouted Judah.

"An evil doer who should be put to death!" his brother John agreed.

"You will now have to go to Ammon to do that," Mattathias sighed. "This Joshua—this Jason, as he paraded himself among the Greeks—has taken refuge among the Ammonites."

"Then let us march beyond the Jordan," said Simon, another of the sons of Mattathias.

"Let us concern ourselves first with the scoundrel who has replaced Jason in the Temple," said the aging priest. "This Menelaus must be dealt with. I believe that the predicted time of desolation may already be upon us. Thus we must plan and prepare. We must be ready to defend the honor of Adonai!" he cried.

"Then let us raise an army to restore Joshua," said Japheth. "I have heard that he seethes with anger and lives for the day when he can overthrow his cousin."

"Let him boil," said the priest. "I would not fight for this Jew who only pretended to be a Jew—this Jason. He was no better than Menelaus. They both bribed the king for the office of high priest."

"Joshua is the brother of our late lamented Onias," said Japheth. "He is a member of the priestly family."

"As am I!" Mattathias declared. "I am a descendant of the tribe of Joarib."

"Could it be that you, Mattathias, wish to become high priest?" Japheth whispered.

"No, my friend." The priest smiled. "No. It is given to me only to serve Adonai as a priest, not as high priest. I wish no power for myself nor such

212

power for any of my sons. I wish only glory for Adonai and the purification of His Temple."

"Then what must we do?" asked Judah Maccabee. "How do we give glory to the Almighty and cleanse His Holy Place?"

"First we must spread the word throughout the land," said Mattathias. "All of Judea must learn that there is a false priest and an evil prophet in the Temple. We must declare the truth about this Menelaus—about who he is, how he obtained his office of high priest, and what he has done."

"I could speak to the Sanhedrin," said Japheth.

"The Sanhedrin has become a Greek *gerousia*," Judah interrupted.

"Calm yourself, my son," said the priest. "The Sanhedrin is the true council, and Japheth would do well to plead our cause—Adonai's cause!—there. There are still many good and pious Jews in this land who will not countenance or condone this blasphemy and treason. There are many of them in the Sanhedrin itself."

"It will be done," said Japheth.

"Would you consider one thing more?" asked the priest. "Would you—and, perhaps, others from the Sanhedrin—go to Antioch itself and speak with the king?"

"Can Antiochus be trusted?" the elder replied. "Consider the plot against Onias and how easily he displaced Joshua."

"But if he knew the truth about Menelaus, would he want such a man in so great a place of power?" the priest persisted.

"I do not know the king's mind, Mattathias. I will

discuss the matter with the Sanhedrin, however."

The men looked nervously at each other.

"We must prepare for the worst, my brothers and sons," said Mattathias. "We must establish a loyal band as did Gideon of old. It will do no harm for Japheth to counsel with the Sanhedrin. It might do good to meet with the king himself. But I believe the time has come for us to prepare ourselves."

"How shall we do this, my father?" asked Judah.

"We must secure arms, and we must learn how to use them. We must find brave men who will be willing to defend Adonai when the appointed day arrives. That day will come, mark my words!" the priest affirmed. "The day will come to extirpate the evil in our midst!"

18

King Antiochus paced the floor of his royal chamber in bristling anger.

Menelaus, that ambitious and corrupt high priest from Jerusalem, had delayed payment of the required tribute. He had been summoned to Antioch to either bring the tax or an explanation. The king desperately needed the gold and silver.

Rome was again fighting the house of Antigonus in Greece. It was the third time that the Romans were pushing their way eastward, breaking treaties and alliances. If they conquered Antigonus, Rome's former ally, nothing would keep the Romans from attacking Eumenes in Pergamum, across the Aegean, who was another Roman ally. And if Pergamum fell, only the Taurus Mountains would stand between Rome and Antioch.

Antiochus had remained diplomatically correct with Rome and its senate. He had periodically sent

emissaries with official greetings and gifts. However-
er, even setting aside the threat to his own kingdom,
Antiochus did not want to see Rome conquer Greece.
Antiochus was first of all himself a Greek, and he
felt a great love for the land of his forefathers.

He had demonstrated that love by sending unprece-
dented and expensive gifts to Athens. He had paid
for a Gorgon head to be placed on the Acropolis. He
had commissioned Cossutius—the Roman architect
who had completed many marvels in Antioch—to
complete construction of the massive temple of Zeus
in Athens. He had long ago promised himself that
he would do that thing for the city of which he had
been made an honorary citizen in his younger days.
It was proving to be a costly promise, but he wanted
to see that great thing achieved. He refused to think
of Romans occupying his beloved Athens.

But, more importantly and more immediately, he
had to deal with Egypt.

He struck out in anger as he paced the marble
floor.

An alliance was essential to both countries. It
would be good for Egypt as well as Antioch. His
overtures had been ignored. His sister Cleopatra—all
Egyptian queens would henceforth be called Cleopatra—had sent him a sarcastic note suggesting that
Antiochus concentrate on the affairs of Antioch and
not those of Alexandria.

There would have to be a confrontation. Antiochus
would demonstrate to the world who was king not
only in Syria but in Asia. He clasped the burning
amulet in his hand. The kingdom was his by divine

217

right. Or, was it, he wondered, because he was rightly divine. He smiled sardonically at the twist of words.

Menelaus was announced and entered the king's chambers.

"I bring you greetings, Matchless Serenity, from your subjects in Antioch-Jerusalem!" he declared, bowing to the floor with a broad sweep of his hands. Antiochus, watching his performance, conceded that the rogue was a superb artist.

"I complement you upon your promptness," said the king.

Menelaus again bowed.

"I do expect an explanation for the delay of the tribute," Antiochus declared. Menelaus was not affected by the harsh tone of the king's voice.

"Your Majesty will have the tribute in his hands tomorrow," he said, "and I do bring an explanation."

"Why must it be tomorrow?"

"That is part of my explanation, Excellency."

"Then explain!!" commanded the king.

"Your Majesty is aware of the treasury of the Temple. Many people—some of them only modestly endowed with wealth—have deposited their treasures with us in the Temple."

"I know that," said the king. "Continue."

"Somehow, word reached the people that the tribute to Your Majesty had been increased. There was fear that we might 'borrow,' shall we say, from the Temple resources. These people—far more than I wish were the case—then withdrew their treasures. Our treasury was depleted, you see."

"You should have informed me sooner, Menelaus!"

"It was an inexcusable lapse, Majesty," Menelaus

218

agreed with a bow. "On the other hand, I did not wish to preoccupy the king unduly."

"You have the tribute with you?"

"It will be delivered tomorrow, sire."

"If you have it why not deliver it today to my treasurer?"

"Forgive me, Excellency, but it is better for both of us if I withhold the details of the matter." Menelaus smiled as though he had not a care in the world. "I regret the secrecy, truly."

"But the tribute will be made?" the king insisted.

"In full, Majesty!" said Menelaus. "In fact, there will be something in addition! Our merchants in Jerusalem are aware of your need, most excellent sovereign, and they have sent an advance on the taxes that are soon to fall due."

The king was pleased with the news.

"Is Judea peaceful?" he asked.

"Quite serene, Majesty," Menelaus replied. "There is some bickering, but a little of this can be tolerated."

"And your cousin, Jason, how fares he?"

"I have no communication with my cousin. He lives beyond the Jordan."

"I have heard rumors that he seeks to raise an army and reclaim his position in Jerusalem."

"I have not heard even rumors of this nature," Menelaus said warily.

"There are times, Menelaus, when I am less and less fond of you Jews. You are not a populous race. You occupy only a small corner on what is a major trade route. But your people remind me of flies that sting horses."

"Socrates once said he was such a fly upon the horse politic."

"Did he? I fail to see a connection," said the king.

"Perhaps the Jews would like to think they exert an influence far beyond their numbers and wealth," said Menelaus slowly and carefully.

"Just be certain, high priest, that you Jews do not goad me or sting me beyond endurance. Horses survive long after flies have departed this life."

Menelaus did not reply.

"I am curious," said the king. "Who is in charge of the Temple during your absence?"

"My brother," said Menelaus. "His name is Lysimachus."

"Is he a priest?"

"He is as much a priest as I," said Menelaus seriously.

The two men looked at each other and then broke into laughter.

"You take many liberties in the king's presence," said the king. "You are a brave man. Be careful, sir, that you do not overstep into brashness." The king escorted the Jew toward the door. "I will see you on the morrow. Be certain you bring the tribute."

Later that day a delegation from Jerusalem requested an immediate audience with the king. Antiochus, having just seen Menelaus, was surprised and curious.

Three men appeared. They were well-dressed and gave the appearance of prosperity. Their spokesman was a man who said his name was Japheth.

"We are grateful to Your Majesty for agreeing to

220

see us so quickly," he said.

"State your business," said the king without preliminaries.

"We are here to protest the actions of our high priest," said Japheth.

"You speak of Menelaus," said the king and the men nodded. "What exactly do you protest?"

"We are aware that Menelaus is in Antioch and that he brings tribute to Your Majesty."

"I believe that is our concern and not yours!" said the king with cold irritation.

"Begging your indulgence, Excellency, the manner by which the tribute was obtained is very much our concern."

"Proceed!" the king exclaimed.

"We have reason to believe that Menelaus told Your Majesty that he brings not only his personal tribute but also a portion of taxes due to you from our merchants."

The king remained rigid and silent.

"Menelaus brings no taxes," said Japheth.

"Do you have proof of this?" asked the king.

"My friends, here, are merchants in Jerusalem, members of the high council. They provided no advance on taxes."

"Is this true?" asked Antiochus.

The men nodded that it was.

"But it is only your word, and you are only two merchants among many," said the king. "Your word is not enough."

"Your Majesty can make inquiries through his new governor, Sostratus."

"Why would Menelaus deceive me in this manner?" Antiochus asked.

"Perhaps, sire, the man seeks greater favor."

The king's face darkened. "You reflect upon me as well as Menelaus," he declared angrily.

"We speak only of Menelaus, Excellency," said Japheth calmly.

"If what you say is true, then whence does Menelaus find this extra money?"

"The answer to that question is the real reason for our being here, Majesty. Menelaus has robbed our Temple!"

"Indeed?" Antiochus laughed. "Menelaus has robbed your Temple?" The idea seemed incredible.

"This man has stolen the silver and the gold—the ornaments, the vessels, the decorations. He sold some of these in Tyre, but he carried so much treasure with him that the merchants in Tyre refused to buy all of it. He is on this very day attempting to sell the rest of it to merchants here in Antioch."

Antiochus pondered the accusation. Kings had robbed temples many times, but would a priest—even a spurious priest such as Menelaus—do such a thing?

"Why should this matter concern me?" the king asked. "How your high priest raises his tribute is his concern, not mine. Nor is it yours!" he admonished the men.

"Your Majesty," Japheth continued, "the Judeans will not allow the despoiling of our holy Temple. Once the deed of Menelaus is fully known, there will be uprisings and violence. This, then, will become a concern for the king!"

The king granted the point but resented the reminder from these Jews.

"And do you have a suggestion for me?" he asked with muted sarcasm.

"Command Menelaus to return the sacred objects to the Temple, sire. Insist that he pay his tribute from his private treasury! Menelaus is not a poor man; he is wealthy in his own right and becomes wealthier with the passing of each month."

That is interesting intelligence, thought the king.

"O King," Japheth continued, "your father, the Great Antiochus, promised Onias, our high priest of blessed memory, that our Temple would never be invaded and that its treasures would never be touched. Your Majesty could reaffirm what your father promised and what is known to all of our people. Your declaration would calm our people, and there will be peace in the land."

The man had gone too far.

"No one instructs Epiphanes," Antiochus said in a low, ice-cold voice. "Especially Judeans."

The audience was ended, and he waved them out of the room.

As he had promised, Menelaus returned the next day, bringing his tribute and the additional sum of an advance on taxes from the merchants of Jerusalem.

"I was informed that you sold some of the Temple treasure to provide this one," said the king.

"My enemies saw the king!" Menelaus said sadly. "It is merely a family dispute, Majesty. There are some who wish to have another as high priest. Your Excellency should not be concerned."

"I become weary of you Jews and your family disputes. You fight each other, you connive against each other, your religion affects everything you do and say." The king felt such a lecture was long overdue. "Did you rob the Temple?" he asked.

Menelaus appeared to be embarrassed by the direct question.

"I merely borrowed a few items, Majesty." He hesitated. "There is so much more treasure in the Temple that a few items will not be missed. When these Jews visit the Temple they will still see vessels of gold and silver, and they will not believe the words of my detractors." Menelaus had regained control of himself. "Besides, Your Grace, does any of this truly matter? The treasure is here, in your hands, to use as Your Highness wishes."

The Jew was right, Antiochus decided. Of course Menelaus had robbed the Temple, and it did not really matter whether it had been done by Menelaus or by himself. In fact, it was probably better for the king for Menelaus to be his agent in the matter. Antiochus needed that treasure, especially now, and he would not quarrel about how it had come into his hands.

"The treasure will be used wisely for the benefit of the kingdom," said Antiochus, rather pompously. "I commend you for your diligence to this matter and to our person. I wish you safety on your return to Jerusalem."

As soon as Menelaus had left, Antiochus summoned the captain of the palace guard.

"Do you remember the three Judeans who con-

224

versed with me yesterday?" he asked.

"Yes, Your Majesty," the captain replied.

"Can they be found, do you think?"

"Of course they can be found, Excellency," the captain declared. "Whether they remain in Antioch or are already on the road southward to Judea, they can be apprehended."

"Do so," commanded the king.

"Does the king wish them returned to the palace?" asked the captain.

"I desire them to be killed," Antiochus declared. "Do it wherever it seems best. I will inform Gorgias, your commander."

The captain nodded.

"It will be done as you command," he said, saluting in Roman fashion as he retreated from the room.

Antiochus again began pacing the floor, no longer as angry as he had been the day before, plotting, now, next steps and action.

First of all, the Jews from Jerusalem would be taught a lesson. If the lesson was not learned, more instruction would be required.

Antiochus decided to put the Jews out of his mind.

It would be Egypt's turn to learn what a kingly wrath could truly mean.

19

Antiochus was resting with his troops within the shadows of the pyramids. His commander, the Macedonian Gorgias, was nearby, as was Appolonius, who now served the king as a counselor.

It had not been a tiring or even a dangerous journey. In fact, Egypt felt very little of the kingly wrath Antiochus had expected to expend.

"This is the strangest war I have ever fought," said the Macedonian. "It has been a war without fighting."

"Tomorrow we march toward Memphis," said the king.

"What do our scouts report?" asked Appolonius.

"The city is quiet, and there will be little resistance," said Gorgias.

"And Memphis is the ancient capital itself!" said Appolonius with amazement.

"We are not yet finished with Egypt, even when

Memphis surrenders," said Antiochus. "We will still have to deal with Alexandria. That is where we'll find the seat of government, and I expect to meet some resistance."

The expedition against Egypt had gone far better than he had hoped. His armies had marched along the coast through Gaza to Pelusium and then southward and westward toward Memphis. He had created surprise and confusion with the rapidity of his movement, and the opposition had strangely melted away. Antiochus held firmly to his amulet, trusting without question this lord who was so easily summoned and who had instructed him along the way. Antiochus believed that success was inevitable.

The reasons for the lack of opposition became clearer as they came closer to Egypt. Cleopatra, his sister, had died, and the royal house of the Ptolemies was in disarray. There were two sons and, of course, the oldest, although a mere youth, was now king.

Two generals—Eulaeus and Lenaeus—named themselves regents for the boy-king Ptolemy the Sixth. They had spirited him away to a sacred island, but the new regents did not know that for several days Ptolemy was already in the hands of Antiochus. His navy was based in Cyprus and had quickly captured the lad.

The generals tried to govern but were ignorant about governing. They then decided to name the youngest Ptolemy, named Euergetes, Pharaoh, believing they could better control the country through him. The result was dissension, confusion, and chaos—all of which worked to the advantage of Antiochus.

"You see what has now transpired," said Antiochus to his two military leaders. "Because I rescued the elder Ptolemy I am, in effect, his regent. I am certainly both his uncle and his defender—while those Egyptian generals support the child *pretender* to the throne, Euergetes."

"Call him *Physcon*, Majesty!" Gorgias laughed. "That's what the Egyptians call him."

" 'Fat Paunch'?" asked the king, disbelieving.

"Have you ever seen him, Excellency?" the general asked.

"No. But you did, Appolonius."

"Not since Ptolemy's coronation. He was a mere infant then."

"Well, I dare say he lives up to his name. He is said to be a fat, ugly brat. Physcon!" Gorgias again roared with laughter.

The Seleucid troops entered Memphis in triumph. Antiochus was officially declared the regent and protector of the sequestered young Ptolemy Philometor. The citizens of Memphis responded with a day-long celebration, shouting and parading, ending with a coronation of Antiochus himself. As he rode through the city, he shouted his greetings and whoever responded in Greek was thrown a gold coin.

"Do you realize," Antiochus said to Appolonius, who was at his side, "that I am the first Seleucid to be honored in Egypt? Not even my father was able to accomplish this!"

They marched up the Nile toward the coast and

Alexandria. Even here there was not a battle worthy of the name, although there were a few skirmishes. The casualties were slight. The Seleucid navy blockaded the port, and Antiochus knew it would be only a matter of hours before the city would surrender.

"We must take care," warned Appolonius. "Egypt now ships much grain to Rome, and if our blockades delay those shipments, Rome will be aware of our presence."

"The Senate knows I am here, Appolonius," said the king with a beaming face. "I sent Heraclides to Rome with an official document saying I was coming to Egypt to insure the throne for its rightful heir. Rome is fighting her own battle, still, in Macedonia and must have stability in Egypt. Rome believes I am doing her a favor by being here!"

"But if the ships do not sail?" asked his counselor.

"A delay of one or two days will not matter. The Romans will blame the weather. And the siege will be over within two days at most!"

Antiochus was correct. The Egyptian generals sent word that they wished to sue for peace.

The Seleucid king was not impressed with the regents. Eulaeus had been chief eunuch in Egypt, and there was a prissiness about the man that Antiochus did not like. Lenaeus, Antiochus was surprised to learn, was Syrian, a renegade who had hired himself years before as a mercenary to the Ptolemies. Antiochus judged both men to be weak and susceptible to bribes. He did not expect the negotiations to extend many hours.

"I have no desire to govern Egypt," he began. "I

wish only two things. I want the rightful king, my nephew, to be on the throne. By virtue of our victory here I accept the responsibility of being protector to Ptolemy Philometor. If you continue as regents you will be accountable to me. The second thing I desire is that our two kingdoms work closely together, that we cooperate and coordinate our affairs, so that our present frontiers will be secure and inviolable."

"Your Majesty does not negotiate," said the eunuch sarcastically. "You merely make demands in the manner of the Romans."

"Perhaps that is because I have had some experience in observing the Romans," Antiochus replied with equal sarcasm. "But take care, Eulaeus," he warned. "There may be Roman agents about, and you would not want them to hear your disparagement of them."

"But in truth you do demand and do not bargain," the eunuch persisted.

"If you had wished to bargain," the king said, "you should have marshaled your arguments in better fashion on the battlefield. I demand because I can."

"If Your Majesty wishes security," said the Syrian Lenaeus, "he must control the Jews in Judea. We have heard of much unrest—even uprisings—which affect the well-being of both of our countries."

"What you say is worthy," Antiochus agreed, "but not your concern. I return to Antioch by way of Jerusalem to see conditions for myself."

There was little more to be discussed.

Documents were signed and sealed that very day. The legitimate Ptolemy was returned and installed again as king of Egypt. And Antiochus left Alexandria not only victorious but much richer. He was followed by ten large wagons full of gold and silver ornaments and vessels, removed, for the most part, from the temple to the Sun in Memphis.

Gorgias accompanied the treasure to Antioch while Appolonius went with the king to Jerusalem. A small contingent of soldiers journeyed with them.

They did not immediately enter the city.

Instead, they surveyed the Judean capital from a hillside overlooking the Hinnom valley.

"Do you miss living in Jerusalem, Appolonius?" the king asked.

"No, Your Majesty," he replied. "There is too much intrigue, too much piety."

The king was amused. "It is a pretty place—a city nestled within and around hills. It almost reminds me of Rome, except Rome is so much bigger, of course."

Antiochus had heard that there had been an uprising after word circulated that Menelaus had indeed robbed the Temple of many of its treasures. The murder of the three Jews was also known. It was difficult from this vantage point to see any damage, but the king was determined to find out if there was widespread discontent.

The king was studying the outer wall of the city.

"That, of course, is the Temple," he pointed. "Tell me, where did their famous king David live?"

"There, to your right, Majesty. It is near a pool that is called Siloam."

"And the mountain beyond us? What is its name?"

232

"The Mount of Olives."

The king had decided to enter the city unannounced. He wanted to surprise both Sostratus, his new governor, and Menelaus, the high priest. Antiochus, Appolonius, and the soldiers began marching quickly toward the city.

"I think I should warn you, Majesty."

"About what, Appolonius?" said the king.

"The name of the gate we enter is called the Dung Gate."

"That does not offend me. Should it, Appolonius?"

"No, sire," his counselor said with a smile. "On the other side of the wall—to the east—is the Horse Gate. To the north is a Fish Gate and a Sheep Gate."

"So it is a matter of 'in one gate and out another,'" Antiochus joked. "It's a bit like the hearing of a certain high priest we shall soon see. With him, I think the king's declared wishes are 'in one ear and out the other!'"

The king first heard from his governor, Sostratus. There had indeed been a rebellion after Menelaus had returned to Jerusalem, just as Japheth, the dead Jew, had predicted.

Several buildings had been burned, and stones from streets torn up and made into barricades. The Jews who had become aroused avoided the garrison and the soldiers but did attack the guards of the Temple. Several persons had been killed. Sostratus thought there might be as many as sixteen or seventeen.

"And how do you view the city now?" the king asked his governor.

233

"I truly do not know, Majesty," Sostratus replied. "The people are secretive, and our spies have not provided us with much information. I believe we must simply keep alert and, if possible, Your Majesty should provide us with more troops. There will be safety in numbers."

"It will be done," said the king. "Now let us summon our high priest and hear how he interprets what you have reported."

Menelaus did not immediately offer an explanation.

"Things did not proceed as you promised, Menelaus," said the king. "You said the people would not be aroused, that enough treasure had remained in the Temple. Did you remove more than you told me? What did happen, Menelaus?"

Menelaus looked at Sostratus, hoping for a clue on how to answer. The governor remained absolutely rigid and gave no sign.

"There were a few dissidents," Menelaus finally answered. "But, Excellency, everything has been settled. The rebels are dispersed. Antioch-Jerusalem is secure!"

"There was a serious rebellion, high priest!" Antiochus shouted. "I must hold you responsible, at least for the time being. You are the leader of the Jews, and Jews were the ones who caused the insurrection. My governor does not know if there will be another uprising. Do you?"

"One cannot predict," Menelaus mumbled in reply.

"Listen to me, high priest. If there is any further disturbance, your usefulness to me—as well as your office in the Temple—is ended. Is that understood?"

"I understand, Your Majesty," Menelaus responded quietly.

"A lesson must be taught these Jews," said the king, "and I have decided upon three things. First, I want you to select fifty hostages, both from the ranks of the rebels and from the merchant class whom you always defend. There must be fifty persons. Can you do this?"

"Yes, Excellency," Menelaus declared. "Are they to be taken to Antioch, Majesty, and, if so, for how long?"

"They will be taken to the citadel, here in Jerusalem, and they are to be executed."

"Then they will be prisoners, sire, not hostages."

"You will secure hostages, and they will be called hostages!" The king was in a fury.

Menelaus closed his eyes for a moment and nodded.

"Secondly, as of today, taxes are to be doubled."

"That will work a hardship upon many people, Majesty," said the priest.

"It may be a hardship for you, too, priest!" the king continued. "Because the third thing I require is that your own tribute to me be doubled."

The king turned to Sostratus.

"You will see that my orders are carried out. Hostages—taxes—and tribute!"

"Yes, Your Majesty," said the governor.

"There must never be another insurrection in Jerusalem," the king said harshly to Menelaus. "See to it, high priest, or you will be neither 'high' nor 'priest.'"

Antiochus had three reasons for rejoicing.

The enlarged section of Antioch was to be called *Epiphanea*, in honor of himself. In time, there would be more cities bearing this name. There were dozens of Alexandrias and Antiochs throughout Asia. There would be dozens of Epiphaneas as well.

Second, a new coin had been minted. It bore a much more flattering image of himself, and each coin now had this inscription:

ANTIOCHUS THEOS EPIPHANES NICATOR.

The last name was new. Nicator meant "victor" and had been used by only a few Seleucid kings. The title was now his to claim.

Thus, his third reason for happiness was the victory over Egypt. It did not matter that there had been no great battles. What did matter was that an alliance had been formed and the southern borders were safe. He believed he had also induced enough fear into Menelaus that there would no longer be any problem with Judea.

He was again admiring his new coin when Appolonius entered.

"There is bad news, Excellency," he said.

"Then tell me your news, Appolonius," said the king with a frown.

"We are being attacked all along our southern borders."

"By Egypt, of course?"

"Yes, Majesty."

Antiochus exploded with an oath. "What happened to our truce, to our agreement?"

236

"The two sons—the two Ptolemies, Philometor and Euergetes—will rule together."

"Philometor and Physcon. And with the same regents."

"But of course, Majesty. This is obviously a scheme of the eunuch and our Syrian traitor. They are the ones who wish to rule."

"Then they will have to answer to me," said the king. He found himself reaching for the amulet inside his garment, needing its warmth, seeking the wisdom it would bring.

"We have no choice," the king said with quiet firmness. "We march again against Egypt. And this time blood will be spilled."

20

This time the march toward Egypt was no charade.
Although Gorgias and Appolonius were literally
at his side, Antiochus was commander-in-chief and
led his forces quickly and imaginatively.

His ships moved rapidly from Tyre to Cyprus and
to Pelusium, at the mouth of the eastern branch of
the Nile. His troops simultaneously pushed southward by land along the coast to Pelusium and soon
occupied it. Antiochus continued with other troops
to Memphis and, northward again, toward Alexandria.

Everything he possessed was dedicated to the battle. He maneuvered troops and cavalry and elephants.
He used siege towers and catapults. Scythed chariots broke the ranks of the enemy. He had learned
from the Romans, and his strategy had a flexibility
that soon overwhelmed the Egyptians and astounded
his military colleagues.

Blood was spilled on both sides of the Nile. Of Antiochus's 50,000 soldiers, one-fourth were killed. Egypt mounted an equal force, but half of its troops died in the fray. Antiochus himself killed again and again, believing in the power of both his amulet and his sword, convinced that the lord he now served would give him the victory. In witnessing and sharing the blood-letting he felt an energy and an elation that drove away all fear. At times he felt he himself was in an arena, in mortal combat with superior and stronger gladiators, and winning.

The Egyptian insurgents were defeated. Antiochus knew it was only a matter of time until a delegation would present itself, requesting peace. And this time the king of Antioch would not be satisfied with installing a puppet Ptolemy king. He would insist upon guaranties and a formal alliance. He would demand territory as compensation. He would abandon neither the island of Cyprus nor the port of Pelusium. The presence of Antioch would remain and be felt in Egypt.

Antiochus and his troops waited in the plain of Eleusis, on the banks of the Nile, only a few miles from Alexandria. In the distance they could see the *Pharos*, the famous lighthouse maintained by priests, which was indeed one of the seven wonders of the world. A fire burned throughout the day and night, and the two-hundred-foot tower emitted smoke by day and flame by night, signaling the entrance to the port to those both on land and sea.

For the first time in many weeks, the king was content and felt peace.

Antiochus did not yet know that in this same month of September, Lucius Aemilius Paullus, consul of Rome, had defeated Perseus in a battle at Pydna, across the bay from Thessalonica. Twenty thousand Greeks had been slain, and six thousand prisoners had been taken.

Nor did he know that his military activities had not been overlooked. A delegation was stationed on the island of Delos, a large slave market, midpoint between Rhodes and Thessalonica, gathering intelligence and awaiting instructions.

The Third Macedonian War had come to an end and, with it, the royal house of Macedon. Without further pretense, Rome intended to make the Mediterranean into its own private sea, *Mare Nostrum*.

The delegation crossed the plain of Eleusis slowly and cautiously.

There was a light mist in the early dawn that softened and disguised the figures in a shimmering haze. Antiochus thought there was something strangely mysterious and magical about the scene and that he was seeing it through an orange-colored curtain of sheer silk.

Official word had been received the night before that the Egyptians wished safe conduct for a small delegation. There were no more than six people, but the king assumed that the Egyptian troops were close by and watching, just as his own soldiers were guarding him as he and his companions progressed.

One of the figures was that of a person dressed in white. As he came closer, Antiochus saw that the

241

man was wearing a toga. He was white-haired, and he appeared to be a Roman senator. Antiochus had the feeling that he knew the man, that they had met somewhere in the past. The tricks of light and mist diffused his focus, and he could not be sure.

As the man came closer, Antiochus realized who he was. He was the senator who had befriended him so many years before in Rome. He was Publius Popilius, the father of Lucretia. Antiochus smiled. He had not thought of Lucretia in many years.

As he continued to stare at the approaching group, the king reconsidered. Surely Publius, the senator, must now be dead.

The sun was higher and the mist briefly lifted.

Suddenly, Antiochus recognized the Roman.

"Gaius!" he shouted, rushing with arms outstretched to greet his old friend. Gaius did not look like his father, the senator. He was bald and the fringes of his hair were white. There was no question. It was Gaius Popilius Laenas, the friend with whom he had shared so much in Rome.

"Gaius, my dear friend!" Antiochus exclaimed. He turned to Appolonius who had followed him. "Imagine! Here in this place I meet the man with whom I spent my youth!" The king smiled and sighed. "I never thought I would see you again."

Gaius held the arms of the king but did not truly embrace him.

"We do meet again, Antiochus," Gaius said. "And how different are the circumstances."

"What joy it is to hear Latin as you speak it, Gaius!" Antiochus beamed. "What good fortune that you are here. We have so much to recount to each

242

other, it will take us a week! The gods have indeed smiled upon us!"

"You were only a prince when I last knew you," said Gaius. "Now you are a king, and you have fought a good battle."

"Thank you, my friend! And we shall quickly dispense with the affairs of state. I want to visit with you!"

"Affairs of state sometimes cannot be dealt with quickly," said the Roman quietly.

"They will be today, my friend, Gaius," said Antiochus. "My terms are few, and there should be no disagreement. I have won the battle, but I will be generous!"

Gaius removed a scroll from a cylindrical container that had been attached to his waist.

"Come, Antiochus, let us speak privately for a moment," said the Roman. His brother, Titus, had said Gaius had become a soldier. He appeared to be in charge. He had not yet introduced anyone from the group of Egyptians. "Before we discuss anything else, there is this communication which you are to read. It comes from the senate itself, Antiochus, and I have rushed here from Delos to deliver it to you."

Antiochus was now puzzled by the formal manner of his old friend. He unrolled the scroll and began to read, at first incredulous, and then with intense anger. The senate had sent an ultimatum. Antiochus was to withdraw from Egypt and return to Antioch. The Ptolemy kingdom was not to be molested. Antiochus could retain Coeli-Syria but was not to occupy any former Egyptian lands, including the island of Cyprus. Antiochus was to take no further military action anywhere without informing the senate in Rome.

Antiochus looked up and saw that the Egyptians who had accompanied Gaius were laughing among themselves. Evidently, Gaius had already informed them about this directive from Rome. It galled him that the eunuch and the Syrian traitor might be among them.

"Gaius," the king pleaded, "my lands were attacked. I fought an invader, and I have now won victory in battle. I cannot be denied!"

"You have read the communication," said Gaius.

"My dispute has not been with Rome. It has been with the Egyptian leaders who used the Ptolemies for their own purposes. My southern borders must be secure!"

"Rome supports the Ptolemies, Antiochus," said Gaius.

"And Egypt attacked Idumea!" Antiochus shouted.

"You maintained a garrison in Pelusium, on the Nile itself. We believe that Egypt was provoked. Furthermore, Antiochus, you only pretended to support the oldest of the two sons. You really wanted to extend your kingdom."

"That is utter nonsense!" said the king.

"The senate has spoken."

"Gaius, how can you—you of all people!—do this to me? We were friends in your father's household. We watched the gladiators together. We drank and wenched together. You—you, Gaius!—introduced me to your own sister."

"Time changes us all, Antiochus," said Gaius. "Some of us, it appears, change more than others."

He paused. "My sister has been dead for five years."

Antiochus swallowed and was silent for a moment.

"Rome cannot enforce this edict!" the king pleaded. He knew he was angry, and he was trying desperately to control his emotions.

"Antiochus!" Gaius said gently. "You know better than to say that. You know the power of Rome and our determination. The war is over in Greece and Macedonia. We know what we want, and we are now free to enforce our will."

"These are shocking demands," said Antiochus, shaking the scroll in his hand. "I must have time to reflect, to think about these matters. I came to this meeting this morning to accept surrender, not to surrender myself." Antiochus began to move away.

"Stay!" shouted Gaius. "Stay exactly where you are." Antiochus turned in surprise.

"But I must have time to think. Give me that much, Gaius!"

Gaius Popilius Laenas did not reply. Instead he took the walking stick he had been carrying and began to draw a circle in the sand, around Antiochus.

"You will have sufficient time to think," Gaius said. "But you will give me your answer before you step out of this circle."

Antiochus shook his head in disbelief.

"The morning has arrived," said Gaius. "The sun and the heat will help you to decide."

"Gaius!" Antiochus called to his former friend, who was already walking away. "I deserve better than this. You humiliate me before my generals and my enemies. I am a king, Gaius. A king! A victor in battle. More than thirty thousand men have been

245

slain! I came to this place in good faith. I gave you the safe conduct—and now you treat me again as a hostage, as a prisoner, as one who is vanquished."

"Consider *all* that you have just said, Antiochus," Gaius thundered from the distance that now separated them. "Consider all of the possibilities before you step out of that circle." Gaius turned and rejoined the Egyptians."

Antiochus felt his heart beating more rapidly, his blood pounding through his veins, and his head pulsating with hammer blows.

If he defied Rome, he would likely never leave this spot alive. If he accepted the ultimatum, he could leave and he might be able to survive, at least for a time.

Clearly, Rome would now seek to control the world. The king could only buy a little time, to preserve what he had. Antiochus suspected that Rome would encourage Egypt to regain its lost province of Judea—but that was something he could thwart. He would do everything in his power to retain Judea as a buffer, as a defense against the Roman-supported Ptolemies. Judea was never more essential to the security of Antioch as now. No longer was it the stepping-stone to Egypt he had once planned. It was now a bulwark, a fortress, to be kept at all costs.

He reached for his amulet. He felt the gods were fickle this day to allow a single man, representing a nation hundreds of miles away, to turn his victory into defeat. The amulet felt warm and comforted his spirit. As he gazed at his friend—his former friend—Gaius, he felt a billowing hatred for the Roman and his country.

He turned to stare at his feet and at the circle surrounding those feet. He glanced toward Appolonius and Gorgias, who must have heard some of the conversation and who were understandably perplexed. But they could not help him to decide. Gaius had made it quite clear. Antiochus must decide for himself, and soon.

The king weighed the possibility of attacking Gaius. He felt for his sword. He knew he could kill the Roman, his former, now traitorous, friend. But what then? Others would be killed—perhaps even Antiochus himself.

He still possessed a kingdom and a son. His was not an insignificant kingdom. It might be short-lived, but perhaps his lord would yet allow his son to inherit it.

Antiochus removed his sword from its sheath. Gorgias immediately removed his own sword but replaced it when he saw the king shake his head.

He stepped out of the circle and, with his sword, drew two lines across it. He then thrust his sword in the sand, where the two lines intersected.

The king motioned to his men to follow him. He turned his back upon Gaius and the Egyptians. He walked with shoulders erect and head high, marching toward his troops who were awaiting him at the delta.

He walked steadily, his contingent of men beside him, tears pouring profusely and unashamedly down his face. He heard laughter and ridicule from the Egyptians and Antiochus noticed out of the corner of his eye that Gorgias and Appolonius were also weeping. They marched with the precision and self-control of soldiers of Antioch.

He found himself holding the talisman tightly. The frustration and shame of tears changed into a seering white flame of returning anger. Antiochus felt the resentment and the hatred shoot through his entire being, from his head to the extremities of his feet.

"Someone will pay for the shame of this day," he murmured. His companions did not hear the words. "Someone will pay!"

21

The word spread like a wildfire throughout Jerusalem and Judea. Antiochus Epiphanes was dead!

There had been a confrontation with a Roman emissary at Eleusis, outside Alexandria, it was said. Antiochus had been forced to give up the lands he had won in Egypt. As he retreated, he had been attacked and killed.

It was the moment for which many Judeans had been waiting.

The supporters of Jason, the deposed high priest, sent word to him in Ammon to return, while they marshaled their forces to overthrow the renegade Menelaus.

There were skirmishes between supporters of the two priests and scattered attacks upon the Seleucid garrison at the citadel and tower gates. What had begun as a celebration of the death of the tyrant was changed into an ever-widening civil war and rebellion.

In Modein, two days' distance from Jerusalem, on the road to Joppa, Mattathias was eager for information but less enthusiastic for battle. His sons did not agree with him.

"Now is the time to rise up against the usurper!" Judah cried.

"We must still be patient, my son," counseled his father.

"How long must we allow the Temple to remain desecrated?" he asked.

"The time of desecration has not in fact occurred," Mattathias answered.

"How can this be?" asked Simon. "The heathen king entered the Temple. That was desecration enough!"

"You yourself said this, Father!" Judah Maccabee persisted.

"I did not perceive the prophecy as I should," said Mattathias.

"Why must our lives always be governed by what the prophet says or doesn't say?" Judah was in a rage.

"Daniel speaks of things which, in truth, have not yet happened. Then will come the time of weeping and the moment for our action." The priest spoke calmly, hoping his manner would quiet his sons.

"Always the prophecies must be fulfilled!" Judah was not satisfied with his father's words. He was now a tall and sturdy man, strong from work in the fields, especially from hauling large boulders from the fields. "Is there some special blessing in waiting, or does Adonai help those who will defend His holy name?"

"Hush, my son!" Mattathias ordered. "I, too, wish to see the false prophet thrown down from his throne. But the time is not yet opportune. Believe me, my sons!"

Judah shook his head in resentment. His brothers appeared to agree with the Maccabee.

"Listen to me, my sons," said the old priest. "If we attack Menelaus we support Jason. Do you truly wish to see Jason again serve as high priest? He was as much usurper as Menelaus."

"At least Joshua belongs to a priestly family," Judah said sullenly.

"Do not call him Joshua!" Mattathias commanded. "Call him Jason, by his adopted Greek name. He Hellenized our people as much as Menelaus. He groveled before Antiochus as much as Menelaus. And did he not intrigue himself against Onias, of blessed memory? Is this not true, all of it?"

Judah had to agree that those were the facts.

"We are but a tiny remnant," said Mattathias. "While Adonai will be served by this remnant, it must be protected, and its strength must not be wasted. We can still add to our numbers. And we must train ourselves more diligently. These are the things we can and must do, my sons. But for now, we must be patient. And we must wait!"

Antiochus, of course, was not dead.

The king learned about the uprising in Jerusalem as he journeyed along the coast northward to Antioch. He immediately ordered his troops to change direction, to march eastward toward Judea.

Antiochus burned with a silent, smoldering anger. He conversed only rarely and issued few orders. There were moments when Appolonius feared for the king's health and sanity, but he kept his distance, sensing the king's profound despondency and irritation.

The shame of Eleusis festered like a sore. The harsh action of his old friend Gaius was a sting that had not yet been removed from his soul. The king had won so much. He had consolidated the kingdom, accomplished what his father had not completed. There was the promise of peace and prosperity for years to come, with no need for further adventures on the battlefield.

Now everything was changed. Rome had ordered him to return to his kennel. Rome had treated him as a mere dog.

Now the Jews were fighting his soldiers and fighting each other. At the very moment he required stability in Judea, peace had vanished. Jason had returned and now appeared to be in control, and Antiochus suspected that Jason's true sympathies might now well lie with Egypt. Menelaus had taken refuge in the citadel.

Antiochus thought: *If I am a dog, then these Jews are my fleas. No*, he decided. *Fleas merely irritate. These Jews are parasitic ticks and feed upon my very blood.*

He had vowed that someone would pay for his humiliation at Eleusis. His troops would soon be in Jerusalem, and that payment would soon be exacted. The Judeans would soon learn that they had a king and that he was very much alive.

He ordered his troops to clean out the city, to root out the rebels, and to restore order. Antiochus went directly to the Akra, where the citadel was situated, to consult with Sostratus, his governor. He also hoped to find Menelaus there.

His high priest was a very frightened man.

"You have not been a faithful steward, high priest," Antiochus shouted. "I warned you about any recurrence of a rebellion."

"Your enemy is Jason, Majesty, not I!" Menelaus protested. "When the rumor spread that you were dead, Jason returned from beyond the Jordan. He and his adherents rose up. Surely I cannot be blamed for that."

"I have many enemies, Menelaus," said the king moodily, "and many of them are within my own house. I am alive, as you can see." He found himself clasping the amulet. "Jerusalem will know how very much alive I am!"

Sostratus reported that Jason had attracted hundreds of supporters and that most of those appeared to be Jews who were loyal to the old Temple ways. The Jerusalemites hid and fed them. It was difficult to apprehend the rebels in the narrow byways of the city.

"They must be rooted out!" Antiochus demanded.

"May I suggest a tactic, Excellency?" Menelaus inquired. He had regained some of his composure.

"Say on," said the king.

"As the governor reports, the followers of Jason are pious Jews. Tomorrow, sire, is the Jewish Sabbath. In fact, it begins tonight, at sundown."

"And what has this to do with stopping this rebellion?" asked the king.

"Loyal Jews are commanded to do no work on the Sabbath, Your Majesty."

"Do you mean to say that Jews would not fight on the Sabbath?"

"I believe it would be so, Excellency."

"Then we will wait until sundown and then complete our task," said the king. "If you are correct, Menelaus, and these Jews do not fight, your assistance will not be forgotten."

The king saw that the priest appeared to relax.

"But your service to me must change," Antiochus continued. "I have learned something from all of these Jewish intrigues and uprisings. I have learned that there is only one way to insure tranquillity for Antioch in this city and that is to eliminate the Jews."

"There are too many of them, Excellency," said the governor. "That cannot be accomplished."

"Perhaps you are correct," said the king. "In that case, there is something else to be done. We can eliminate the Jewishness of the Jews."

Sostratus and the Seleucid officers were puzzled. Menelaus smiled a half-smile as though he understood.

"Menelaus, in the hours before sundown, I wish you to counsel me on how this might be done."

The massacre began at sundown and continued through the night into Saturday. The loyal and pious Jews did not take up arms or fight, as Menelaus had predicted. Those forces of Jason that remained in

254

the city were exterminated, and those who harbored them were also killed.

It was reported to Antiochus that since his armies had entered the city more than forty thousand Jews had been slaughtered. Antiochus thought the total to be too high, but as he walked to the Temple with his two aides and Menelaus, and saw the dead bodies piled up along the gutters of the streets, he began to agree with the estimate. The city of Jerusalem on this Sabbath was almost painfully quiet.

"Begin to remove the bodies beyond the walls of the city," Antiochus directed his lieutenants. "Burn them or bury them. They must not be allowed to remain in the city."

"Today, Majesty?" asked Sostratus.

"We do not observe the Sabbath, do we?" said the king. "The work must be started today."

Other orders were issued as they walked.

"Issue a call to the people who remain. They must gather before sundown outside their Temple!"

Antiochus quickly marched into the Temple, followed by Menelaus, Sostratus, and Appolonius. The king remembered the configuration of the various chambers from the tour Jason had given him only a few months before. His soldiers already occupied the building.

He headed first for the room to which he had previously been denied entry. He entered the "Holy of Holies," the room he had been told only the high priest could enter once a year. He was disappointed with what he saw—or, rather, what he did not see. There was a slightly raised platform, but otherwise the room was empty.

There was an elaborate drapery that separated the room from the Temple sanctuary.

"Remove the veil!" commanded the king. "It must be sent to Antioch."

The soldiers began their work.

"Remove whatever else is of value. I want all of the gold and silver, all of the sacrificial vessels, the candelabra, the candlesticks, the ornaments—everything!—removed and sent to our treasury."

"It will be done, Majesty," said Appolonius.

They walked on to the high altar of burnt offerings, smoldering with a few dying coals.

"Bring the image of Zeus that we carry with us," said the king. "And bring me also a pig."

"This is Judea, Excellency," said Sostratus. "Swine are forbidden to the Jews. A pig will be difficult to find."

"Others than Jews live in Jerusalem. You will find a pig. Bring it to me. It must be done quickly!"

He stirred the coals and ordered more wood to be placed upon the altar. His soldiers were busy throughout the sanctuary, removing and stacking treasure, folding the heavy drapery, fulfilling his many commands. Antiochus sat beside the altar and waited.

He looked at the simple walls and high-beamed ceiling. It was an adequate Temple, he supposed, but he himself had built more elaborate ones. He had heard of a Jewish king named Solomon who had built a much more ornate place of worship, but it had long since been destroyed.

He recalled the story of Heliodorus. He wondered

256

if the horsemen had attacked him in this room or the one behind. He had both doubted and believed the story. There had been no witnesses, and the people who had spoken about it were dead. Onias had been killed. Heliodorus had probably died. So many people were dead—especially today, in Jerusalem, outside the walls of this holy place.

The king picked up the amulet and looked at it. So much had happened to him since Amphion had first given it to him in Antioch. It had brought him wealth and success. He did not blame the talisman for what had occurred in Egypt—nor even the uprising in Jerusalem. One was due to the treachery and arrogance of Rome and the other to the perversity of a strange and proud race. He gazed reverently at his talisman. He had been blessed. He still had a kingdom, and it would be preserved at all costs.

He rubbed the amulet as he had done many times before. It felt strange to do so in this public place, in this Temple built to honor Adonai, whom his lord hated.

The reality of his lord appeared, as it always did when he held the talisman in this particular way.

"Do I follow your command, my lord?" he asked. "I am here as you decreed. You know what shall next transpire. If I have misunderstood, tell me now!"

The personage before him did not speak, but smiled and nodded. He remained for several moments and then vanished.

There was no question in the mind of Antiochus about the words of the command he had received. Now, he was reassured. Now, he felt a calm he had not known for many days. Finally, in this holy place of the accursed Jews he knew he was truly Epiphanes, he was truly God. Jerusalem would soon know it.

His officers returned, and the soldiers brought in the image of Zeus and the swine.

"Are the people being assembled?" the king asked.

"Yes, Majesty," said Sostratus.

"Bring them into the courtyard, in front of the pillars and steps. I will address them in due time."

He ordered the image of Zeus to be placed on top of the Jewish altar. The coals were again blazing, and the soldiers had to be careful not to burn themselves.

Antiochus then walked to the corner where animals were killed and asked that the pig be brought to him. He had sacrificed many swine to Greek deities during his lifetime. With the aid of a soldier, he took his new sword and quartered the animal. Half of it was placed upon the glowing coals. The fat began to burn almost immediately, and the aroma of burning swine flesh began to permeate the room.

He called for a basin with water and had it placed upon the altar as well. The remaining parts of the pig were placed in the basin to simmer and cook.

He stood for several minutes, silent, lost in his thoughts and no one dared to interrupt him.

He gestured to Menelaus.

"Bring me the sacred writings!" the king commanded.

"All of them, Majesty?" Menelaus asked.

Antiochus reached into the memory of his youth and remembered that Benjamin, his slave, had called the writings by a special name.

"I wish the Torah to be brought to me."

Menelaus bowed and left the sanctuary. The king remembered that the Torah—the first five books of the Jewish leader Moses—were considered to be the holiest of all Jewish writings. The Torah contained the law, given by Adonai Himself, he had been told.

The caldron was boiling furiously by the time the scrolls were brought to him. The king spread them out upon the floor.

"Bring twenty of the Jews who are gathered in the courtyard," said the king. "I want Jewish witnesses to what will be performed."

The Judeans were brought as Antiochus directed. All of them seemed frightened. Two of them, smelling the odor of burning pork in the sanctuary, vomited where they stood. Some beat their chests, some wailed, and some tore their garments. Every Jew showed his revulsion at this uncleanness within the holy Temple.

"Silence!" shouted the king.

Antiochus now ordered the soldiers to carefully remove the caldron and pour the hot broth upon the scrolls. The pious Jews began to chant and cry, and several of them fainted.

Antiochus then knelt before the altar of burnt offerings, bowing to the image of Zeus, and savored the smell of the sacrifice. The deed was done, even as he had been commanded.

He stood, smiling, feeling his strength and superior power. "Are the people assembled outside?" he asked. He was assured that the people were waiting and would greet him. "Appolonius," he said, drawing his counselor to his side, "after today I return to Antioch. I anticipate no further trouble, but I would like you to remain for a few days. Sostratus will stay on as governor, but I appoint you mysarch of all Coeli-Syria, of all El Beka, including Judea. Will you stay?"

"Your Majesty honors me greatly," said Appolonius. He would serve the king as his adjutant, as a ruler in the area. He was proud of the appointment. "I serve the king however he wishes," he said.

The assembly was small, but the Jerusalemites cheered, prompted by the prodding of sword and soldier. Antiochus wondered how many Jews remained. So many had been killed.

"Citizens!" Antiochus began. "Order has today returned to Judea and this city. That order will be sustained! Your former high priest Jason, whom many of you followed, has fled. My governor, Sostratus, remains, and the garrison will be strengthened. I today appoint Appolonius, who once served here as governor, as ruler of all Coeli-Syria. Thus, the presence of Antioch will be seen and felt daily and hourly in this place. Once again you will be known as Antioch-in-Jerusalem, but it will now have greater meaning than ever before."

There were a few scattered cheers.

"Your Temple is now the temple of Zeus. I myself have offered the first sacrifice—and this has been witnessed by some of your people. A new altar will be built and a new image erected. But no longer is this the Temple of Adonai. It is now the temple of Zeus, the paramount god of the Greeks!"

There were no cheers, despite whatever prodding his soldiers attempted.

"Your king, Antiochus Theos Epiphanes Nicator, today issues these decrees to the Jews. Hear them well. Observe them well. Break them upon penalty of your lives.

"First, daily sacrifices to Adonai will cease. There is to be no worship of Adonai, no reading of the Torah or the sacred writings.

"Second, the Sabbath will no longer be observed as a holy day. We decree this particular change on this particular Sabbath!" The king tried to make a joke about it and then grew serious. "Your holy days and festivals will be those that are celebrated in Antioch.

"Finally, Judeans, I decree that no longer will you circumcise your male children. No sign must distinguish you from your brothers. Beginning today, we will be one people, living and worshiping in the same manner, everywhere. You will worship as Greeks, from this day forward and forevermore!"

He called Menelaus to his side.

"Behold your high priest!" he shouted. "He continues to be the high priest, but he serves me and will perform his duties as I decree."

Menelaus smiled for a moment and then raised both arms in a blessing, looking directly at Antiochus.

"Long live the King!" he exclaimed. Then, turning to the people, he shouted, "Long live Epiphanes!"

The soldiers picked up the chant and onlookers were urged to join. Jerusalemites had arms twisted, fingers pulled back, and hair at the back of the neck pulled. Some of the soldiers were too energetic with their swords and some drew blood.

The chant became louder. The people had no choice.

"Long live Epiphanes! Long live our divine king!"

The king stood erect, rigid as a statue. He closed his eyes, drinking in the words, absorbing the glory of this great moment. He wanted to remember it forever.

22

It was now the eighth year of the reign of Antiochus. Mattathias entered his home in Modein slowly and with visible pain. The door did not open easily. He had five sons; one would think that someone would find the time to strengthen the hinges. His walk from Jerusalem—a long walk of two days—had left him exhausted. His youngest son, Jonathan, guided him to a chair.

His other sons were in the field. Despite all of the troubles in the land, crops still had to be planted, cared for, and harvested. The men had to eat as well as train themselves for battle. Mattathias sighed. The lads had seen him coming and would soon join him. The priest smelled food cooking, and the meal would bring them together. He would not criticize the boys about the door. They had so many other and so much more important things to consider.

Boys. They were no longer boys, none of them.

They were men, sons of whom any Jewish father could be proud.

Elizabeth brought him water. "Drink, husband," she said, "but drink slowly. The water is freshly drawn from our well and is cold."

"Thank you, goodwife," he said. "The waters of Modein are refreshing. I know how King David felt when he thirsted for the water of his youth."

Elizabeth smiled and returned to her cooking. The priest could not remember whether she was a year older or younger than he. He was bothered about this recurring loss of memory. They were both growing old, but they had shared a good life. Mattathias was proud of Elizabeth. She was a good mother and wife. More importantly, she was a good mother in Israel, pious and wise. No one lit the candles and recited the Sabbath prayers as well or as fervently as she.

His sons returned from the field.

"The door needs fixing," said Eleazar.

"I noticed," said the priest. "The door has required attention for the past six months," he added with a smile.

"I have never seen you so weary, my father," said Judah Maccabee.

"My feet feel heavy, but my heart is heavier," said Mattathias. "My heart is breaking."

"You should not have gone to Jerusalem, Father," said Simon.

"It was necessary to go. It was ordained that I see the desecration so that you and those who will follow you will know the truth of the matter. Blessed be the Almighty, I have witnessed more than I wished to see, but I am the servant, still, of Adonai."

"You will renew your strength, my Father," said his oldest son, John. "As it is promised. You will renew your strength as the eagles renew theirs. Would you like to rest? There will be time to tell us of your journey."

"No," Mattathias declared in a firm voice, pulling himself erect. "There will be an eternity to rest when Adonai calls me to Himself. I must speak with all of you, without delay."

He recounted the descration of God's holy Temple. He had been one of the twenty who witnessed the pouring of swine broth by the king himself upon the sacred Torah. He had seen the small image sitting astride the altar of burnt offerings, where the flesh of the unclean pig was roasting.

His sons and their mother were aghast.

"Then the desecration has truly come," said Judah.

"It is the abomination of desolation," said the priest, with a sob in his voice. "But this was only the beginning."

He then reported to his family the decrees that Antiochus had announced—that Jewish worship would cease, the Sabbath would not be observed, and that there be no more circumcision.

"They may close the Temple in Jerusalem," said Judah, "but they cannot enforce these decrees in our villages!"

"Let us pray that it may be so," said the priest. "The king, however, is strong. He has his soldiers, and he has Menelaus."

"He stood with the king on the Temple steps, you

say?" asked Simon incredulously.

"He now openly serves the king who calls himself a god. Menelaus is high priest to Epiphanes. He himself began the chant of cheering for the king."

"He must die!" said Judah. "He is a traitor and blasphemer."

"He will die one day," said his father, "as all men will die."

"No, my father," said Judah. "He must not be allowed to die as all men die."

"You remained in Jerusalem longer than you planned, is it not so?" asked John.

"We were worried!" cried Elizabeth.

"I could not leave until Antiochus left. I wanted to be with my brethren, to comfort the pious Jews, especially the priests with whom I had served. It was good that I stayed on." He turned toward his wife. "I regret that you were worried, Elizabeth."

"Tell us of what occurs now in Jerusalem," Judah pled.

"Workmen are removing the altar of burnt offerings. A new and larger altar is to be built inside our Temple. A larger image of this Greek god called Zeus is to be placed above this altar. Gentiles enter and leave the Temple as they wish. No longer is it a house of prayer. Our Temple worship has ceased." Mattathias was crying. "Instead, it has become a house of ill repute," the priest continued. "Prostitutes have been brought in. They live and ply their trade in the priestly chambers."

"It is truly an abomination," said Simon.

"What a cleansing the Temple will require!" Eleazar exclaimed.

"Yes, my son," said the priest. "Eleazar, do you remember the old teacher for whom you were named?" His son nodded. "He lived in Antioch for a time, but he returned to Jerusalem. He is a very old man, much older than I."

"I remember him, Father," said Eleazar. "I remember him as a kindly and devout man."

"He was a kindly and devout man, my son."

"He no longer lives?"

"He is now in Abraham's bosom," the priest replied. "I was not there, but I was told about the celebration in honor of his ninetieth anniversary when the soldiers of Antiochus entered. They had learned of the party, and they knew Eleazar. They brought their gift—a gift of pork, which they commanded him to eat."

"They would do such a thing to a teacher of the law!" Judah exclaimed in anger.

"Listen to my story, my son," said the priest. "Eleazar's friends feared that the soldiers meant to make an example, to have their own way. They whispered to the old man to eat some lamb, which they would place in his hand, and simply pretend that he was eating the pork they had brought."

"Eleazar would not do this!" Jonathan declared.

"No. This is what he replied, as I heard from one who was there. 'I will pretend nothing. I will not disgrace my years. I will not lead our youth astray. I will uphold the law. Even though I might live for a time by doing this thing, I would never avoid the mighty hand of the Eternal!' "

The sons of Mattathias were deeply moved and were weeping.

"Eleazar said these words in Greek, so the soldiers understood. They then forced the pork meat into the old man's mouth, which he promptly spit out into the faces of the soldiers."

"How did he die?" asked the son who bore the name of the old priest.

"He was taken outside and flogged to death."

"I have heard enough!" Judah Maccabee shouted. "Father, we must not stand idly by while such evil exists!"

"I must tell you about one other occurrence, one that I saw with my own eyes." Mattathias struggled to control his emotions as he recalled the event he had seen.

"It is forbidden, now, to circumcise our children," he continued. "Two Jewish mothers in Jerusalem disobeyed that decree. According to our law, after the prescribed eight days following the birth of their sons, they took them to Abijah, a pious and loyal priest, and their sons were circumcised. Somehow the soldiers learned about the event. The mothers were arrested. The legs of the babies were tied together with a thin rope, and each child was placed around the neck of his mother, as though he were a necklace. The mothers were stripped to their waists. Then they were paraded through Jerusalem, accompanied by soldiers. Each mother, bare-breasted, carrying a naked, crying, recently circumcised baby boy! It was a terrible sight," sighed the priest. "I saw it with these eyes, my sons."

"Heathen!" shouted Jonathan, his youngest son.

"The mothers were then marched to the hill over-

268

looking the Kidron. Together with their screaming infants, they were pushed over the precipice. The four of them are also now in the bosom of Abraham."

Elizabeth and the five sons sat silently in shock and horror as they visualized what they had just heard.

"New decrees are being added to those Antiochus announced," Mattathias said. "Everyone is to celebrate the festival of Dionysius, whom the Romans call Bacchus. It occurs once a year and becomes nothing but a drunken orgy. Everyone is to participate, says the decree, drinking and parading in the streets, waving images of the phallus. It is public perversion. A disgrace! And everyone must wear those abominable ivy wreaths the Greeks enjoy so much."

"Not everyone will participate, my Father," said Judah firmly.

"What is worse, there is to be a celebration each month. We are to commemorate the king's birthday, not once a year as an anniversary, but once a month. Sacrificial entrails are to be offered to Zeus. When they have been burned we are to eat them in honor of this Epiphanes."

"I will not soil myself with such uncleanness," Simon declared. "It is forbidden."

"My sons, as I walked slowly and in sorrow from our holy city, I thought about the prophecy and the meaning behind these terrible events. I believe there is only one purpose in the mind of the king and the evil priest, Menelaus, who now serves him. I believe this madman will force everyone to worship him. He calls himself Theos Epiphanes—'God Manifest'

269

—may Adonai forgive me for even repeating the blasphemy. His new coins show the image of Zeus, but it is the face of Antiochus. And now the decree to honor his birthday once a month in a rite of sacrifice is the beginning of required worship of his person."

"You comprehend well, my Father," said John.

"Recite for me the first four commandments, which describe our covenant with Adonai," commanded the priest. "John?"

" 'You shall have no other gods before Me.' "

"Simon?"

" 'You shall not make for yourself any idol, or any likeness of what is in heaven above or on the earth beneath or in the water under the earth. You shall not worship them, or serve them; for I, the LORD your God, am a jealous God, visiting the iniquity of the fathers on the children, on the third and the fourth generations of those who hate Me, but showing lovingkindness to thousands, to those who love Me and keep My commandments.' "

"Judah?"

" 'You shall not take the name of the LORD your God in vain, for the LORD will not leave him unpunished who takes His name in vain.' "

"Eleazar?"

" 'Remember the sabbath day, to keep it holy. Six days you shall labor and do all your work, but the seventh day is a sabbath of the LORD your God; in it you shall not do any work, you or your son or your daughter, your male or your female servant or your cattle or your sojourner who stays with you. For in six days the LORD made the heavens and the earth, the sea and all that is in them, and rested on the seventh day; therefore the Lord blessed the sabbath day and made it holy.' "

"You do well to hide God's Word in your hearts," said Mattathias, wiping another tear from his eye, but this one brought by joy. "We are attacked by an evil enemy who will not be satisfied until he destroys both Jews and Jewish faith. This wicked man and his priest attack the two things that distinguish us from the rest of the world, the things that kept us faithful as Jews throughout the exile and our many wanderings. We are forbidden by Antiochus to worship Adonai on the Sabbath. And now we must not show evidence of our covenant with Adonai through circumcision. Take these two things away from our people and you take away all that we are before men and before the Almighty."

"That is clearly the purpose behind these decrees of Antiochus," said Simon.

"But he will not prevail!" shouted Judah. "That is also prophesied."

"Indeed it is, my son," said the priest.

"Father," Jonathan interrupted. "May your youngest son remind you of the fifth commandment, which all of your sons believe and follow?" His father motioned him to continue. " 'Honor your father and your mother, that your days may be prolonged in the land which the Lord God gives you.' "*

The father embraced his sons, and Elizabeth joined them.

*Exodus 20:3–12.

"That commandment will have special meaning to each of us in the days ahead," his youngest son added.

"*Shemá Yisroel!*" Mattathias cried out.

All of them repeated the sacred words together, in covenant with each other and with their God.

"Hear, O Israel: The Lord our God, the Lord is One!"

23

Forty thousand Jews were indeed killed in Judea in what can only be described as a holocaust. Thousands were taken prisoner and forced into slavery, distributed throughout the kingdom of Antiochus. A new Jewish exile had begun.

Many of those Judean slaves were brought to Antioch.

Many Jews decided, at least outwardly, to conform to the king's decrees, some of them convincing themselves that in survival they might preserve some of their heritage and faith.

However, there was a remnant—a relatively small group of Jews—who knew they would never submit. They would never bow down to false gods.

Antiochus knew that such dissidents had to be confronted and public examples made if his decrees were to be fully observed. He wanted no more Jews nor Jewishness. More than ever, he would demand worship of himself as the human incarnation of Zeus.

He spent much time alone with the amulet those days. From it he gained strength and confidence. To it he gave attention and reverence. Through it he communicated with and worshiped his lord, who now directed his total life.

Some said that the king had aged and looked ill. Antiochus felt the flabbiness of his face and body, saw the wrinkles etching his forehead and eyes, but he felt healthy and vibrant. He did not appear in public as much as before, but that was fitting for a king who was divine. Laodice, his sister and queen, was dead, and Berenice no longer fascinated him. There was Lysias, however, who was still counselor, tutor to his son, and a companion who lived with the king in the king's own quarters.

On this day, in Antioch, he would appear in public.

Eight Jews had been brought before him—a mother and her seven sons, ranging in age, he had heard, from ten to twenty years. She was a woman past her prime, and her sons were scrawny. They were not the stuff of heroes. They were slaves.

"Where is your husband, woman?" he began.

"In the bosom of Abraham," she answered, in Greek.

"What does that mean?" demanded the king.

"It means that my husband is dead. He was killed in Jerusalem."

"You will address the king as 'Excellency' or 'Majesty'!" commanded Lysias, who stood beside the seated king.

"Excellency!" the women added. Antiochus noted

the sarcasm. There were moments when he admired the raw courage of these Jews. But he would not allow that admiration to overwhelm his judgment.

"It is reported to me that you and your sons did not celebrate the king's birthday in the approved manner last month," said the monarch. "Is this true?" The king fondled a well-tooled leather whip in his hand. It looked to him as though the oldest of the sons before him had already felt the sting of some-one else's lash.

"I now congratulate His Majesty," said the woman without smiling.

"The approved manner of celebration is to eat of the sacrifice offered to the king," Antiochus said, smiling.

"We do not eat pork or the guts of animals," the aged woman declared. "Excellency!" she added quickly as the king raised his whip and struck the floor a foot in front of where she was standing.

"We are prepared to die rather than break the laws of our ancestors!" shouted the oldest son, stepping in front of his mother. The king now saw that the man had indeed been whipped; there were welts on his neck and forehead as well as on his arms.

"Are you prepared to die?" asked the king with a snarl. He stood. "I wonder if you are even prepared to suffer."

The king clapped his hands and several slaves appeared.

"Bring meat!" he commanded. "And see that the coals on the altar burn brightly. Place the caldron upon the altar."

The meat, a savory roast pork, was brought to the

king who himself took the platter and passed it under the noses of the eight persons standing before him. He handed the platter to the slave who followed him, took a piece of meat in his hands and walked to the eldest son, who stood beside his mother.

"Eat!" he commanded. The man's jaws were clamped shut.

The king gestured to two soldiers. "Open his mouth. Force it open if you must!" he directed. When the Jew's jaws were pulled apart and held open by the soldiers, the king threw the piece of pork into his mouth.

"Now close his mouth and keep it closed. Cover his nose. He will have to swallow it!"

The king waited until he saw the cartilage in the man's throat rise and fall.

"There. That wasn't too difficult, was it?" The king sneered, nodding to the soldiers to release their grip.

The Jew gasped for air and then spit directly into the face of Antiochus. "Great is Adonai and greatly to be praised!" shouted the young man.

Antiochus slowly wiped his face with his sleeve and then quickly gave the man a heavy blow on his face with the palm of his hand. He struck hard enough to cause pain to his hand.

"This Jew does not serve the king well with his tongue," Antiochus said. "Take him to the next room and remove it."

The king said nothing more until screams were heard from the adjacent room.

"I will not force this meat upon you," said the

king above the noise of the cries. "You will simply request it. You will not be as foolish as the witless eldest son whom you now hear."

The screams were no longer human but sounded like those of a wild and wounded animal. Then there was silence.

"What have you done to him?" shouted another son, pushing his way toward the king. The soldiers restrained him.

"Allow him to see for himself," said Antiochus.

The soldiers escorted the lad to the doorway, pushing him inside. The boy froze at what he saw. The blood drained from his neck and face, and everyone saw him turn and retch, and then heave.

He was returned to the group standing before the king. The sour bile of his breath permeated the air. "Forgive me, my mother," he said.

"What did you see?" she asked.

"Please, my mother," the lad remonstrated. "I must not tell you."

"Tell me!" she cried.

"Tell her!" commanded the king, pushing the handle of the whip into the boy's stomach.

"They are killing him."

"But tell your mother how we are killing him," the king ordered.

"They have cut him up as an animal," said the son, hesitating.

"We have placed his parts in the caldron," said the king, "and the vessel is upon the coals."

The mother cried out.

"They are frying my brother to death!" said the boy, admitting more than he had wished and once again yielding to his nausea.

The king pointed to the platter of meat the slave was holding. "You may request your portion whenever you wish," he said.

Each Jew turned from the sight, but otherwise there was no reaction.

"Then let the memory of what you have seen and heard remain with you!" said the king. No one was fully certain of what he meant until they saw Antiochus grab the boy—with the aid of two soldiers—and then place both of his thumbs into the young Jew's eyes, pressing until blood and fluid emerged and the boy was blinded. "Hand me a blade!" Antiochus shouted, and the king then silenced the boy's screams with the dagger.

"The king has gone mad!" whispered the mother.

"Does anyone else wish to lose his tongue?" the king asked. He shuffled about, livid with anger, his face contorted with an intensity that was frightening.

A third son stuck out his tongue and tried to hold it with his fingers in a show of bravery. The king excised it.

"You have courage despite your foolhardiness," he said.

Each of the older six sons was tortured and mutilated.

"The King of the Universe will raise us up!" shouted one of them, as the knife flashed in his face.

"You will be punished for making war against the Almighty!" screamed another.

The marble floor was soiled with blood and vomit

and urine—stark evidences of death and fear. Even hardened soldiers turned their eyes from the spectacle of sheer butchery. Six of the brothers were ultimately killed, taken away to be burned upon the pagan altar.

Only the youngest son and his mother remained.

"I do not know how you came to bless me in my womb," she cried softly, speaking in Aramaic, a language Antiochus did not fully understand. "I gave you birth, but I did not give you life or breath. It was the Creator of the world who gave you life and who will do so again!"

Antiochus put his hand on the ten-year-old's shoulder, but the boy withdrew quickly. He tried to speak kindly.

"Lad, there is no need to pretend that you are as brave as your brothers. Besides, what good will dying do? If you do as I say—if you simply taste this meat—I will protect you. I will make you rich—and powerful! Everyone in this room is witness to this promise!"

The boy remained silent.

"Speak to him, woman!" said the king angrily to the boy's mother. "Make him understand! Do you wish to lose all of your sons?"

"My son, have pity upon me," she said in Greek but then began to whisper softly in Aramaic. "My son, my dearest son, I carried you nine months in my womb, and I have nursed you and fed you and clothed you. Do not forsake your brothers or me. Do not fear this executioner. Fear only Adonai! Be worthy of your brothers and of the Covenant!" They embraced each other violently and with tears.

279

"Well, lad?" asked the king.

The boy brushed the tears from his eyes and took a deep breath.

"I will obey the law of Moses, O King," he declared. "Our God is one God."

Antiochus waved to one of the soldiers who ran forward with a piece of rope. The boy was garroted and his lifeless body taken to the altar room.

"Well, woman," said the king, "are you satisfied with your seven sons?"

"Oh, I am very satisified!" she said, tears creeping out of her eyes as she smiled.

"Say, 'Excellency!' " Lysias commanded.

"Never again will I say that word," she exclaimed. "Never will I say 'excellency' to this vermin." She spat in the king's face. "Only Adonai is Excellent, may His name be praised."

She was about to continue, but Lysias drove a sword into her belly, and she slumped to her death.

Antiochus turned away from the scene of carnage, not in disgust but with a flush of warmth and success. Again he clasped the amulet and whispered, "Thank you, lord and master, for the gift of granting life or death."

Antiochus decided he would put Jerusalem and the insufferable Jews out of his mind. The decrees had been issued, examples had been made, and surely the stubborn race would learn who was king. The time had come to play.

A year had passed since he had announced new Olympic games to be held in Daphne. Participants had been invited from every Greek city in Greece and Asia to the month-long celebration. New arenas and temples had been built in Daphne, the beautiful resort city ten miles south of Antioch, situated high in the hills among the fragrant eucalyptus trees.

Daphne was in readiness, and so was the king. No longer would he remain a hermit in the island palace.

One year ago he had been victorious in Egypt. Then the truce had been broken, there had been the second expedition followed by a second victory, and then the ultimatum from Rome.

Antiochus would not be deterred. The games had been announced before the Roman intervention, and the games would be held. In fact, the king intended to go beyond the sports events. Now that a huge *triumph* had been held in Amphipolis for the consul Lucius Aemilius Paullus, who had defeated Greece at Pydna, he had decided to have his own triumphal parade.

There had been displays and parades in Antioch but never a *triumph* in the true Roman manner. Not even his father had accomplished that. Antiochus felt that his time had come; he would honor himself and bring greater glory to the games.

With great humor, Antiochus had also decided to invite emissaries from Rome, and the senate had accepted the invitation. Antiochus not only wanted Rome to observe the event; he wanted the emissaries to view his military strength. He knew that he was in no position to threaten, but he wanted Rome to know that his was still a strong kingdom in Asia, despite the forced retreat from Eleusis in Egypt.

He had a victory to celebrate. Judea was firmly in

his hands. Never again would the Jews rise up in rebellion. The wealth from their Temple had built the new temple to Apollo in Antioch, and it would also pay for the celebration. Tiberius Sempronius Gracchus, whom the senate said it was sending from Rome, would be duly impressed.

The Romans—and hundreds of other guests—were indeed impressed.

The parade began in Antioch and moved southward to Daphne. It was led by five thousand troops, the elite soldiers of the realm, dressed in Roman armor, shouting with every fourth step.

They were followed by the battalions of mercenaries. There were five thousand Mysians, three thousand Cilicians, and four thousand Thracians and Celts. They dressed as Greeks, with golden-brimmed helmets, white tunics, and crimson pleated kilts.

Next came the Macedonians—the heart and muscle of Antiochus's armies. There were twenty thousand of them—half carried golden shields, the other half shields made of silver and bronze.

The royal gladiators followed the Macedonians. They did not march, they strutted and joked and joshed. There were 240 pair of them today. They were professionals, who knew many of them would die in the new arena in Daphne, but they walked without fear.

Then came the cavalry—first, the famous equestrian company of a thousand Nicean riders, sporting golden plumes in their helmets, riding white Arabian steeds. These were followed by other horsemen

282

in silver-plated armor, wearing purple cloaks.

A hundred chariots passed the reviewing stand, some with knives mounted to the sides of their wheels, others carrying pikemen and drawn by two or even four horses. Two huge battlewagons were pulled by elephants.

Tiberius Sempronius today had proof that Antiochus indeed had restored a corps of elephants to his arsenal. There were thirty-six of them carrying wooden platforms and armored troops. Antiochus glanced at the Roman as the elephants were passing. Tiberius appeared to be overwhelmed.

The military part of the parade had taken six hours, but the spectacle was far from over. Slaves now appeared, cleaning the pavement as they went. Antiochus hoped that the Romans would notice the similarity of the road to one of theirs.

The remainder of the parade was to be ceremonial and entertaining.

The men and the women marched separately. The men wore white robes and thin gold crowns. The women were also dressed in white and wore garlands in their hair. All of them were young and handsome, and their marching often gave way to dancing. Both the men and the women were assigned to various temples in Antioch and Daphne. Their purpose in life was to give pleasure.

As the day grew longer and darker, torches were placed in stands along the streets and some of the marchers themselves carried lighted candles.

During the lulls and gaps between groups, a lone clown would criss-cross the streets, riding a decrepit nag, shouting orders to the marchers, and often falling off his mount directly in front of the paraders, as though to tease them into missing a step. The antics of the clown were hilarious, and the crowds roared with delight.

Only the stablemaster knew that the clown was the king. Antiochus slipped out from the royal box several times during the day, donning and removing his disguise, enjoying the joke he was playing.

Every triumphal parade Antiochus had seen in Rome included a public display of the royal treasure, usually calling attention to its most recent additions. The king would not be outdone by the Romans.

The treasure was carried by slaves, male and female, which was proper since slaves were themselves part of the treasure.

A thousand silver vessels were displayed, six hundred gold vessels, and eight hundred ivory tusks. The great veil from the Temple in Jerusalem was carried by its edges by fifty slaves; following the games, Antiochus planned to send the tapestry to Athens as another gift to its temple to Zeus. Other slaves sprinkled scented perfumes and oils onto the crowd.

As the parade finally drew to a close, participants in the sports events marched in single file. Three hundred different cities had sent representatives to the Daphne games, and there were several participants from each city. The cities were separated by a citizen carrying the banner of his respective polis. The line of sportsmen extended itself for more than a mile.

Night had come, and the torches outlined the

avenue for as far as the eye could see.

Antiochus again slipped down from his royal box, this time not to play clown but to appear himself, as king.

The procession of deities had begun. The number of statues representing the various gods and goddesses was beyond counting. There were deities honoring the seasons, the times of the day and night, the gods of individual towns and cities, the deities of ancient stories, images of harvests and fertility and war. Some of the images were carried in litters with silver or gold supports. The images themselves were made of gold or other precious substances and stones. Many were garbed in finery that would befit a king.

The end was in sight, but it would long be remembered.

A chorus of five hundred persons raised their voices in chant and song.

They were followed by eighty musicians, marching in rows of five, whose bugles emitted a constant royal fanfare.

Then came Antiochus.

He stood erect, with arms folded on his chest, looking neither to left or right, riding in a white gilded carriage drawn by six black stallions.

It was customary for the king to conclude such a triumphal parade, but on this day, Antiochus wanted everyone to note that it was he, the king, who followed and completed the procession of deities. The world must know that he was more than a king. He was *Theos Epiphanes*.

The parade had lasted fourteen hours. No one had ever seen anything to match it.

"You looked magnificent, Excellency," Lysias told the king later.

Antiochus was pleased.

"Your Majesty will forgive me," Lysias continued, "but there seemed to me to be a strange resemblance."

"To what, Lysias?" asked the king.

"To the standing figure on the shoulder of the face that we see on the mountain."

"The *Charonion*, you mean?"

"Yes, Your Majesty."

"You say I looked like the smaller figure on the mountainside?"

"Indeed," affirmed Lysias, "especially as you stood in the chariot."

"As I grow older it should be anticipated," the king replied vaguely.

"I do not understand, sire."

"Do not try to understand, my dear friend," said Antiochus. "You would learn my secret if you did!"

The games continued for thirty days and included all of the events that had become customary. New records were established, and new champions were crowned. Antiochus attended the games and the gladiatorial contests, which became the highlight of each weekend, but he was no longer excited by them. He was more concerned with how the games began and would end. The extravagance and the spectacle of the opening parade, with its demonstration of power and wealth, had brought him his greatest joy, and he thought it had made the greatest impression upon both his guests and his subjects.

The conclusion of the games would be another opportunity for spectacle.

The final banquet, held in the Great Room of the palace, honored the winners of the Olympic events. It was a lavish feast with dozens of meats and vegetables and wide variety of bread and fruit. The food was served in what seemed to be an unlimited quantity, accompanied by a comparable ceaseless flow of wine.

Antiochus greeted many of the guests personally. This greatly surprised but also pleased them. There would be a final surprise that only he could have designed.

After the meal, actors appeared in a final dramatic episode.

The actors carried an enshrouded figure that looked like an Egyptian mummy. As the musicians began to change the tempo of their music, the figure was lowered to the ground. As this was done, the figure appeared to come alive, shedding its shroud and tape, and joined the actors in a sensuous dance. The actors circled the mysterious figure and then broke away. The spectators saw that the previously enshrouded figure was now totally naked, dancing with a precision, and even some grace, that soon changed from being merely erotic to openly vulgar.

Suddenly someone recognized that the naked dancer was the king. After his name was shouted there was an embarrassed silence, which then gave way to nervous chatter and sniggering, and finally exploded into a roar of laughter and applause.

The dance ended. His royal robe was brought to him, but he did not immediately put it on. Antiochus felt no shame. After all, the images of his many gods stood naked in this fashion. The dance would be remembered and was a fitting climax to a month of unforgettable excitement.

He finally put on the robe, bowed to his fellow actor-dancers, and bid his guests farewell.

The Roman, Tiberius Sempronius, approached him.

"I have meant to ask you," the king began, "whether there was a Lucius in your clan? I remember a Lucius Sempronius who was the centurion who accompanied me to Rome."

"He was my brother," the Roman responded.

"He no longer lives?"

"He was killed in Pydna."

"A pity, sir. He thought we might meet again. What was his rank at the time of his death, may I ask?"

"He died a centurion, Your Highness."

Later, the king reflected that some men were destined to be too kind and too good to advance in the affairs of men. Lucius was one of those gentle, now forgotten persons, killed in the battle that was decisive in Rome's affairs.

Antiochus would never be forgotten. He was grateful to his lord for this past month, which had pushed aside the memory of Jews, their Judea, and their Adonai.

He felt some pain in his left side and at the base of his skull. He had heard the occasional mutterings that he should be named *Epimanes*. He was not mad. He was growing old, but this was a small price to pay for what he had just experienced. He was neither mad nor meek. He was *Epiphanes*!

24

When Heracles and his men arrived in Modein, Mattathias and his five sons were wearing sackcloth and ashes, the traditional Hebrew garb for mourning. Hidden within the sackcloth garments, however, were daggers and knives.

Heracles had been in Modein before—a month before, to be exact—when he and his men had built an official altar and shrine to the king. This had been done in dozens of towns throughout Judea, at the king's command.

Heracles was a captain in the army of Antiochus, who reported to Sostratus the governor. He was a huge man, about thirty-five years old. He was named for the originator of wrestling, and this Heracles himself looked like a champion contestant.

"Heracles has ordered everyone to the marketplace," said Simon.

"We must obey," said Mattathias. "But let us stand

in the fringes of the crowd. It is safer that way." The priest had grown more feeble in recent weeks, but today his voice was strong and his face had a ruddy color. "Are we armed?"

"Judah has seen to it," said John.

"What do you mean?" asked the priest.

"The weapons are safe, Father," said Judah Maccabee, smiling. "They are hidden in the hills."

"Good!" said the priest. "But I asked if *we* were armed."

His sons patted their hips and nodded.

"And I have mine!" Mattathias declared, removing his knife from its sheath and then replacing it. "I have named it 'Vengeance of the Lord!' " he said as he patted it.

His sons laughed.

"Retribution is not a matter for jest!" remonstrated their father. The sons smiled cautiously to each other. Mattathias was growing old. Their father was unpredictable; his temper went up and down like the hills and valleys that surrounded them.

"Let us see what this Heracles has to say," said Mattathias.

Heracles saw the latecomers, even though they tried to infiltrate the outer edges of the crowd.

"Mattathias, come forward!" commanded the captain.

The priest approached the king's representative, accompanied by his sons.

"This altar has been built for more than a month, Mattathias," said the captain, "but, as yet, it has not been used."

"Then the altar will not wear out from frequent

use!" said Mattathias. The crowd roared with laughter.

"You are correct," said the captain, trying to humor the people, "but an altar has only one purpose and should be used."

"I have no need to use this altar, captain," said the priest calmly.

"It is the king's birthday, Mattathias, and it is time for the monthly sacrifice," said Heracles. "Mattathias, be the first to make your offering."

"Why should I be first?" asked the priest.

"For many reasons, sir," said the captain. "Because you are an elder in Modein, because you are a respected leader, and because, of course, you desire to honor the king."

"I honor the king in my own way."

"But the king has decreed that sacrifices be made."

"And thus you ask me to make a sacrifice to Antiochus, who calls himself Epiphanes," declared the priest.

"It is being done everywhere, Mattathias. Your Adonai has not struck down His Jews who made this small sacrifice to honor the king."

"It matters little to me what is done elsewhere," said Mattathias.

"But, Mattathias"—Heracles smiled—"if you make the sacrifice, the villagers will follow your example."

"I know."

"Then the king will honor you with many gifts, with gold and with silver." Heracles beckoned to the priest. "Come. The coals are ready."

Mattathias shook his head.

"Why must you be so obstinate, old priest!"

shouted a man called Joseph. "You arrived late. You did not hear what this captain of the king's army promised us if we did not make the sacrifice today!"

The priest walked over to the man. "Joseph, you are a Jew!" he said.

"I want to live in peace," Joseph replied.

"Your father was Japheth, my son. Japheth who himself went to Antioch to speak to the king, Japheth who was a member of the Sanhedrin. You are his son!"

"And I became an orphan because my father went to Antioch." Joseph clasped and unclasped his hands. "We can all be killed today. Make the sacrifice and be done with it, Mattathias. Adonai will forgive us."

The priest stood staring at the young man and began to shake his head.

"Mattathias?" The captain pointed to the altar.

"As for me and my house, we will serve Adonai!" the old man declared. "That is my answer."

"Continue to serve your Adonai, Mattathias!" coaxed the captain. "Serve your god, but give homage to the king."

"It is not homage that you ask. It is worship."

"One may worship many gods."

"There is only one God!" declared the priest in a firm, calm voice. There were murmurs of approval from the crowd. "I do not care if everyone in every town and nation in this kingdom bows down to this king. I will not do so. I will not forsake the law of my fathers. I will fulfill the Covenant with Adonai!" he shouted.

Joseph rushed passed him. Mattathias grabbed his sleeve.

"Where are you going, Joseph?" he asked.

"To make the sacrifice! Someone must do it."

"You are mad, Joseph!"

"What are we asked to do, Mattathias? Merely to sacrifice the entrails of a sheep! An exception was made! Not a pig, not a swine. A *sheep*, Mattathias. What is wrong with that?" Joseph pushed himself away from the priest. "Jews are told that entrails are unclean, that we are not to have anything to do with them. These are only sheep guts, old priest! I don't want them, and the king may have them in his sacrifice!"

He broke away, but Mattathias again held his arm.

"You will make a bad example to the young and the weak among us. You break the first and the second commandments. If you make this sacrifice, you will worship an idol!"

"Let go of my arm, Mattathias," Joseph shouted and pulled himself free. "This has to be done for our people, for Modein!"

Mattathias caught him at the altar.

"Joseph, you must not do this," he exclaimed. "I command you!"

"I will not listen to you," said Joseph, stooping to prepare the sacrifice.

Mattathias removed the knife from its hiding place, pulled up Joseph by his collar, and plunged the knife into his heart.

"No Jew will make a sacrifice to Antiochus!" cried the priest. "Not in Modein. Not as long as I am elder and priest."

Heracles fell upon him, but Mattathias still held the knife in his hand. He slashed wildly at face,

293

arms, stomach, at whatever moved. The priest fought in a frenzy, and the huge man, who looked like a wrestler, fell backwards upon the glowing altar. He did not move because he was dead.

Fighting erupted between Heracles's soldiers and the townspeople.

"There is your sacrifice, great and mighty Antiochus!" Mattathias shouted above the turmoil, pointing to the lifeless form of Heracles. Waving his bloodied knife in punctuation, the priest turned to the crowd of Jews around him. "Let everyone who loves the law and stands upon the Covenant follow me!"

The priest and his sons fought against the invaders and slowly made their way to the edge of the crowd, and then ran for the hills as they had planned. Several of the townsmen followed them. Those who ran left all of their possessions behind them.

Word of the defiance to the king's decrees in Modein spread throughout the land. There was no general uprising, but there was a growing discontent. Some Jews talked of compromise with Antiochus and were fearful for their lives. Many wondered what new reprisals would come because of the slaying of Heracles.

However, the remnant, about which Mattathias had spoken so often, did exist throughout Judea. Those were the "godly men," the "pious ones," the *hasideans*. Some were being called *Perushim* and in a later day would be known as Pharisees. Others who remained in the hills established isolated communities and called themselves *Essenes*. Centuries later, when Jews faced new terrors and persecutions, a remnant would resurrect the name of *Hassidim* for themselves.

The few who loved the law joined Mattathias in the hills. Since they expected retaliation from Antioch, they continued to train themselves and to recruit more fighters for the battles to come. While they trained, they carried out brief forays into surrounding villages. They destroyed every altar they could find that had been built to honor Antiochus. They further defied him by circumcising young Jewish males, according to the law of Moses. And they kept the Sabbath.

The first major battle occurred in Jerusalem, but Mattathias and his band had no part in it.

Jewish loyalists attacked a contingent of Macedonian soldiers, returning to their garrison in the Akra. A dozen soldiers were killed. Sostratus, the governor, ordered all of his troops to pursue the rebels.

The insurgents were living in a huge cave, south of Jerusalem, near Bethlehem. Counting wives and children, there were nearly a thousand people living in crowded and uncomfortable circumstances.

Sostratus and his soldiers soon found the hiding place.

"Listen to me!" Sostratus shouted toward the entrance of the cave. "There has been enough bloodshed. Why should we resume foolish fighting? Do as the king demands, come forth, and you will be spared!"

"How do we know that we will be spared?" a loud voice questioned from inside the cave.

"Because I give you my word! I am Sostratus, the

295

governor. I speak for the king!"

While the rebels continued to discuss the offer, Sostratus ordered his men to gather dry brush and firewood and to stack them at the entrance to the cave.

"Come back another day," shouted a voice from inside the cave. "We will not come forth since this is our holy day, our Sabbath!"

Sostratus had forgotten that it was the Jewish Sabbath since it was no longer observed in Jerusalem in any special way.

"Again I offer you life!" he shouted. "Come forth and be spared."

"We will never profane the Sabbath, and we will not obey the king's command!" Many voices from inside the cave shouted affirmation.

Sostratus ordered the soldiers to light the bonfire.

The smoke entered the cave, and within minutes, women and children began to pour out of the cave, clutching their throats and rubbing their eyes, coughing uncontrollably. They were killed by Sostratus's men as they left the cave. The warriors still remained inside.

When the fire had subsided and cooled, Sostratus ordered his men into the cave. Sostratus had remembered another Sabbath day, in Jerusalem, many months before. He hoped that it was still true that the Sabbath, for Jews, was indeed a holy day.

Mattathias was furious when he learned of the event.

"Our men did not throw a single stone!" he shouted. "They did not barricade the entrance. They did nothing!"

"It was the Sabbath, Father!" said Judah. "They did try to save the women and the children."

"And it became a slaughter," his father replied.

"Hearken to my words, all of you," Mattathias continued in a soft but firm voice. "I know it is written that we are to keep the Sabbath day holy, and the Torah teaches us how that is to be done. But I say to you today that Adonai will forgive us if we honor Him on the Sabbath with the sword. If anyone attacks us on the Sabbath day, whoever he is, wherever we are attacked, we will resist!"

His sons and their companions murmured approval.

"There is no one left to resist, to defend the cause of Adonai. We will not defile the Sabbath by attacking others on that sacred day. But if we are attacked, we will, hereafter, resist! We must not be killed as our brothers were in Jerusalem. Listen to me. If we are killed—when we are killed—it will be as courageous Jews in battle, fighting for the law and for Adonai!"

Six months passed, and the skirmishes increased in number. The soldiers of Antiochus were surprised that the rebellion not only continued but seemed to be gaining strength. The small band from Modein was becoming an army.

Mattathias was older and weaker, and one day he called his sons before him.

"The army of Adonai grows strong while I become more frail," he said. His sons protested, but Mattathias waved them to silence. "It is appointed.

I must soon join my fathers. It is the will of the Almighty!" He propped himself up on an elbow and gestured to his sons to seat themselves beside him.

"I have much to say to you. Listen carefully, because the time is short." The old priest coughed for several seconds.

"Simon," he said, "you are a man of sound judgment. You are next to the oldest, but I want you to take your father's place."

Simon looked at John, the oldest of the sons.

"It is all right," said John, "Father and I have already discussed it. There are other things I must do."

"Obey him, my sons," the priest continued.

"Judah Maccabee, you are the strongest and the bravest of my sons," he said. "I appoint you commander of our forces. It will be given to you to lead our people to victory in this war against the heathen."

Judah, the tallest and biggest of the brothers, had bowed his head. His broad shoulders were shaking, and his brothers saw that he was quietly weeping.

"All of you must hold fast to the law," said Mattathias in a voice that was now much weaker. "Remember to seek vengeance for Adonai. The Torah has been destroyed throughout the land. Preserve the copies I have made. Make copies of them. See to it that the Torah is restored and studied. The Temple has been desecrated. It must be cleansed. The stones of this new altar of Antiochus must be pulled down and removed. Build a new altar. Destroy the idols. Purify the Temple, according to the word of the Torah. Onias had a son. See if he lives, and, if he does, protect and instruct him. If you cannot find him, then, you, Simon, are best versed in the law and you must serve as high priest."

Simon appeared struck with fear of what might truly be asked of him.

"Adonai will give us the victory," said the priest. "I shall not live to see the day, but one day all of you will again be able to sing 'I was glad when they said unto me, let us go into the house of the Lord!' "

The five sons placed their hands upon their father's thigh. In the ancient way they swore before Adonai that they would do as he asked.

"My sons, you live to see the prophecy of Daniel fulfilled. It is now so clear to me. Since the death of Onias there has not been proper sacrifice made in the Temple. Daniel says that two thousand three hundred evenings and mornings will pass, and then the holy place will be properly restored." Mattathias spoke with a sweet, mystical timbre in his voice. "Count the days from the death of Onias, from the time we ourselves left Jerusalem for Modein, because no longer could we worship Adonai in the way the Scriptures command. Count the days, my sons, and take heart. There is meaning in the number of days! There will be an end to the struggle. Adonai will be glorified and worshiped. The Temple will be restored!"

Mattathias closed his eyes, but his lips were still moving. The five sons leaned closer and heard the words, which they recognized as the closing words from the sacred book their father had loved so much.

" 'Those who have insight will shine brightly like the brightness of the expanse of heaven, and those

299

who lead the many to righteousness, like the stars forever and ever. . . . Many will be purged, purified, and refined: but the wicked will act wickedly, and none of the wicked will understand, but those of you who have insight will understand!' " The priest opened his eyes for a moment and smiled. " 'But as for you, go your way to the end; then you will enter into rest and rise up again for your allotted portion at the end of the age.' "*

Mattathias shook himself, and, for a moment, seemed to have regained his former strength.

"My sons, be men!" he said fervently. "Be men! Be brave for the law!"

He smiled, looked a moment at each of his five sons, and then he died.

At night, secretly, his sons buried their father in Modein, the village of his birth, where the final rebellion against Antiochus had begun.

The battle ahead would be long and hard, but at its end the Maccabees would revive the worship of Adonai and would restore the kingdom to the Judeans. The Hasmonean dynasty—begun with Mattathias—would survive until Pompey would claim all of El Beka for Rome. The Temple would be cleansed on the third anniversary of its desecration on the twenty-fifth day of Kislev. That cleansing is still remembered and celebrated through eight days of rejoicing called *Hanukkah*.

*Daniel 12:3, 10, 13.

300

25

Antiochus was being tossed about in the back of a wagon, somewhere in Persia, beyond the Euphrates. The wagon was much more practical than a chariot because it did allow room for him to lie down. But the vehicle was hard and unbending. The king was alive but very sick, and he wondered if death might not be preferable to the pain he was suffering.

"Drive more slowly!" he commanded.

The two soldiers nodded, and the horses immediately slowed their pace.

When he became ill, he decided to return to Antioch without delay, leaving his troops to return later. Dorymenes was a trusted commander and would protect and deliver the treasure safely.

He had entered Asia because he needed treasure. The games at Daphne had been an extravagance, and the war in Judea was going badly. He went to Media and Parthia to make an official appearance, to check on satraps and governors, to insist on payment of tribute and taxes, and to rob a few temples.

There had been no battles in the eastern provinces, but he had encountered some insubordination. He had not given enough attention to the eastern portion of his empire because of his preoccupation with Egypt and Judea. There was so much wealth in the East, and he had often pondered on this journey whether in the future he should better pursue commerce rather than war.

The world required writing materials, but why should the two sources be papyrus from Egypt or parchment from Pergamum? There was a demand for cattle and for leather. He had seen vast grasslands where animals could be grazed and fattened. There was bitumen in the Dead Sea; perhaps it could be found elsewhere. Bitumen was useful in improving harvests in vineyards. On this very trip he had learned that there was pitch to be found on the banks of the river Oxus, just to the north of him. To accomplish such commerce would require people, but he had slaves and would secure more slaves. He sighed. He also required time. How much time would he be given?

He could not avoid warfare, much as he might want to do so now. The kingdom was in shambles. If he did not survive, Antiochus would leave very little to his son to govern. So much had gone wrong.

Judea had been the key. He had known that from the very beginning.

This Judah Maccabee had become an amazing general, with an army of ten thousand Jews. Antiochus had heard how they fought their battles in new

302

ways—using spies, infiltrating the ranks of the king's armies, attacking at night, using small groups of soldiers to attack and divert the Seleucid troops while mounting major offensives from the rear.

Sostratus had been killed.

Appolonius was also dead.

Appolonius had also become a good general, Antiochus mused. He had chosen his men well. The king recognized ability in Appolonius when they had fought together in Egypt and Judea. Now he was dead. Judah Maccabee not only had defeated his general but had personally killed him and removed his sword as well. Antiochus had heard that this Maccabee took much pleasure in showing off that great sword of Appolonius.

So much had changed, and Antiochus was often wearied of sorting out the names of his subordinates, a few who were old, so many who were new, untried recruits.

Lysias was the man in charge during the king's expedition to the East. He was guardian of young Antiochus, the prince, and chief governor. Lysias was supposed to be in Judea, the king thought, to restore order. Lysias was loyal. He was also affectionate, the king recalled with a smile.

Phillip managed affairs in Antioch and taught the young prince.

Gorgias, the veteran of the war with Egypt, still lived. Seron was the new governor of Coeli-Syria. Gorgias, the king had heard, had been beaten badly at a place called Emmaus.

The king again bristled at the memory of Judah

303

Maccabee. It was rumored that this Jew was even trying to make an alliance with Rome, behind Antiochus's back. It was said that the Romans might try to return Demetrius to Antioch. The king struck the floor of the wagon with his hand and felt pain. His nephew, Demetrius, son of his murdered brother, had a legitimate claim to the throne. He should never have let him live this long in Rome. The old senator would have seen to it, once, a long time ago. The king knew that people said he was cruel and mad. He had not been cruel enough. What king, in his right mind, would allow a rival to live? Perhaps he was mad, as people said.

Antiochus felt a sharp stab of pain, closed his eyes, and, when he opened them again, saw a cluster of trees ahead of his wagon.

"Let us rest at the oasis," he said.

When they came to a stop, Antiochus sat up and looked about. It seemed to be a pleasant-enough watering spot, having date palms and a few clusters of grass.

"Do either of you know this place?" he asked his soldiers.

"I believe we once passed this way, Majesty," one of them replied.

"I see a small river yonder. Do you know its name?"

"If this is the place we passed through on our way to Parthia," said the soldier, "then I was told the river's name is *Lethe*."

"How strange," said the king. He remembered an ancient story told by the Greeks. *Lethe* was the river of oblivion, the river to the underworld.

"Is Your Excellency hungry or thirsty?" asked the other soldier.

"I feel feverish, and I would like some water," the king replied. "And perhaps some dates would be good, if you can find any."

The men scampered away, leaving Antiochus alone with his pain and his thoughts.

His head was now pounding with a hammering he had not felt before. It seemed to be inside his head, at the base of his brain. He knew he was not hearing as well as he once did, and his vision was even now quite blurred. He did not see the trees clearly. His greatest discomfort were the sores, the chancres enveloping his groin. He dreaded the pain of passing water, so he drank as little as possible, despite his thirst.

"It is a swift-moving stream, Majesty," said the soldier, who returned with a gourd filled with water. "The water is fresh and good!"

The king moistened his lips and drank just a little of the liquid.

"Does the king wish more water?" asked the soldier.

"No, this is enough," said the king. "Assist your comrade." The other soldier was climbing one of the palms.

"It is beginning to cloud," said the soldier. "We may have a storm, Majesty."

This arid land would be a strange place for a storm, Antiochus thought, as he removed the amulet and slowly rubbed its inscription.

There was a rumble of thunder in the distance.

Perhaps a storm was coming. Antiochus could not see clearly.

"You were too lenient!" said a voice.

"Is it you, my lord?" Antiochus cried.

"Your Majesty calls?" shouted one of the soldiers.

"It is nothing!" replied the king. "Carry on with your work!"

"It is indeed your lord," said the voice. "You have failed me, Antiochus."

"How have I failed you, Excellency?" asked the king.

"You did not destroy the Jews," said the voice, "as you were commanded to do."

"I killed thousands, Majesty! I destroyed their Temple. For good measure I even went to Mount Gerizim and made the temple of the Samaritans a temple of Zeus Xenios!"

"You took slaves. You did not kill all of them, and now, again, they raise the banner of their God."

"I tried, Majesty. I tried my very best to do your will!" said the king in fear.

"You failed, Antiochus!" declared the voice. "You showed much promise, but you failed."

The sound of thunder was closer.

"Is it also Zeus Keraunios, the god of thunder?" Antiochus cried out.

"It is only I," said the voice, "and you hear my displeasure. You have failed me, Antiochus. I could have thwarted the purposes of Adonai Himself. But I will not fail. Others will follow you. Others will take your place. Through them I will carry on my dispute, and, one day, I will win."

A thunderclap exploded close by, and the horses

were frightened by the noise and began to run. Antiochus remembered that he was alone in the wagon, that there was no one to control the beasts.

He struggled onto his knees and in great pain climbed over the front seat of the cart and managed to grab the reins.

He fought his way to his feet, swaying with the wagon, pulling as hard as he could on the reins. He thought he saw the two soldiers running from the trees toward him.

The king pulled and shouted, but the animals were in fright and ran as though they were possessed by demons.

The river was just ahead.

In his blurred vision, Antiochus saw that it was not a wide river but just a stream. But as his soldier had said, it appeared to be a swift-moving stream.

The horses plunged into the water, which was deeper than either the animals or Antiochus had expected. The horses were now thoroughly frightened and fought each other and their harness restraints in panic. The wagon began to break up.

Antiochus felt himself being thrown up into the air. He was still tightly clasping the talisman and was staring at the heavens when his body hit the water.

The soldiers found pieces of the wagon and recaptured the horses.

They searched for more than an hour on both sides of the stream that one of them thought was named the *Lethe*.

Shrugging their shoulders, they mounted the horses and continued westward.

Epilogue

He strode through the corridors as though he owned them.

He did own them. He owned the corridors, the offices on all seven floors of this building, as well as the expanding underground of the headquarters of Orcus Enterprises Unlimited, the building that housed his computers and the management team that ran his empire.

"*Buon giorno*—good day!—signor Festo!" greeted a security guard.

Signor M. M. Festo merely nodded. He was glad that the corridor was almost empty.

As he walked toward the elevator bank, he smiled pensively but confidently as he thought of the 557 employees who worked for him in this building. Each was a skilled technician or specialist. Each had been carefully screened before employment. Each was well paid—far better than anyone else in Rome with comparable technical status and ability. For the most part, he thought his employees were loyal. He smiled again, ruefully this time, amused at how often during recent days he had felt it necessary to qualify his thoughts and statements.

He entered the private executive elevator, which would take him directly to the seventh floor. He glanced at his watch. He had at least ten minutes to spare before he was scheduled to call his staff meeting to order.

He entered his private office through an unmarked door. Only rarely did he appear in the outer office. He enjoyed his privacy. In fact, he thrived upon privacy. He did not grant many interviews, and editors around the world had to search carefully for a recent photograph of him.

His private office was huge, and signor Festo approved of its vastness. It was large enough for board of directors' meetings, although none had been or would be held here; there was a special room for that purpose. The furniture in his office was starkly modern and functional, yet clustered in arrangements that provided an intimacy and a warmth for the many smaller meetings and conferences that were held in this place. The luxury of space and the aura of power pleased him.

He signaled Maria, his secretary, on the intercom, to indicate that he had arrived. He knew that she would be at her desk. She always waited there until he arrived. He told Maria he did not wish to be disturbed and would go directly to the staff meeting. He would not take any calls.

He sat in the slim, ebony judicial executive chair, sniffing and absorbing the aroma of the prime leather that always created for him a sensual excitement and a sexual awareness.

He turned his chair toward the wide picture window and gazed at what was always a spectacular view of the Eternal City. Below him was the Piazza Venezia, with its outflowing arteries of *corsos* and *vias*. Only an occasional taxi or bus was moving. Rome had changed. Perhaps the petroleum crisis had finally brought order to the traffic of this city.

He smiled and sighed, observing the history within his sight. The Forum. The Colosseum. The Pantheon. San Angelo's Castle. And, to the west, beyond the Tiber, St. Peter's and Vatican City, the enclave that still pretended to be a state within a state.

The executive indulged himself, now smiling broadly, as he looked at the aging and graying monument to Vittorio Emanuele in the plaza below him. Victor Emmanuel. The last of the empire's kings. Signor Festo knew that Victor, of course, had not been a true Caesar; Mussolini had seen to that. But Victor Emmanuel was the last of his line—or so most people thought.

The man undid his tie and unbuttoned his shirt, turning his chair again toward his desk, determined to relax before the important meeting to come. He reached inside his shirt and felt for the medallion he had worn for many years as a sort of good-luck charm.

It was more than a charm, although it had brought him much fortune. He sensed a power there, a power that extended far beyond the Rome he had just

311

observed through his window. That power would soon shake the world.

M. M. Festo. He smiled. That was not his real name, but that no longer mattered.

He caught his reflection on the well-polished surface of his desk. He was well tailored, well groomed, comfortably youthful and slim. He could not see his eyes in the reflection of the desk, but he had noted some lines around them this morning in the mirror of his bathroom at home. They were hard, perhaps even cruel lines, he thought. Few people had seen them. He fostered the notion of being a wealthy recluse and mystery man. The low profile image suited him and his purposes.

M. M. Festo.

He himself had chosen the name. His mother was Syrian. His father, unknown to him, perhaps even unknown to his mother, was either Italian or Spanish or Portuguese, according to the gossipers. He was not bothered by his uncertain origins.

Mahoud Manuel Festo.

"Mahoud" was adequately Arabic. The rest of his name was a kind of joke or pun. The rabbi had encouraged him in the jest to be perpetrated upon a naive and unsuspecting public.

"Manuel" was sufficiently Mediterranean. In earlier days, a few associates had nicknamed him "Manny." He discouraged the practice, but for a time it did not hurt his business relationships with his Jewish friends. He was "Manny" to the Jews, "Mahoud" to the Arabs. He enjoyed playing both factions against each other.

312

Put the name together, however, and one had at least two interesting combinations. "M. Manuel" was obvious, and the rabbi had explained its meaning to him. *Emanu-El*. "Manny Festo" had a similar meaning. It all suggested a revealing, an appearing, a manifestation. Festo had long felt that he was destined to be part of some magnificent revelation. He was not completely certain of all its ramifications, but he felt inklings of expectation and anticipation.

The intercom buzzed.

"I said I was not to be disturbed, Maria."

"I thought I would remind you of the time. sir. The staff has gathered in the board room."

"I am aware of the time, Maria."

"Yes, sir." The intercom clicked off.

Signor Festo was rubbing the amulet. He looked again at its characters. The rabbi had explained them to him. He was not sure what the numbers meant, but one day the rabbi might explain more fully.

"It will be a good day, Mahoud," said a voice. "And don't concern yourself now about those numbers!"

"I am glad you answered," said Festo.

"Don't I always answer?" replied the voice.

"Yes," said the executive. "We make the decision today."

"Yes, I know."

"I have gone over each point, as you suggested. Everything has been assigned. Today I hear the reports."

"Excellent."

"May I ask a question?" asked signor Festo.

"You are already late for your meeting."

"Surely the leader may be late, if he chooses."

"Ask your question."

"Must the declaration be made in Rome?"

"You have asked that question before."

"So I ask it again!" said Festo impetuously.

"Do not become impertinent, Mahoud!" cautioned the voice.

"Forgive me," said the man. "Perhaps I am only apprehensive."

"Very well, I will go over the matter once more," said the voice, coldly. "Listen carefully."

M. M. Festo nodded.

"Rome is the center of the world."

"Some would argue the point. It is the center of Europe, there is no question about that."

"It is the center of the world. A few years ago, no one would have dreamed it would be so. Italy was in turmoil; its political parties offered no solutions. But today the power base has shifted, has it not? The industrialized nations of the past now huddle in brown-outs and quiet cold. Rome has become the center once again—this time of communications, finance, commerce, and industry!"

"It is true."

"A major religious body resides here."

"That is also true of Geneva."

"Surely it is not the same, Mahoud, even though you have your links with Geneva."

"True," said Festo.

"Most importantly, I suspect, is the psychology of the event," the voice continued. "For us it is both historical and psychological. Few people will admit publicly that the vision of a Roman empire still burns. But it does. We both know that it does, especially with the revitalization of the Mediterranean countries. All roads once led to Rome. Again, it is true. This is where the declaration must be made. Believe me!"

"I would not be here today if I did not believe you," said Mahoud Manuel Festo.

"Mahoud, there is much history within you as well," declared the voice. "You do not *know* this— you only *feel* this."

"That is true."

"Within you are found the genes of Alexander, of the Seleucids, of the Caesars and Herods, and even the Huns."

"It is not possible biologically."

"I know whereof I speak."

"Forgive me. Of course, you know such things."

"Consider *Emmanuel*, although I have much hesitation in using that name, as we have discussed. The crucified Jew's other name is one I will not repeat. Consider, then, *Epiphanes*."

"*Epiphanes?*" Festo repeated with an excited shudder.

"There is a similarity in name and meaning. You have studied the lives of all the great leaders, the truly outstanding ones who served me. There is also a similarity of service."

"I have studied this, my lord. Is there a connection? Could it be that, in some way I do not yet comprehend, we belong to each other?"

The voice did not immediately respond.

315

"Are you prepared for your meeting, Mahoud?"

"You have not answered me!"

"Are you prepared?" insisted the voice.

"I am ready."

"Then go to your meeting. Be calm and proceed as we agreed. We have a plan, a timetable. You must not rush into things. That is where the others always failed."

"Yes, my lord," Mahoud whispered.

"I am with you. Remember that."

"*Shalom*," said the executive.

"*Shalom*, Mahoud? There will be no peace. No *shalom*."

"Then, *bon chance. Buona fortuna.* Can you wish me that?"

"Yes, I can wish you good luck, signor."

The room was silent.

Festo ran a comb through his hair, rebuttoned his shirt, and tightened his tie. He breathed deeply to overcome a sudden nervousness and left through his private exit for the staff meeting.

The meeting began as soon as the chairman sat down.

Festo called for reports, following his prepared agenda. There would be no preliminaries and no jesting today. There was important business to transact. He saw that the rabbi was observing him keenly.

As each staff person reported, Festo jotted down the key facts for later review and follow-up, should that be necessary.

The Parliament of Europe was in recess in Strasburg. The Eurodollar remained relatively stable during the week but could fall quickly and suddenly. The price of gold was still artificially high.

Scandinavia was without oil reserves. Britain relied on its North Seas sources, but supplies were insufficient. Electricity was rationed throughout most of Europe. There were still a few functioning nuclear facilities, but most generators burned coal.

Communications media were operating, but on a reduced basis.

It was reported that the United States of America, which had long since ceased to be a major industrial nation, was expecting a good harvest. The USA was struggling to remain the world's breadbasket, but its agriculture was now less technological and more labor intensive, and production was on the decline.

The USSR was North America's chief competitor in agriculture. Neither the US nor the Soviet Union were the major military powers they had been in the past. Their military equipment had not been destroyed but had been placed in mothballs.

Signor Festo was most interested in the report on oil. The Orcus interests possessed contracts for the last remaining oil reserves in the Arabian Gulf. The report stated that oil reserves in Nigeria, Mexico, and Venezuela were at an all-time low, and their governments were curtailing pumping. Orcus interests had adequate supplies and would benefit from spot sales. It also had made excellent progress in manufacture of simple solar energy devices, which it had long been researching. The Orcus fleet of partially wind-driven tankers and freighters was "on line," ready to sail with oil or solar generators.

The firm's computers had increased both capacity and compatibility with every other international computer system. Linkages had been arranged—sometimes through under-the-table maneuvers—but linkages were assured. Secret police files, beginning with Interpol, were no longer secret.

Festo showed his pleasure. He knew that for all practical purposes, every human being on earth was now registered somewhere, somehow, with a number. International agencies, governmental programs of welfare, social security, and tax units, as well as the commercial systems of insurance and credit all provided the potential for a comprehensive data bank to monitor every being on earth.

He learned that the new super computer, installed on the three floors below ground level in this very building, was operational. It would become the hub for the international monitoring and control just as soon as the signal for interlock would be given. Festo smiled. It was a formidable new underworld.

The reports turned to political alignments.

Political leadership everywhere—whether of "right," "left," or "centrist"—agreed upon the necessity to resolve the world's energy crisis and fiscal chaos.

Signor Festo heard that all possible groups and alliances had been contacted. Support was assured from all religious and minority groups.

It had taken more than a year to develop such a consensus, but success was now in sight. Unveiling this gigantic coalition might well turn out to be the crowning achievement of the day. After all, coalitions existed to allow diverse groups to work together for some common goal.

M. M. Festo listened carefully and asked only an occasional question for clarification.

Each person who reported was an expert on his or her field. Festo doubted whether anyone in the room other than the rabbi and himself comprehended the significance of the reporting, how everything fitted together, how the facts supported and complemented each other. The so-called Third World of generations past had promoted the idea of a "new international economic order." It had never come about. But Festo—and the rabbi—knew how close they were to its achievement, in ways never imagined.

He checked his written notes against the agenda.

"According to my notes everyone has reported. Is that correct?" Festo asked. No one raised a voice. Festo stood. "I thank you for your excellent work. All of you have worked long hours, far beyond the normal call of duty. I want you to know that I personally appreciate it."

Everyone appeared to be smiling, grateful for the affirmation.

"In the kind of high-level business management consulting and development work that Orcus Enterprises does, we delve and probe into areas that must often appear to be irrelevant or confusing to you," the board chairman continued. "Let me assure you that this is never the case in Orcus Enterprises Unlimited. That last word in our corporate name is important. We are not limited in what we investigate or analyze. And the work on which you have reported to me today will soon prove my point."

He had gathered up his papers, and it was clear that there would be no questions.

"Thank you, again," signor Festo said. "Announcement will be made in due time about our next meeting."

He waved a general good-bye but did not remain to visit. He left the room quickly, followed by the rabbi.

"They are ready for us in the media center," said the rabbi. It was only a few doors down the hall from Festo's executive suite. The media center contained a small television studio, a control room, tape and videotape recorders, and a small conference room, fully equipped for every kind of audio-visual presentation.

"Coffee?" asked the rabbi.

"Yes, thank you," said Festo. The rabbi poured and passed a ceramic mug; Styrofoam cups had long since been abandoned because of the petroleum shortage.

"Your staff does good work," said the rabbi. "Those were excellent reports. Concise. Accurate."

"It is expected of them," said Festo. "And they are paid extremely well for it."

The rabbi smiled, poured himself a mug of coffee, and sat across from his superior.

Rabbi Gershon ben Judah.

Mahoud Manuel Festo quickly reran a mental tape of the unusual man who sat in front of him. He had met the rabbi five years ago on a trip to the Middle East. The rabbi had become Festo's advisor and alter ego, up to a point. There were private matters Festo would never share with the rabbi.

Gershon was—or had been—a legitimate rabbi.

His scholarship and knowledge of world religions and sacred literature were among his greatest assets. He was equally at home discussing Christian, Eastern, or Judaic beliefs, but he himself was a man of no particular belief. He was scientifically astute and something of a technocrat in his own right. Festo knew that Gershon believed no more in a traditional Supreme Being than he did.

The rabbi knew of the master plan. In fact, he had helped in its design and implementation. He and Festo consulted frequently, testing ideas and assumptions with each other, arguing, parrying, and analyzing each other's theories and plans as only two people with great respect for each other could do. Most people probably considered them friends. That was not their precise relationship, Festo believed. You could have a great respect for someone and not be friendly. They were simply respectful colleagues. Festo often saw an intrigue and a callousness in the rabbi that surprised him and forced him to be cautious, even when he had wanted to be on more friendly terms with the Jew. Festo laughed inwardly. He ought to be able to recognize intrigue and callousness in others; he saw enough of both in himself.

"We proceed with the plan?" asked the rabbi.

"Yes. Everything is in order. The timing is right."

"Then, shall we review the drill?" asked the rabbi.

"You sound like a retired British sergeant!" Festo laughed.

"There was a British occupation in my homeland once, as you may recall."

"That was years ago, Gershon—way before your time!"

"I may well be ageless, signor," said the rabbi coldly and deliberately. "Perhaps you are, too," he added. "What is the plan presently?" he asked.

"First, I am to make the declaration," said Festo. "After the announcement is made, linkage with all computer systems will occur. A bank holiday will be declared, and all banks and stock exchanges will be closed until further notice. Our shadow organization will surface and assume command at every level of national and international government. The decrees will then be issued, in the series and on the schedule we have already determined. Is this your understanding, thus far?" Festo asked.

"Yes." The rabbi scratched his balding head; he had long ago given up wearing a yarmulke. "I have a few worries, of course."

"For example."

"You see no possibility of military interference?"

"Do you?"

"Frankly, no. But can we be certain?"

"Who is able to challenge us militarily, Gershon?" asked Festo. "Eventually, there might be problems with the communist bloc. But it would take years for them to regroup, and even they have to go along with us for now. They also need the energy we can provide."

"Trouble is prophesied."

"Oh, come now, rabbi!" Festo laughed.

"You do not wish to hear the prophecy of Daniel?"

"You've read it to me. Besides, it's not prophecy;

322

it was history written at the time of Antiochus Epiphanes."

"I don't agree. Neither do many scholars. I think it's prophecy."

"You're an unbeliever! How can you believe in prophecy?"

"I accept many things I do not believe."

"You speak in riddles."

"Then let me read to you from the Revelation of St. John the Divine."

"No!" Festo was angry. "I want to act without fulfilling someone's notion of someone's ancient prophecy."

"So it begins." The rabbi sighed.

"It begins when I give the word. It begins with an alert to all wire services, to all the television networks, to all communications media that a major announcement will be made at the restored Roman Forum."

"Will they come?"

"The release bears the masthead of the European Community of Nations. It is major news. The media will be there."

"The choice of the Forum was sheer genius, Mahoud."

"It is where all great announcements were made in Rome, where the senators watched their triumphs, where temples to all of the ancient gods were built. Now that Rome has reconstructed the area to look exactly as it once did, it is the perfect spot for us."

Both men sat silently for a moment, reflecting upon history past and history soon to be made.

"The declaration you recorded yesterday is ready for you to see," said the rabbi.

"Good," said Festo.

The rabbi picked up an intercom telephone and gave instructions. "You will be amazed at what the technicians have accomplished."

The rabbi pushed a button, and the lights in the room were dimmed. Suddenly, a figure entered and stood before them. It was absolutely remarkable: the figure appeared to be a twin of Mahoud Manuel Festo. He knew the explanation. They were seeing a new system of electronic imagery, using principles of holography. Laser beams recreated a three-dimensional figure of Festo, using three separate videotape tracks which, since they were on a single moving tape, would never be out of synchronization. He looked exactly as he had yesterday, when the video-tape was made.

"Incredible!" Festo exclaimed.

"Quiet. You're about to speak," cautioned the rabbi.

"Citizens of the world!" Festo heard himself speak. "We face, together, problems the like of which the world has never seen. Thousands of us are hungry and starving. Tens of thousands of us are freezing. Factories are idle. Transportation does not move. Harvests may not be harvested. Our money is without value. There is chaos!

"Citizens, we are without food and fuel. We have reached the ultimate crisis of our planet.

"Our governments have sought solutions, but to no avail. Our international bodies have floundered and failed. Anarchy has raised its head—but anarchy, too, has shown that it offers no solution. We lack food and fuel, and no one can provide it—or even promise it."

The laser-induced figure paused.

"That is, no one could promise a solution until today. This is why I am here, in this place, today, making this statement. Few of you know me or have ever seen my face. However, governments and corporations have known me for many years. My profession is to rescue organizations from bankruptcy and chaos. Some of you who see me know what my organization has accomplished and how we have succeeded. And we shall succeed once again, to the benefit of all of us!"

The figure waved a document.

"This document is official authorization from the Parliament of Europe for my organization to effect and carry out a plan to rescue all of us from the disaster that has already begun. This document is a contract between the parliament and Orcus Enterprises Unlimited. The United Nations Security Council, in secret session, has agreed to add its support. My company is being given sixty days in which to prepare a plan, using all of our skills and computers, and expertise, to bring back a style of life in which hunger and cold and inactivity will disappear. The contract calls for sixty days. My friends, we will not require sixty days!"

"Now comes your bit of piety," said the rabbi.

"I come to you with confidence and hope. I am a man of faith. I believe that God wills good for His world still. Throughout history, the great Source of Life provides prophets and leaders who can change

325

history. In all humility, I know that God has given me this exceptional opportunity to be of help."

"Bravo," said the rabbi sarcastically.

"There is only one God. All of the world's great religions know this. Thus, mine is not false modesty or humility. I declare to you today that I know I can help each one of us, each one of our nations, to achieve that one world of prosperity and abundance for which we have prayed—and dreamed!"

The figure paused as though waiting for applause. Suddenly it shuddered, as though hit with an object, and then collapsed to the base of the rostrum. Festo had rehearsed the fall several times yesterday.

"That is when you will be shot," said the rabbi. "We will have a live sharpshooter using an actual rifle."

"With live ammunition?"

"No. But the blank will be loud and real enough."

"Are we certain that the television cameras can reproduce holographs? Will it look authentic? Will it be real?" This problem had long nagged Festo's mind.

"We've tested it," said the rabbi, "and it works. Of course, on TV it will be a flat image—none of this three-dimensional realism. But it will work." The rabbi pushed a button, and the room lights brightened. "We'll pretend to carry you off—our backs will be toward the cameras—and within minutes you will reappear. But, this time, it will be you, in the flesh."

"You're sure we'll have enough time?"

"Mahoud, this is a staged media event," said the rabbi. "The television commentators will be in shock.

326

So will the reporters and photographers. You've just announced a contract to govern the world, and you are shot. There will be utter confusion, and we'll add a few sirens. There will be enough time for the TV types to stutter and flounder and speculate, in a dozen languages. And then you will reappear."

"I complete the declaration, confirming that 'God' literally raised me up for such a time as this."

"No one will ever forget it—nor will they doubt you. That's why we're staging all of this."

"And that will be our miracle."

"A rather impressive one, don't you think?" asked the rabbi with a chuckle. "Think of it. The event will be carried by satellite transmitters and seen by millions around the world. It will be repeated dozens of times, ad infinitum, on national and local television newscasts, in every country, of every ideological persuasion. You will promise precisely what people need—food and fuel. And a man who is killed and raised from the dead before one's very eyes must have the power to do that! It will be on television, don't you see? If it's on television, it's got to be true!"

"It looks foolproof," said Festo. "The technicians did do a good job."

"I'll tell them." The rabbi picked up the telephone, thanked the engineer, and said that Mr. Festo and he would be going to Mr. Festo's office.

"It's going to work!" signor Festo said, after they had returned to his office.

"It must work," said the rabbi. "Our master will see to that."

"Our master?" Festo asked in surprise.

"The lord whom we both serve."

"You know about *him*?" Festo could not believe it. This was one of the private matters never discussed with the rabbi.

"Signor, I know more than you dream. I said I was ageless, and I was not joking. Neither did I jest when I suggested that you, too, were ageless."

"I don't understand."

"I know all about the amulet with its three sixes, remember—the one you never remove. We must talk more about that special number."

Manuel Festo felt that he should have guessed that this rabbi was no mere mortal he had met accidentally in Israel five years ago.

"Mahoud," the rabbi said, "there is unlimited power behind us. We must not be afraid. You know, as well as I, that our lord's plan will not be completed today or next week or next month. It will take years. And the day will come when we work not for the good of the people but for the good of our master."

"I know," Festo said quietly. "It has been told me that one day I will complete the work of Antiochus Epiphanes."

"And you will have Menelaus beside you."

"You are Menelaus?" Festo whispered incredulously. "Menelaus was buried in a barrel of ashes. That is what I heard."

"Did they ever find his body?" asked the rabbi. Festo was silent. "No more than they found yours," the rabbi concluded.

Mahoud Manuel Festo felt overwhelmed by the mystery, and yet today he had the impression, the feeling, that everything would be explained and fall into its proper place.

He relied upon his lord.

"Come," he said to the rabbi, almost casually. "We must make the final preparations. It will soon be time for my appearing."

Moody Press, a ministry of the Moody Bible Institute, is designed for education, evangelization, and edification. If we may assist you in knowing more about Christ and the Christian life, please write us without obligation: Moody Press, c o MLM, Chicago, Illinois 60610.